Ignoble

Matt Elham

Matt Elham

There were enough Matt Jreses
already in the publishing world!

For Selena.
Without you, this would never have happened.

Chapter One

The smelting building was a small, unimposing structure which at first glance was just one of the many service huts scattered around the mine site. Made from wood, it was raised on stilts around eighteen inches from the ground. It was heavily weathered both directly from the tropical rains and indirectly from the mud kicked up by the frequent tropical deluges.

Those with an educated eye would notice some key differences in the design of this particular building, if they took the time to inspect the structure more closely. It was constructed at virtually the lowest point of the mine's support site. Gravity fed the gold-laden cyanide solution downhill to a large storage pond, which was logically located at the very lowest point of the area, outside of the mine itself.

The smelting building was located adjacent to this pond, and the gold-laden solution was then pumped into the building though pipes which ran underground from the pond. These pipes entered and left the smelter concealed in the building's supporting stilts so as to not draw excessive attention to the building's true purpose. When this design feature was pointed out to visitors, they noticed that the stilts supporting this building were indeed more substantial than those supporting other buildings.

Structural engineers might also notice that the building's wooden frame was actually a veneer, covering a very sturdy, cinder block structure underneath. The windows were shuttered, as was the case with most buildings on the mine, having been designed to withstand the driving rain. However this building's shutters lacked hinges, a small detail that revealed the important detail that these shutters never opened.

The final giveaway was the multiple air-conditioning units mounted to the sides of the buildings. The smelter needed to reach two thousand degrees Fahrenheit for the gold to liquefy, allowing it to be extracted from the slurry. This heat was created by a double walled and insulated furnace, but the ambient heat produced by the process needed to be aggressively disbursed to make working conditions in the room bearable.

The mine's designers were smart enough not to build ostentatious fencing around the hut, which would have drawn excessive attention to the building and its true importance. So ostensibly, the building was a storage hut for maintenance supplies for the cyanide ponds. Site maps supportively described this as the building's purpose. The ponds themselves were surrounded by some serious fencing, emphatically adorned with warning signs describing some the worst effects of cyanide poisoning. The signage and the pervasive smell of bitter almonds was generally enough to keep inquisitive mine hands away from the area.

The hut was three hundred yards downhill from the administration area, a distance Lucas and Amber covered quickly. The anticipation surrounding their illicit adventure created an unfamiliar rush of adrenaline, not common to them from doing their day jobs.

They slowed as they approached the smelting hut, a building whose function they'd deduced from a schematic of the mine site they'd studied at the start of their fieldwork. They understood the mining process well enough to know there had to be a smelter somewhere, and a process of elimination and exploration had left this building as the only realistic candidate. They understood the benefits of the subterfuge.

Lucas covered the last few yards to the building with an exaggerated tip-toe, as he'd been instructed to do by countless movies. He pressed his back tightly against the side of the building, attempting to stay invisible in the lengthening evening shadows. The most rudimentary of surveillance systems would have detected him in an instant, but considerations such as that were not on his mind as he led Amber bravely towards their evening's excitement.

Amber pressed herself tight to the building beside Lucas, fighting to suppress a grin that was threatening to form on her face from her amusement at Lucas's antics plus the unfamiliar thrill of being naughty. She looked expectantly at Lucas, waiting for his next move.

Lucas smiled back and motioned for her to follow him. He peered around the side of the building towards the door but instantly recoiled. Amber, who was right behind Lucas, was bumped by his sharp retreat, causing her to emit a sharp exclamation. Lucas held his breath and indicated for her to back up and resume their tight formation against the building. As they did so, a security guard walked into view.

Fortunately, it appeared that he had not seen or heard them, as he continued his patrol without faltering. He wore what looked like an Army uniform, complete with a military cap. No rank or insignia were displayed on his sleeves, and the uniform looked very old. As Lucas held his breath, he randomly speculated whether the guard was actually the first user of this particular outfit.

The most notable thing about the guard, and the thing that immediately drew Amber's eye, was the large gun he was carrying, slung over his shoulder. More experienced African hands might not have been too concerned about the weapon. They would understand the myriad of ways in which the gun may not represent a threat. Poor maintenance may cause the firing mechanism to lock. The guard may not have been trained on how to fire it. Or it may be something as simple as the guard not having been given any bullets. But to Lucas and Amber, it was a big, scary gun.

The guard continued his patrol past the smelting building and turned a corner beyond the cyanide pools, passing out of sight behind the pond's fencing.

Lucas released the breath he'd unconsciously been holding as the tension relaxed from his muscles.

Amber whispered to Lucas: 'Jeez, that was some gun. Do you still think this is a good idea?'

Lucas embarked on a short but turbulent struggle between, on the one hand, the imperative of self-preservation, and on the other, the desire to look strong and authoritative in Amber's eyes. Amber was staring at him with a look of excitement and dependency, which made this decision a relatively easy one. After all, they were legitimate guests of a legitimate mine, just out for an evening stroll. No-one was going to shoot them on sight. Come on, get a grip, he thought.

'Calm down,' he said, trying to not allow the nervousness to show in his voice. 'They're not going to shoot us. Come on.'

Lucas looked back around the corner of the building. Seeing no-one, he cautiously tip-toed around the corner, keeping his back closely pressed to the wall. His eyes pivoted rapidly to his left and right, alternately checking the door he was heading for and the direction in which the guard had departed. Amber silently followed his lead, also remaining as close to the wall as she could.

Lucas moved slowly which he hoped would result in progress that was both quiet and undetected. He continued to remain alert to the guard's return as he inched along the wall towards the door. Checking that Amber was still in close formation behind him, he turned back towards the door and reached for handle.

As his fingers drew inexorably closer to the handle, the door flew violently open, missing his outstretched knuckles by mere inches. Three security guards absolutely flew out of the building, guns and voices raised.

'On the ground,' one of the guards shouted. 'Get down. Now!'

'Get your hands where we can see them,' amplified a second guard, as he and his third colleague pointed their weapons towards Lucas and Amber in a way which left no doubt of their intentions.

Lucas and Amber threw their arms in the air and sank to their knees in shock.

"Oh, shit," Lucas whispered as he closed his eyes.

Chapter Two

Davie Eason leaned nonchalantly against a wall at the corner of Seventh Avenue and Thirtieth Street in central Manhattan. His eyes swung lazily from left to right, from uptown to downtown. He was alert, but unless something went badly wrong, he knew things would stay quiet for another hour, perhaps two.

He'd been in position for a good few hours now, moving every five minutes or so and taking an occasional break from the chill evening wind in the Staples store a block farther down seventh. He didn't need to be available every second of every hour, but he liked to minimize his time off the street. Every interaction he missed was an opportunity wasted.

He was happy with his progress in the organization but was ambitious for more. He'd spent a tough few months at the lowest level of the organization, doing those really shitty jobs that were menial and tedious, not to mention risky. He'd been the type of guy he was now waiting for. But he'd worked hard, kept his nose clean and his abilities had been quickly recognized, resulting in a promotion to the role he now held.

In this new role, he was close to making the minimum wage. Davie smiled to himself, thinking that breaking minimum would be a landmark to be celebrated. But he knew that wasn't the point. The point was to be good, to get noticed and to get to the next level in the organization as quickly as possible. Then he needed to remain reliable, not mess anything up and eventually he'd find himself in a position where he could make really good money. He knew he'd quickly forget the months spent earning a pittance when the big bucks started to flow. Few people ever reached those heady ranks and there were hundreds applying each day to get their place on the greasy pole, so Davie understood that it was a numbers game. It's wasn't like his wage was being taxed anyway, which he knew meant that his take-home pay was above those poor souls greeting customers for hours on end at Wal-Mart.

So far that shift he'd collected a little over three hundred dollars. He did some quick mental arithmetic and figured that he'd get about twenty-three dollars of that, a little over seven percent. Not that he was working for a percentage. He was paid six bucks for each hour he was on duty so the nearly four hours he'd worked had earned him twenty-three bucks. He knew that the collections would increase as the night went on, which would make his percentage drop. He'd probably end up making around two or three percent. That was what he was averaging over the eight weeks or so he'd been doing this particular job.

He liked doing mental arithmetic like this as he was interested in the economics of the business. Not that he'd advertise this to anyone, but the mental gymnastics helped keep his mind active during the long hours of boredom. Leaning against a wall for hours on end wasn't a mentally taxing job. He'd figured he'd made less than one percent of the take doing his entry-level job, and he now knew that there were two or three of them for every one of him. So the street team was taking perhaps five percent of the pot as wages.

His current job carried considerably more responsibility than his previous one, so certainly merited the pay rise he'd received. He'd worn clean through the soles of a pair of sneakers covering the miles in that previous role. It had required no discernable skill beyond maintaining a decent level of physical fitness. Not having holes in your pockets was another key requirement, Davie thought with a smile. A percentage of recruits inevitably went bad, but the system was structured so that no one person could damage the organization financially. Davie was interested in the risks of the business as well as the economics.

Chapter Three

The plane was a sleek corporate jet, a Cessna Citation, registered in Nassau under the name of GoldRock Mining. It contained space for just eight passengers and was able to fly from New York to Los Angeles without refueling. Its passengers travelled swaddled in a luxurious, yet surprisingly quiet cabin given the size and power of the twin jet engines located just feet from their ears on the sides of the fuselage.

For most people, it only took a few seconds after climbing the steps into the cabin for many of their preconceptions about private jets to be dispelled. Most assumed that corporate jets offered unlimited space and luxury. Certainly, everyone got a window seat, upholstered in the finest leather. Certainly every passenger could gorge themselves on the fine food and wines prepared to order by the attentive cabin assistant. But once passengers had contorted themselves into their seat, the lack of headroom, elbowroom and turning room meant that they were strongly inclined to remain seated until disembarkation.

The plane was thirty minutes northwest of Ghana's only international airport, and was only ten minutes away from the small jungle airstrip that was their destination. The three passengers could not have had more differing attitudes towards the flight.

Carlos Vasquez, the host for the flight, had lost count of the times he'd made this journey. While to others it might have seemed inconvenient to have to fly between meetings, he knew that forty minutes of calm, coddled comfort in the aircraft was infinitely preferable to the dusty and dangerous five hour drive which provided the only alternative. He did not need to worry about bringing liquids on board, or taking the coins from his pocket. He also didn't have to worry about flight delays as the plane's departure could only be delayed by his actions. He was one of GoldRock's most senior executives, representing them throughout the region, and as the host of the flight he'd taken the front starboard seat of the aircraft. He was dressed all in black and stared resolutely ahead, not feeling any great desire or obligation to engage his guests in meaningless small talk.

In contrast, Amber Marshall was making this particular trip for the first time. Her eyes were intently fixed on the view from her window, as she sat in awe of the magnificence of the scenery passing beneath her. The exoticism and vibrancy of the rainforest presented a stark contrast to the industrial landscape she was far more familiar with seeing from the window of the commuter shuttle from La Guardia to Washington.

Her right hand concealed a small camera, held low and discreetly in her lap. She had realized with a little embarrassment that she was actually scared to use it, fearing she'd surrender some of her already fragile credibility by acting like a tourist. She knew she worried too much that her youthfulness and good looks might undermine people's perception of her professionalism, and she worked hard to avoid doing anything that might validate that fear. She'd trust her excellent memory to capture the view. She was a professional, first and foremost, and this was a business trip. Besides, the flight back would probably not require Carlos's supervision and so would give her ample opportunities to take photos. In her other hand was an old-fashioned notepad and pen, as she knew that preparedness was everything.

Lucas Steadman was also taking this trip for the first time, but as Amber's boss, he was focused on projecting a strong and authoritative image to both her and Carlos. He tried to resist gazing out of the window in case Carlos became inclined to initiate a conversation, but found himself unable to ignore the spectacle of the magnificent tropical landscape. He'd noticed Amber holding a camera so had wrongly assumed he could get copies of her photos. Lucas sat across the aisle from Carlos, with Amber seated directly behind him.

Since leaving Accra, Ghana's capital, the uniformity of the canopy had been total. After a few moments, by concentrating hard, Amber's eyes had begun to discern clearings in the canopy, revealing small villages. It was difficult to distinguish details as the settlements were also predominantly green in color, from the dark green thatching of the huts to the lighter green grass which filled space between dwellings. An occasional road also could be seen, usually a greenish brown track.

Lucas and Amber were both shocked when the plane reached their destination – the GoldRock mine. The landscape instantly changed from a dappled, tropical green to a dirty, industrial brown, as the trees and undergrowth had been cleared to facilitate the exploitation of the mine. The monotony of the brown earth was broken by occasional mounds of gray-brown rock. After flying across this new landscape for little more than a minute, Amber was able to make out a runway. Still brown in color, but with a definition that suggested regular maintenance and straight edges that never occurred in nature.

As the plane began banked to continue its descent, Amber eye's noticed a change in elevation that seemed disproportionate to what her ears were telling her as the pressurized plane descended. Her first thought was that the plane must be climbing, but she quickly ruled that out as they were obviously only moments from landing. She quickly realized that what she'd sensed wasn't the plane rising, but was actually the earth falling away from their plane.

As Amber's eyes and ears reconciled the sight that was being revealed to her through the window, she realized she was looking at a monumental blemish on the face of the earth. In fact, she was looking into a monumental blemish. A man-made blemish in the form of an open cast mine.

Chapter Four

Davie's vigil continued. Three Runners had now passed by, and each time Davie couldn't help but reflect on his time in that role.

The entry level position of any organization was rarely great, and Davie's current employer was no different, except it was also a very risky job. You never had anything particularly incriminating on you, but you operated as a bridge to the Talent in the business. And Talent was always volatile. Davie had heard some stories about the Talent that made his toes curl. There had been one guy Davie had heard about who'd been very ambitious. He thought that he would build respect by pissing on a Runner. Literally urinating on him. Some of the Talent's support team had held the Runner down while the Talent pissed on him. Davie had no proof that the episode had ever really happened, but the story had quickly become an urban legend around the organization and had been repeated to him on numerous occasions. Although that perpetrator had earned some short-term respect from doing this, Davie had heard that he was quietly moved out of the organization the next month. That kind of story created publicity, and publicity was to be avoided. Davie had quickly figured that out.

The real risk of being a Runner was simply that you were new. Untrusted. Unproven. It was very easy for the Talent to blame things on the Runner. It was a reasonable conclusion. Talent was established, Runners weren't. Talent had a customer base, an established book of business, and so they had a real value to the organization. Runners brought nothing and could be replaced overnight. The couple of stories Davie had heard all ended with the Runner getting the blame. Davie had spent some time analyzing the various stories he'd heard and could see how blame could easily have fallen on the Talent. But the Runners always took the fall. Davie was glad his running days were over. He'd worked hard, been personable and had got through his apprenticeship without incident. Being a little older than the typical recruit probably hadn't hurt either, as he brought a maturity, respectability and discipline to the role that youngsters lacked.

The real challenge of his current position was that it required a level of record keeping. He was required to keep a record of who'd brought each dollar. Memories couldn't be trusted, he'd been told time and time again. Those making the drop-off needed to know that the transaction had been accurately recorded. Davie had thought about this a lot during his time as a Runner and it made good sense. It was a good control, to spread the knowledge of the cash flow between multiple people. Davie was interested in the psychology of the business, as well as the risks and the economics.

In his current job, there was more cash in his hands at the end of a shift than any of the Runners would ever see. But he'd earned the trust. Still, if someone in his position went rogue, the organization wouldn't go broke overnight. The best night he'd ever had resulted in him passing a little over seven thousand dollars up the chain. He'd made point-seven percent that night. He was sure he'd see ten grand one day, and if he ever did and decided to run off with the cash he wouldn't exactly be retiring to Rio. Plus it had been made clear to him during his training that they'd send their Recovery Team after him if he skipped out. They regularly reminded him that they'd know from the Runners exactly how much money had been passed up the chain so would know how much to tell the Recovery Team to collect. Plus they'd add an "Inconvenience Fee", Davie had been told. Davie had quickly figured out that he didn't want to spend time with the Recovery Team.

Glancing at his watch, he decided it was time to spend a few minutes warming up in the Staples.

Looking out of the plane's window, Amber's eyes widened as the mine descended deeper and deeper. She knew it had to be a man-made phenomenon from the clearly defined ridge she saw spiraling around the edge of the depression. It was not something that could have formed naturally, and she quickly realized that it had been designed to provide vehicular access to the depths. Peering closely, she could make out very small but brightly colored vehicles crawling along the narrow ridge. The vehicles seemed impossibly small from the viewpoint of the Cessna, but Amber knew she was actually looking at some of the largest industrial vehicles ever built. The scale of the mine simply dwarfed the vehicles.

Amber had read about what she was seeing before embarking on this journey, and she had seen lots of photographs, but nevertheless she realized how unprepared she was for the sheer scale of what she was seeing. What she was seeing was the remnants of a pristine wilderness that had been sacrificed to provide access to the precious metals lurking beneath. It was truly shocking to see what mankind was capable of doing to its own planet in the pursuit of profit.

Across the aisle of the plane, Lucas's professional facade had cracked a little. He'd not has as clear a view of the site as Amber, but had still found the aerial view so compelling that he couldn't help but gawp at the sights unfolding below him. Detecting the descent, Carlos had also broken his forward gaze to glance at his guests. Seeing they were fully engaged by the view from their windows, he resumed his impassive forward vigil with a barely perceptible shake of his head.

Lucas finally broke the uncomfortable silence that had held since they'd left the airport in Accra, recognizing that he now had something meaningful to talk about.

'You're forty percent complete?' Lucas strived to suppress the incredulity in his voice, but failed. Picturing the mine at two and a half times its current breadth and depth was a difficult task.

'Correct,' Carlos responded curtly, turning in his seat to address Lucas directly. 'We're already the largest mine in western Africa by excavated volume. When we reach eighty percent completion, we will be the biggest in the world.'

Carlos was hard to age, but people usually guessed that he was around forty. He clearly came from Hispanic stock, with a bronzed and weathered face which was bordered by closely cropped dark hair. An athletic physique clearly lurked beneath his black clothing, but it was his eyes that commanded the greatest attention. Gray and steely, they seemed to be older than the surrounding face. People assumed this sense of age came from Carlos having spent too much time outside, squinting to minimize the harsh effects of the sun. Rarely did people feel they knew Carlos well enough to ask.

He spoke English fluently with a trace of an accent, which was not strong, but which brought an exoticism to his speech patterns that certainly was unusual for a mine executive living in western Africa.

Amber broke her study of the view and looked at Carlos, blinking as her eyes re-accommodated to the relative gloominess of the cabin.

'Wow. It's absolutely huge,' she said. 'When do you expect to reach eighty percent completion?'

Carlos turned his head to look at Amber. 'Another four or five years of blasting. We speed up if gold prices rise. We slow down if they fall.'

He held his gaze on Amber, a gaze which she returned evenly. She realized that Carlos was examining her, looking through her exterior in an attempt to evaluate her character. By no means was it a threatening gaze, but she knew that its intensity might be unsettling for many. She sensed that Carlos's eyes could really motivate someone if that was his goal.

Amber was no stranger to receiving stares from men and had on occasion also received them from women. She was in her mid-twenties and was taller than average at five feet eight inches, with soft hazel eyes and shoulder length chestnut brown hair. All in all, she was widely regarded as being a very attractive human being. Not that she'd ever admit this; those who know her well felt that her indifference to her own attractiveness actually compounded her appeal. Amber was far more concerned about making her mark in her profession, so she swatted away any suggestion of beauty. She worried that if she yielded and acknowledged the label, it would be easy for others to use it against her as an explanation for her success.

She was wearing jeans and a smart linen shirt. She was not averse to dressing well and looking good, as looking good was the professional thing to do. That day, she had carefully selected attire that was comfortable to wear when travelling, but which still looked elegant. She would never admit that she would select clothing that flattered what was clearly an attractive physique, even if that was often the case.

'While we're over the mine,' said Lucas, 'why don't you give us an overview of the mining process? If you'll forgive the pun.' His interjection broke Carlos's gaze, not that Lucas was aware of it as his eyes had been locked on the scenery below the plane.

With a final glance at Amber, Carlos responded: 'Certainly. I instructed the pilot to do a few circuits of the property before landing.'

Lucas settled back in his seat. He knew what was coming, but his interest was in how Carlos would describe the process. He also thought that the briefing would help Amber, who he assumed would not be familiar with this particular type of mine operation.

Lucas was coming to terms with being in his thirties. He was good looking in a bookish kind of way, with a single man's taste in clothes. He was educated and informed enough to be able to identify and purchase high quality, well-fitting items of clothing, but he lacked the higher-level skills required to combine those items into effective ensembles. At five ten, he was a few inches taller than Amber, with dark brown eyes and light brown hair that was slightly unruly from being a little too long.

Lucas approached life with an openness and honesty that was certainly endearing, but which sometimes made onlookers question the depth of intelligence behind his attentive, inquisitive eyes. Not that Lucas recognized it, but this generally caused people to underestimate his abilities, mostly to their detriment.

Carlos continued. 'We're after one thing and one thing only. Gold. The days are gone when you could just walk along a river bed picking up nuggets – any material that easy to find was harvested a thousand years ago. The gold we're after here is embedded in the heart of the rock in particulate form, with each particle measuring less than one hundred microns in diameter. Which is about the thickness of a human hair. Extracting it from the rock requires some complex engineering followed by a simple chemical process.'

Amber had put down her camera and was scribbling on her notepad. Contrary to Lucas's assumption, she was already familiar with the mine's processes, having researched them thoroughly before leaving the States. Despite this, she felt a need to look attentive by scribbling down the bulk of Carlos's commentary. Something deep within her felt that this would earn her some respect. The tourist in her would have to wait for a better opportunity to sightsee.

Carlos continued: 'Every day we blast another section of the rock to rubble. Engineers set the explosives during the day, which we detonate at six o'clock each evening, when we change from the day to night shifts. This is the most efficient time as no men are in the mine during the explosion.

'This explosion dislodges a few thousand tons of gold-laden ore, which we scoop into trucks. You should be able to see these trucks from the plane, they are very large.'

Lucas and Amber both looked out of the window reflexively. As they did so, Carlos looked discretely at his watch. His delivery was measured but he made little effort to mask his disinterest. He'd done this many, many times before and he'd learned that whilst the story was fascinating to visitors, it was a real chore to deliver. Carlos continued, knowing from experience that a comprehensive description of the process now would save him from answering a hundred tedious questions later.

'Each of these trucks can move around three hundred tons of ore. They bring the material up and out of the mine along the access roads you'll be able to see around the edges of the excavation. The trucks dump their loads back on the surface, which we then scoop onto conveyor belts.

'These belts move the ore to a series of crushers, which break the ore into pebbles of a relatively uniform consistency, roughly the size of your M&Ms. This material is then carried on further conveyors and is added to large mounds of crushed ore. Those are the grayish heaps you'll probably be able to see around the edge of the facility.

'We situate these mounds very carefully. They are built on large expanses of plastic sheeting. We sprinkle a calcium cyanide solution over the ore, which leeches through the material we've gathered. As it passes through the rock, the cyanide bonds with any gold particles it encounters, creating a gold-laden solution, which is captured by the sheeting underneath the mounds. As we position these mounds uphill from the processing tanks, a combination of the sheeting and gravity channels this liquid downhill into collection ponds. We add carbon to this cyanide solution which we then pass through a smelter, which allows us to extract the gold. Simple really.'

Lucas noticed that Amber had covered several pages with notes during Carlos's lengthy monologue. Lucas realized that Carlos's description had been the most succinct explanation of the process that Lucas had ever heard. He made a mental note to get a copy of Amber's note so he could perfect the story himself for future telling. He felt a strong need to compliment Carlos, but before he could do so, Carlos indicated that both the lesson and the tour were over.

Carlos leaned forward and raising his voice shouted towards the cockpit: 'Captain – take us down'.

Chapter Five

At the end of each shift Davie took the money he'd collected to an appointed location. This location changed regularly. He'd receive a text detailing the rendezvous point at the end of each shift. Davie had thought a lot about that text too. The text always came exactly the minute his shift ended. Exactly on the minute. Tonight it would arrive at two A.M. exactly. Not one minute to. Not one minute past. Exactly at two A.M.

Where the Runners would find Davie on the street changed every day too. He received a text message notifying him where to go that day precisely an hour before his shift each day. Precisely on the hour. More often than not, Manhattan. Regularly the Bronx. Once he been sent to Hoboken, which had been a challenge to get to in the hour Davie was allowed to take to reach his pitch.

Davie had thought a lot about the notifications and had decided it was implausible that a human would be so precise each and every day. Which suggested that there was a computer somewhere, which was spitting out the texts. This in turn suggested a level of sophistication he hadn't expected to find in an organization of this kind. But then again, it was a big enterprise, with a lot of associates to coordinate. Davie could understand how it would be simpler, and in the long run cheaper, to have a computer doing this kind of chore rather than having someone on the payroll to do it. Besides, people make mistakes, computers didn't. Davie knew the organization was intolerant of mistakes. Davie was interested in the logistics of the business, as well as the psychology.

The drop-off location was usually some crappy bar with a dark and smelly back room that was used for the count. Occasionally a quiet corner of a Laundromat. Once it was in the back of a Seven-Eleven. But the process was always the same. He'd be positively identified by some hulking slab of meat on the door. He'd take his records and cash into a back room, where his contact would be sitting. Usually Jorge, occasionally Luis. Once a lean, pasty fellow who'd introduced himself as Nigel.

He'd count the cash onto the table and total up the receipts he'd documented. His counterpart would then count the cash again and when they agreed totals, both would initial the document. Initials, rather than signatures, Davie had been taught.

Davie would then be handed his wages and he'd leave. They'd come from the pocket of the person taking the cash, never from the cash he'd collected. Another detail he'd noted with interest. Often there were no words said, as the whole process could easily be carried out in silence.

Davie's cash always balanced. He'd keep a running total in his head throughout the shift and would do a quick pre-count on his way to the rendezvous. They'd warned him not to do this, not to draw the cash out in a public place before reaching the rendezvous point, but he'd figured he'd rather be one hundred percent accurate in front of his superiors even if it meant breaking a rule. Davie had never found it hard to find a restroom or a discrete corner where he could conduct a quick count to verify the total he carried in his head.

Once, early in the process when he was still learning the ropes, he'd been two dollars short. It had been a very easy decision to make up the shortfall from his own funds. A very, very easy decision as he didn't want to give his superiors any reason to distrust him or to retard his progress through the organization. It was only two bucks, but already knew that two bucks mattered to his superiors.

He'd thought about that day for some time, wondering how his total had got out of synch with his records. He was very careful to segregate his own funds from the cash he collected for the organization. But he's only been off once, but taking into account the forty-nine shifts he'd worked, he knew that would benchmark well against his colleagues. His bosses believed he'd been accurate forty-nine times out of forty-nine. Davie smiled as he realized that tonight would mark a half century of perfect counts. Maybe Jorge would congratulate him for this. Pat him on the back. Give him a bonus. Davie smiled. Probably not…

And so the cycle continued, five or six days a week. The only variation came each Wednesday. Jorge was the closest thing Davie had to a boss, and Davie always did his count with Jorge on a Wednesday. After the count, but before receiving his wages, Jorge and Davie would speak for a few minutes. Davie likened it to a continual assessment process you might see in large corporations.

Davie would report on anything he'd noticed on the streets. Specifically Jorge was interested in any Runners that Davie was suspicious of or concerned about. Not that snitching was part of the culture, but Jorge made it clear that part of Davie's role was to keep an eye on the junior associates bringing cash to him. It was made clear that this was a crucial part of the additional responsibilities Davie had signed up to when he'd been promoted.

Jorge made it clear that Davie wasn't expected to act on any concerns he raised. Jorge and others would take care of things. Even so, Davie was still new enough to the role that he hadn't felt the need to set the dogs on any of his street colleagues. He sensed that he'd be expected to offer some criticism of a Runner at some point, as he matured into his role. It would be expected. Not all Runners could be trusted, and it would be a black mark against Davie if it was felt that he was trusting everyone.

Jorge would occasionally compliment Davie on some aspect of his performance. Never his accuracy, as one hundred percent accuracy was an expectation of the job. Congratulating someone for doing their job to the minimum acceptable standard wasn't part of the organization's culture.

Instead, Jorge would often compliment Davie on his appearance or his punctuality. A token compliment to make Davie feel that the organization was pleased with him.

Jorge would usually remind him not to count his cash in public. Occasionally Jorge would tell a story about a Runner who'd gone bad. Inevitably the story ended poorly for the Runner. Davie would nod and smile, thanking Jorge for sharing the story with him, while privately acknowledging that the story was being told for a purpose. As a warning.

Davie knew that the Wednesday chats were his opportunity to develop a rapport with the higher-ups in the organization. What Jorge said didn't really matter, the fact he was taking his time to say it was what was mattered. Davie tried hard to project deference to his superior during these chats, as was required for someone in his still lowly position within the organization. But he tried to blend this with a level of self-assuredness that built confidence. Jorge would be the person to recommend Davie for promotion, as and when the time was right. Davie had been in his current position for only a couple of months, so it was too soon to hope for or to ask for a promotion. But he knew it would come.

Keep your nose clean, Davie boy, he told himself. Balance your counts. Stay out of trouble. The promotion will come…

Chapter Six

Carlos sat behind his modest desk, which seemed small for a man with such weighty responsibilities. Despite its small size, his desk was uncluttered. A laptop computer was the largest object on the desk. A flat-screen monitor sat adjacent to the laptop, with the screen angled carefully so that any visitor entering the room and sitting across the desk from Carlos would be unable to see what was displayed on his screen. A telephone and a small stack of manila folders were the only other clues that the desk was actually used.

The orderliness of the desk mirrored Carlos's office. Given the remoteness of the posting and the challenges of living for months at a time at an isolated mine site, visitors might expect to see photos of home and family providing a link to loved ones elsewhere. They might expect to at least see certificates proclaiming membership of impressive institutions. At the very minimum, keepsakes from happier postings. Carlos's office did not conform to other people's expectations. The only decorations to be found were a number of dull yet colorful topographic maps of the mine and its surroundings, maps revealing details unintelligible to a casual observer but which were essential and perhaps even enthralling to a professional geologist.

Lucas and Amber were settling into the uncomfortable visitor chairs provided across the desk from Carlos. Selecting furniture that was known to be unpleasant to use for any length of time was a tactic deployed by a certain style of leader. Carlos knew that his choice of guest seating communicated a desire for brevity to anyone choosing to sit in them. Regular visitors had learned to be so brief that they rarely even bothered to sit down.

Lucas and Amber had both cautiously glanced around Carlos's office when they'd entered, in an attempt to gain an insight into their host but failing due to the sterility of the room. It was the morning after their arrival at the mine, as Carlos had absented himself as soon as they'd arrived at the mine the previous evening. Lucas and Amber decided to refresh themselves with a good night's sleep after their lengthy journey from the United States. They were now wearing formal business attire, and while it was still early in the day, it was already very warm and extremely humid outside. A noisy air-conditioner mounted to the wall was battling valiantly to counteract the tropical heat, with limited success.

Amber was coping well with the heat, but Lucas had already developed beads of sweat on his temples. He steadfastly kept his suit jacket on, superficially to appear professional but mainly because he was fearful that tell-tales of sweat may already have appeared on his shirt which would undermine the aura of professionalism that was so important to him.

Carlos was still dressed in his customary black, and was clearly unaffected by the heat. He waited patiently as Lucas and Amber shuffled in their seats, in a vain attempt to achieve a level of comfort adequate to get them through the meeting.

On the floor beside Amber was a large brief case, similar to those carried by pilots, in which she had brought the cornucopia of files and notepads needed for the engagement. Amber pulled one of the smaller files from the case and after failing to catch Carlos's eye for approval, she delicately placed it on Carlos's desk, conscious that the Zen-like minimalism of the desk was being threatened by her actions. Hell, what choice did she have? Carlos may not appear to need files, but she and Lucas did…

Their shuffling and general discomfort was forgotten when Carlos spoke.

'You slept well?' A safe opening gambit from Carlos.

Lucas and Amber exchanged a brief glance. Both knew that Lucas would be taking charge of the conversation from their side of the table.

'Yes we did. Thank you. The accommodation is quite comfortable for such a remote location.'

'You are most welcome,' Carlos responded, his deadpan delivery conveying the exact opposite. 'Please indulge me. This is our fifth year of operation, yet the first time we've been honored with a visit...'

Carlos's sentence rather tailed off, as he invited Lucas to continue the discussion. Lucas smiled, recognizing an opportunity to take the lead and occupy familiar territory.

'Yes,' Lucas said, settling slightly deeper into the chair. 'The U.S. Congress recently passed a law requiring that all mines owned by U.S. companies comply with U.S. laws, wherever they are in the world. So we've been hired by your corporate office back in New York to certify that your operations comply with those laws.'

'That's an expensive decision,' said Carlos, deciding to probe a little to see Lucas's reaction.

'It certainly is,' Lucas replied, acknowledging the implicit criticism of the law. 'But it was also a political decision, which turned out to be very popular with the electorate. American regulations are probably the toughest in the world, so are the hardest and most expensive to comply with. But we all share the same earth.'

Lucas smiled gently, knowing as soon as he'd formed the words that they'd be lost on Carlos, as was the case with virtually everyone who made a living from the mining industry.

Carlos did not return the smile. 'Indeed. So you work for your Environmental Protection Agency?'

'Actually no,' Lucas responded quickly, refuting what was a common misapprehension. 'That would be way too much work for the E.P.A. to handle. We work for a private firm accredited by the E.P.A. to conduct these reviews.'

Carlos received this information in silence. His gaze passed to Amber, who returned it confidently. Carlos had known the answer to all of the questions before he'd asked them. In fact the entire conversation had gone according to the script Carlos had developed in his head prior to the meeting. His interest was more in how Lucas and Amber explained their roles. One issue of particular interest to Carlos had been answered, though, with the clear confirmation that Lucas was the senior member of the team. Amber did not appear to have much to offer, beyond brightening the room and taking pages and pages of notes.

Carlos decided to test his hypothesis further, and so turned to Amber as he moved to the next page of his mental script. 'So what will you be looking at?'

Amber opened her mouth to speak, eager to participate and to establish herself as a key member of the team, but Lucas was already answering before she could speak.

'We'll look at the entire process,' he said. 'From blasting through crushing, to smelting. Health and Safety of your employees, that kind of thing. Focusing particularly on your use and control of chemicals, obviously. Cyanide can be nasty stuff.' Lucas's eyes yearned for a smile from Carlos, for acceptance, for some sign of a connection at a human level.

Carlos recognized the gambit, but steadfastly refused to oblige Lucas, preferring to stare back at him without emotion. Lucas was starting to feel that this would be a long project if they failed to develop any rapport with the mine's senior executive. He was all too aware that a consultant sent to review and find fault in operations often trudged a lonely road if the level of human interaction never extended beyond the strictly professional.

'I will tell you now that you will not see the smelting process. The strictest security exists over this very sensitive area,' Carlos eventually replied.

Lucas shot a glance at Amber. 'I understand the security considerations, but it's a critical part of the process...'

'By all means raise it with your superiors. Mine have made it absolutely clear to me. Your visit is not a reason to compromise our security.'

Lucas noted the first hint of a smile on Carlos's lips as he delivered this news. His eyes shared the moment with both Lucas and Amber.

Lucas shifted in his seat. The discomfort he felt from the seating arrangements was quickly being overtaken by the discomfort he felt from the conversation.

The moment of silence dragged on but Carlos was in no hurry to fill the void. Lucas blinked first, looking at the file Amber had placed on Carlos's desk.

'Well, we can come back to that later. Let us walk you through our detailed scope of work.'

Lucas was the first to yield, and as a result lost the battle. Carlos's smile was his first of the meeting, through which he made everyone understand that he knew he'd won.

Chapter Seven

Amber sat on a deckchair outside her guest accommodation. Western visitors were allocated a simple hut which contained a bedroom, a small sitting area, a kitchenette and a bathroom. These were considered to be all of the facilities a western visitor might need to maintain an acceptable level of comfort when the nearest room-service was two hundred miles away.

It was evening and the workday was over. The day had progressed like they all did at this time of year. The first suggestion of sunrise had sent temperatures racing into the eighties en route to the inevitable mid-nineties. By lunchtime, the overcast skies had generated an oppressive fog of humidity, and the threat of an electrical storm built steadily as the early afternoon progressed. By midafternoon, the air could no longer hold the accumulated mass of moisture, which was the trigger for the late afternoon storm that released the pressure from the system. The inevitable rainfall was heavy and lasted around an hour, forcing all but essential staff to take cover. The upside was that it pulled the humidity from the air and dissipated the cloud cover, leaving the mine bathed in pleasant sunshine until sunset.

The beautiful evenings had turned out to be Amber's favorite part of the day. With the work day over and the humidity under control, Amber had come to enjoy taking some time out to watch as the setting sun painted the broad African sky with colors she didn't recognize from her current home in New Jersey or her childhood home in Louisiana.

Amber had brought a full range of clothing with her, and had wanted to put on some shorty shorts to allow the evening sun to warm her legs, and perhaps to tan them a little. But she knew she was still on duty, even if the working day was notionally over. Besides, she'd quickly decided that the testosterone-laden atmosphere of the mine was not an environment for her to be showing any skin. Some of the stares she'd received when wearing a simple pants suit had already verged on the intrusive, in her opinion. As a result she'd decided to wear jeans and a simple t-shirt that evening. Tanning would have to wait.

She leaned back in her chair and closed her eyes as she took some of the waning rays of the sun onto her upturned face. She sighed contentedly – no matter how grim or stressful work had been you still needed to take time each day to grab a moment of joy from whatever nature had on offer.

Lucas emerged from his hut, which was located next to Amber's, his hut being slightly further up the pathway which led down from the accommodation area to the administration block. He carried two bottles of Club beer, a local brew which they both preferred ahead of the competing Star brand. Lucas had listened with interest when the reasoning behind this simple branding had been explained to him. A significant proportion of rural beer-drinkers were illiterate, so the products differentiated themselves by using simple, easy to recognize logos.

Lucas's only other acknowledgement that his work day was over was to shed his suit jacket. His shirt sleeves were rolled up, and there were indeed marks on his shirt where the tropical heat had spurred his sweat glands into action. He'd resolved to shower and change clothes, but the beer came first.

Amber heard Lucas approaching and opened her eyes, squinting into the tropical twilight. She took one of the beers as Lucas sat down beside her.

'Thanks. We've only been here for three days, but it feels like a month.' Amber broke the silence, putting into words something they had both been feeling.

Lucas took a long draw from the icy beer, contemplating his response. 'I know exactly what you mean. This is a tough assignment. At least we're making good progress. We're a good team.'

Amber easily absorbed the compliment. She knew they were a good team, but she welcomed Lucas's acknowledgement of the fact. They'd taken plenty of the time during the planning phase to prepare for the trip. They'd clearly allocated responsibilities and developed a thorough plan, which they'd been methodically working through. They'd been communicating effectively thus far during the fieldwork. Amber had quickly realized that Lucas was an easy boss to work for, even if she felt that he was reluctant to stand up for them as and when contentious issues arose.

Another moment's companionable silence passed as they both enjoyed the rejuvenating effect of the cold beer.

Amber again was the one to break the silence. 'Carlos is an odd one though, don't you think? Never met anyone quite like him.'

Lucas reflected on her comment before responding. 'Yeah. He's very hard to read.' He paused again, then added: 'Plus he's the only guy we've come across who hasn't hit on you.'

Amber's cheek's flushed red at this comment. She swigged from the beer bottle in a futile attempt to conceal her face, realizing that this was Lucas at his most indiscrete. First of all, he'd obviously noticed that she'd been receiving attention, more than was perhaps usual and certainly more than was appropriate. In some ways she felt relieved to hear his comment, as his confirmation meant she'd not been imagining it. But was *he* trying to say something? Or was he just being his usual clumsy self? The beer emboldened her to push the issue and find out.

'You haven't hit on me.' She quickly took another swig of beer as she realized that the pin might now be out of the hand grenade.

Lucas contemplated his response for a moment while he studied Amber's profile. Expecting an answer, she turned her head and met his gaze. Lucas didn't sense that she was challenging him with the look, nor did he feel she was threatening him with her comment. Their eyes held each other for a long moment: neither felt that they were competing in a staring contest that had to be won. Lucas was the first to look away. He knew what he wanted to say, but he also knew that he couldn't say it directly.

'No,' he said evenly. 'I'm your boss. For this project at least. I can't hit on you. Even if I wanted to.'

Lucas looked straight ahead as Amber reflected on his words. The ambiguity left her perplexed. What was he saying? Did he want to? She felt as if a small battle had been fought without a clear winner emerging. She decided to change the subject.

'I've been wondering. Is Carlos Mexican? I don't feel any great desire to ask him directly. He doesn't welcome professional questions so I am sure he doesn't want me asking personal ones. But, if he is from that part of the world, wouldn't that be an unusual background for an African posting?'

Lucas welcomed the conversation's return to safe ground. He'd taken a risk by saying what he'd said, a risk he wouldn't usually have taken, but one he felt comfortable with given the unusual situation they were in. The mine's staff had been welcoming enough, but they'd not expected to develop any real rapport with them. Added to that was the frustration that they were so far away from home that they couldn't decompress with family and friends in the evenings. Lucas recognized that this left them more reliant on each other for emotional support than was usual. Lucas thought he'd probably overstepped a boundary but felt oddly relieved to have done so.

Lucas remembered Amber's question and was easily able to respond, as this topic was one he'd given some thought to.

'He's certainly Hispanic, but I think he's from farther south – Chile perhaps. There are quite a few big open-cast mines down that way. Copper mostly, rather than gold, so the chemistry is different, but the general principle would be the same.'

Amber nodded. Her question had been asked and answered satisfactorily, for now at least.

'Right,' she said. 'That makes sense. So how concerned are we *really* about seeing the smelting process?'

'We have no way of forcing them to let us in, but they should really be co-operating with us. We do have the full force and will of the United States Congress behind us, after all. Not that Carlos seems to be too concerned by that fact.'

Lucas took another deep draw from the beer. He looked down at his watch, as disparate thoughts merged and formed a plan in his head. He realized that the moment presented them with the chance to make some progress with the project, and at the same time he could show some backbone to Amber. Two birds with one stone – time to go for it.

'C'mon. Drink up. Let's go take a look at this smelting room. They won't invite us, so let's invite ourselves.'

Amber was shocked. 'We can't do that! We can't just go and break in...'

Amber's response hovered tantalizingly between statement and question, which only served to embolden Lucas. In that moment he felt more authoritative than ever before, and he enjoyed the feeling.

'Who said anything about breaking in?' he said. 'Let's just go take a look. They're changing shifts so there'll be no-one around. Hey, it'll be an adventure...'

Lucas jumped to his feet. Amber took a further swill from the bottle but stayed resolutely seated, observing Lucas with a mixture of amusement and anxiety. She was seeing a different side of Lucas, a side that she had hoped would reveal itself, but now it was on show she didn't quite know how to handle it.

'I didn't sign up for an adventure,' she said, perhaps a little too indignantly. 'I signed up to protect the environment.'

Lucas was standing beside her chair, and a smirk spread across his face. As Amber observed him for another long moment, she realized that she was teasing him with her resistance. She was surprised to admit that she was doing it deliberately and was shocked when she realized that she was enjoying the control she was exerting over him.

He was waiting for her to act, but was he waiting her approval for him to go alone? Or was he waiting for her to get up and go with him? Would he really not go on his own? Was he that dependent on her? Eventually she broke into a wide smile. Only one way to find out.

'OK, OK. Calm down. Let's live a little.'

Chapter Eight

Lucas opened his eyes, relieved to still be alive but distressed to see that the guards were still pointing their guns resolutely towards them. Lucas flapped his mouth in a vain attempt to speak but couldn't corral his brain into coherence.

Beside him, Amber felt as if several years' of emotions had hit her central nervous system at once, which produced an overwhelming jolt that sent her head spinning.

The three guards were shouting and gesturing wildly, both in heavily accented English and a local dialect unintelligible to Lucas and Amber. Lucas began to realize that there was a near total lack of organization in their actions, with no-one being obviously in command. He suspected that having so easily pacified the intruders without experiencing any level of resistance, the three men did not know what to do next. Their training was nevertheless good enough that they kept their guns steadfastly pointed at Lucas and Amber, which made their broad intentions clear even if specific details remained hazy.

As the first jolt of adrenaline passed, and with growing comfort that the situation had stabilized, Lucas relaxed enough to study the guards in a little more detail. As was the case with the guard who'd patrolled past earlier, they wore old and ratty uniforms, that didn't seem to fit particularly well. Their uniforms bore no insignia to denote rank or function.

Lucas realized that as he and Amber remained mercifully un-shot, it was appropriate and timely to open negotiations. Remember, he told himself, we're authorized to be here and we were doing nothing wrong. If he'd actually touched the door handle, perhaps they'd be guilty of some level of trespass, but as he hadn't got that far, there should be no problem.

'Whoa – we were just looking around.' Lucas said, attempting to modulate his voice in a display of authority and self-assuredness. He was only marginally aware that the stress had made his voice high-pitched and tremulous.

At that moment, two more people arrived. The guard who'd patrolled past them around the cyanide ponds reappeared at a jog, alerted by the hubbub. The appearance of a fourth gun pacified Lucas again. An instant later, Carlos arrived, jogging down the hill from the administration block. Lucas's beleaguered brain noted that Carlos did not appear to be out of breath or perspiring, despite the obvious exertion required to cover the distance in the short time that had elapsed. Carlos instantly assumed command of the situation.

'OK – stand down guards. Good job.'

The guards quickly exchanged glances and deferring to Carlos, they shouldered their weapons, taking a pace or two back from their still cowering captives. Lucas and Amber felt able to relax, bringing their hands down to their sides even if they remained on their knees.

Carlos continued to instruct the guards: 'They're with me.' Turning to Lucas the command was simple. 'Explain?'

Lucas slowly returned to his feet, dusting crusted mud from his knees, breathing hard in an attempt to bring his pulse and his blood pressure down to non-critical levels. He paused for an instant as he prepared his response.

He could assert that they'd every right to be there as representatives of the United States Congress. He could demand that Carlos explain why his guards had acted so aggressively with two unarmed and legitimate visitors. He could demand a full and immediate apology. But Carlos's stern demeanor and Lucas's underlying guilt at what he and Amber had actually been attempting destroyed any bravery he may have initially summoned.

'We were, er, we were going to look at the cyanide ponds. These guys just appeared out of this building.'

Carlos was clearly not impressed by this response, and neither did he appear convinced by it.

'I'm sure,' he said. 'Well you'll no doubt be surprised to learn that you're right outside our smelting room, which is the most secure building in the entire complex, hence the aggressive response. Now you've had the opportunity to see some of the security we deploy to protect this building, you'll understand that I wasn't bluffing.'

Amber had also risen to her feet, and was backing gently towards the building, vainly hoping that Carlos hadn't noticed her. As Carlos explained the significance of the building she felt less comfortable moving towards it, even though its sturdy construction seemed to provide a haven of safety. She felt a desire to speak, to explain, to provide some mitigation that Lucas seemed unable or unwilling to offer. But she smartly concluded that silence remained her best strategy. Lucas continued to take the lead.

'Yes. We've seen,' he said. 'The security is, well, it's impressive. We'd better head off – I think its dinner time back up the hill. We can check out the cyanide ponds another time. Thanks Carlos.'

Lucas nodded appreciatively to the guards, and found himself unconsciously lifting his hand part way to his temple in an amateur salute. Realizing how ridiculous he must look, he quickly lowered his hand. The guards stared back, stony-faced. He and Amber turned on their heels and trudged back up the hill towards the visitors' camp.

Carlos silently watched them depart. Turning to the guards he held each guard's eyes in turn and gave them a clear nod of approval.

Chapter Nine

Carlos sat in his office, alone. He held a cellular phone to his ear, listening to a voice many miles away. His office was as uncluttered as ever, with the door firmly closed.

'Yes. They tell me they are half way through the project,' he said into the phone. 'Apart from the brief excitement outside the smelting room, there is no cause for concern.'

Carlos wore his trademark black, and his body language echoed his lack of concern, as he leaned back comfortably in his chair, clearly feeling he was in command of both the phone discussion and the broader project.

Five thousand miles away, in a boardroom in New York, three men sat listening intently to a speaker phone which rested on a meeting table between them. Their body language could not have contrasted more sharply from Carlos's. They leaned in, intently listening to the authoritative words floating in from Africa, sporting hunched shoulders and facial expressions which fluctuated between concern and anxiety.

The man called John had assumed the role of spokesman.

'As we expected,' he said, glancing anxiously at his colleagues. The quality of the phone connection belied the distance between the participants, as there was only a minimal delay on the line.

Carlos resumed: 'Indeed. They are optimistic that they may actually finish ahead of schedule.' Murmurs of approval travelled back to Carlos's ear from the team sitting in New York.

'Our follow up precautions are in place your end?' he continued.

John retained the role of spokesman. 'Absolutely. Everything is in place. As we agreed.'

Carlos's response was simple. And short. 'Good.' He abruptly ended the call without allowing further comment.

Back in New York, John leaned in to disconnect the call, causing the cluster of red lights on the speakerphone to go dark. All three men then leaned back, gently exhaling as the pressure in the room lifted. The men looked from one to the other around the table, unsure of who was going to make the opening gambit, now they were out of Carlos's earshot.

John Showers was in his mid-forties, hair gently graying at the temples as well as thinning across the dome of his forehead. The thinning had produced a small monk's tonsure at his crown. In the battle between balding and graying, John won a special prize for suffering from both. He had once been fit, running half-marathons and cycling significant distances on a regular basis, but the challenges of an office based role had become a slippery slope down which the calories had flowed. This had resulted in a spreading midriff which was only partially concealed by his smart and expensive business suit. He looked between the other two men and moved to fill the conversational void.

'Phase one is nearly complete. So we can shortly move to phase two.' His words formed more of a statement than they did a question.

The other men were relieved to be able to respond to John's commentary, rather than to lead. They nodded enthusiastically in agreement. After another exchange of glances, they all rose to leave.

Back at the mine in Ghana, another few days passed without incident. Lucas and Amber had learned their lesson and stayed well away from both the smelting room and the cyanide ponds, knowing they'd get nowhere without official approval and a guide.

They'd talked about the episode at the smelting building on a number of occasions and had concluded that it had been a misguided excursion from start to finish. Amber felt that Lucas had been annoyingly apologetic about the whole thing, as she felt he'd pushed her into accompanying him, exposing her unnecessarily to danger. They had concluded that they should just respect the security over what was obviously a very important part of the mining process.

They had continued to ask Carlos about when they'd be able to review the operations within the smelting hut, but all of their enquiries had met with such resolute refusal that they'd grudgingly dropped the subject entirely.

Otherwise, their project had gone smoothly. Their overriding conclusion was that Carlos was running a very tight ship. Every associate that Lucas and Amber had spoken to clearly knew their responsibilities and were able to explain them effectively. They could also readily describe the procedures supporting their areas of accountability. These procedures in turn seemed to be appropriate to their purpose.

With the exception of the smelting process, Lucas and Amber were able to complete their work to a satisfactory degree, and Lucas felt that their documentation was in great shape to be reviewed by their engagement partner back in New York. They actually found themselves ahead of schedule, so even had a day to spare before they were due to leave.

An exit meeting was a traditional formality at the end of an engagement such as this, so Lucas and Amber joined Carlos in the mine's board room to review the work they'd completed and the conclusions they'd drawn. Lucas and Amber sat next to each other on one side of the table, facing Carlos across the table in an adversarial configuration that so often occurred at such meetings.

Aside from the expansive meeting table and the dozen chairs that surrounded it, the board room was otherwise very plain. The now familiar geophysical maps decorated the walls, along with a large clock.

At the far end of the room was a small bureau, upon which sat a yellow cube. Measuring about three feet square, it was made of polystyrene and sat rather incongruously on the bureau without any clear explanation of its purpose. Lucas and Amber had both noticed it earlier in their engagement, but neither had had the opportunity to ask what it represented.

The meeting was drawing to a close, and over the course of the discussions papers and files had been spread liberally over the visitors' side of the table, the output from the dozen or so working days they had put in at the mine. Carlos had brought a legal pad to the meeting, and had nearly filled a page with notes as a token gesture of buy-in. Nevertheless his disinterest in the process was clear.

Lucas had commented to Amber when they'd taken a brief break that it would have been usual for several of Carlos's senior managers to attend a meeting such as this. They'd both been surprised when Carlos had elected to attend alone, and his attitude and curt responses to their comments furthered the impression that he would have preferred to skip the meeting himself.

Amber currently held the talking stick, having led the fieldwork supporting the part of the engagement being discussed. 'So we agree that your plans for reacting to a cyanide spill need improvement and there are opportunities to recycle some of the less toxic chemicals.'

Carlos looked at Amber impassively during her report. Taking a short note, he responded succinctly. 'I understand.'

He looked pointedly at the wall clock. 'So that concludes our agenda.' Once again he showed an aptitude for phrasing a question as a statement, in a manner that clearly discouraged argument.

Lucas leaned forward, conscious of the adversarial atmosphere Carlos was creating. Carlos started to rise from the table.

Lucas held up a hand. 'There is one more issue. We haven't reviewed the smelting and handling of the gold.'

Carlos settled back into his seat with a sigh.

'Despite your best efforts to breach our security,' Carlos added, somewhat aggressively.

'We apologize again for that misunderstanding, and we say again that we were just going to look at the cyanide pond. But we really do need to see the smelter in action before we can complete our report.'

'As I said when you arrived, our security must come first.'

'We understand the need for security. But *you* must understand *our* need to do our job.'

'The strength of our security is the reason you can't complete your job. That's all there is to say. So we're done here?'

Lucas and Carlos locked eyes across the table. Amber could feel the tension building and found herself holding her breath, waiting for someone to blink. The silence prevailed for several seconds, neither man wanting to back down. To Amber's disappointment, Lucas once again conceded defeat by looking down to his notes.

'Yes. We're done,' he said.

The irresistible force couldn't shift the immovable object. All three relaxed as the clouds of confrontation passed.

'Good,' Carlos continued briskly, with a lighter tone to his voice. 'A car will be waiting to take you to the airport at eight tomorrow morning. I am afraid that the jet is otherwise engaged.'

This statement was delivered with the first genuine smile Amber had seen from Carlos since they'd arrived. Amber thought it was a little petty for Carlos to be celebrating the consignment of his guests to a five hour car journey.

Carlos rose once again to leave. Amber halted his departure with a question.

'Before you go – what's that box? In the corner?'

Carlos followed Amber's eye line and looked at the small yellow cube. He surprised Amber by smiling genuinely for a second time.

'That represents the gold we produced in our last fiscal year,' Carlos said. 'Five hundred and six thousand ounces.'

Carlos crossed the room and picked up the cube, which was very light as it was made of polystyrene. Carlos balanced it effortlessly on the palm of one hand.

'If this was made of real gold, it would weigh around sixteen thousand kilograms,' he continued in a lecturing tone. 'Which is about eighteen of your American tons. It would be worth over six hundred million dollars at today's prices.'

With a final smile he gently tossed the cube towards Amber, who easily caught it between her hands, an impressed look on her face. Carlos quickly left the room.

Amber looked at Lucas and they both smiled.

'That's not much volume for such a high value,' Amber said. 'I knew gold was one of the densest elements, but it's almost impossible to believe that such a small volume of gold could weigh eighteen tons.'

'Yeah, it's genuinely impressive,' Lucas replied, taking the cube from her and bouncing it on his hand. 'All this for just that.'

They exchanged another smile and started to corral the paperwork back into the pilot cases. Neither spoke for a moment, both reflecting on the moment of confrontation over the smelting room, but both scared to directly address it. Lucas knew he'd been weak and had hated to be defeated in front of Amber. But he knew that Carlos wasn't going to yield, and nothing Lucas could have said would have changed that.

Lucas knew that the sanctions available to Congress were significant if a mine failed to receive the certification they'd mandated. As it currently stood there was no way that the GoldRock facility could be certified while such a major aspect of the operation remained uninspected. Carlos did not appear to realize the consequences of his actions, or if he did, he did not seem to care about them.

Amber elected to take the conversation in a different direction.

'What do you think they will do with the site when there's no more gold?' she asked.

'Very little material will have actually left the site by the time the mine is decommissioned. There'll be a large hole and an almost equally large mountain right next to it. It's not cost effective to put the mountain back into the hole, so they usually just flood the mine to make a lake. I don't know if this part of Ghana needs a recreational lake half the size of Delaware though...'

Lucas and Amber both laughed heartily. They knew they'd completed a difficult job to a high standard. They'd been operating well behind enemy lines and had suffered no casualties, leaving aside their one near-death experience.

Without expressing it, they knew it had been a bonding experience for the both of them.

Chapter Ten

The next morning, Lucas and Amber woke to their last day in western Africa. For this visit at least.

For Lucas, the joyous sense of freshness he experienced when stepping out of the shower would be short-lived as the humidity would grab him and start to shake the sweat loose from his glands before he'd even set foot outside of his guest hut.

Lucas decided he was still 'on duty' even if the day was going to be devoted to travelling, so he selected his last remaining unworn formal shirt and slipped on his suit pants. Feeling both guilty and rebellious at the same time, he carefully folded his suit jacket and returned it to his suitcase for the journey. To hell with it, he thought.

For Amber, the just-showered freshness would last a little longer into the day, as her southern upbringing brought with it a sterner resistance to the rigors of tropical heat and humidity. Unlike Lucas, she considered her work to be complete, so she unhesitatingly selected a casual shirt and jeans from her suitcase. She was prepared to allow comfort to trump professionalism given the rigors of the journey ahead.

At the stroke of seven thirty, Amber heard a knock on the door. She opened it and greeted one of the Ghanaian office staff who had been deputed to be the official porter for their departure. Beside him stood Lucas, sweat already beading up around the temples but nevertheless sporting a broad smile. The end was near…

Their porter effortlessly grabbed Amber's bulky suitcase, pleased to be able to now counterbalance the weight of Lucas's case already in his other hand. Without a glance behind her, Amber pulled the door to the guest hut closed. For this year, at least.

Lucas and Amber followed their porter down the gentle incline to the administration block, where a four wheel drive vehicle was waiting to take them on the grueling drive to the airport. Lucas and Amber had wondered privately whether the non-availability of the jet to fly them back to the capital that morning was punishment for their unauthorized excursion to the smelting room. After some debate, they had concluded that even Carlos wouldn't be that petty. They knew that Carlos had met with some Government officials in Accra on the morning of their arrival, which adequately explained why the jet had been available for them and Carlos to share when they had arrived in the country.

To their surprise, many of the local staff had assembled by the Land Cruiser to see them off. Friendly faces all, given Carlos's conspicuous absence. Lucas took the lead in acknowledging the gesture and was able to say a few words of thanks for the hospitality. Further embarrassment followed when the appointed spokesman produced two small gifts and passed them to Lucas and Amber, a gesture which was amplified by a spontaneous round of applause from the assembled group.

Fifty yards away, up the slope towards the accommodation units and hidden from sight by the dining block, Carlos watched the display of sentimentality with distaste. He was cautious to ensure he remained unseen, but he had peered around the edge of the building throughout the small ceremony. He found himself wondering how two outsiders who were tasked with finding fault could end up being so popular with the people they were reviewing? Indeed, how could they be so popular that people would buy gifts on their departure? Carlos knew that his team would not be so presumptuous as to request the cost of such gifts be reimbursed by the company, so knew that they must have been funded from their own pockets. Perplexing…

Carlos's attention was snapped back into focus by the slamming of a car door. Just behind him, again out of sight from the assemblage below was another Land Cruiser, into which a large Ghanaian was loading luggage. A considerably smaller white man stood beside the vehicle, quietly observing Carlos.

Carlos never failed to be impressed by Dirk Bekker. Small in height and weight but not in attitude, Carlos and Dirk had worked together on numerous projects over the years. Their relationship was one of mutual respect, forged by a shared complicity in certain unspoken deeds, which allowed Dirk a level of informality with Carlos that Carlos had always quietly resented but knew better than to correct. As long as Dirk remained loyal and efficient, Carlos had resigned himself to accepting the disrespect that Dirk's informality implied. Also, Dirk's fee had not increased in the last three years, which Carlos greatly respected. Their mutual complicity might have given Dirk ample leverage for negotiation if he had so chosen.

The Ghanaian was a local resource called George Mensah, who had previously worked with Dirk on a few projects around the region, but who had not yet left the Dark Continent. Dirk had vouched for George, noting his talent for a certain type of project, and had expressed a willingness to develop him by working together on future projects. The black and white skin combination also happened to suit Carlos on this occasion.

George was large, very large in Ghanaian terms and he would not have looked out of place on the Green Bay Packers' defensive line. He had started his career as a laborer at the mine, but George had shown himself to have an intelligence well superior to his peers, along with an unwavering loyalty which allowed him to take on the more morally ambiguous tasks without question. Most importantly, he had the discretion to keep details of those tasks very much to himself, which was an essential criteria for success in Carlos's world.

Carlos and Dirk exchanged glances. No words were exchanged as the briefing they'd completed the previous day had been thorough. Carlos turned his attention back to the gathering below, in time to see Lucas and Amber climbing into the back seats of the Land Cruiser, accompanied by a local driver and security guard as was the local convention.

White people driving themselves through central Ghana would be too great a temptation for local opportunists out to make a quick buck through extortion or worse. It was not unheard of for newborn girls to be thrown in the path of vehicles driven by white drivers. A baby girl is considered a financial drain to a family over the first decade of its life, so the compensation paid by the guilt-stricken white driver, or more likely by their employer, carried considerably more value to the family than the daughter. Such were the realities of life in the region.

Dirk joined Carlos as they watched the group wave to the car as it departed. Silently, Carlos shook Dirk's hand and watched as George climbed into the driver's seat. Dirk slipped into the passenger seat. The second Land Cruiser pulled away moments after the first.

Ghana's main airport, the Kotoka International Airport was located close to the center of the capital city, Accra. An important hub for air travel in western Africa, it was still rather basic and challenging for inexperienced travelers. Experienced Africa hands much preferred it to the chaos to be found in Lagos or Abidjan, but Lucas and Amber were more familiar with the first world comforts of La Guardia, so approached it with great trepidation and anxiety.

When they had arrived in the country, VIP privileges had been provided by GoldRock such that immigration formalities had been completed in a small, private room close to their arrival gate. This had allowed them to connect quickly onto the mine's corporate jet without having to leave the tranquility of the secure area of the airport. Their arrival that morning at the front doors of the departure terminal came as quite a shock.

Quite simply, it was a scrum. Close to two thousand people were clustered outside the main entrance doors to the terminal, ebbing and flowing in an attempt to see into the building. Barriers had been erected in an attempt to corral the crowds, but they'd been largely dismantled through the day with the result that the crowd now went where it chose. Security guards manned each door into the terminal, scanning the documents of those who had made it through the scrum to ensure they were entitled to enter the building.

This scrutiny became less intense with the provision of a crisp U.S. bank note, at a minimum one bearing the face of Andrew Jackson. This was the generally accepted entrance fee for the crowd of fixers, pickpockets, chancers and outright thieves who made a living from roaming the halls of the airport, preying on whatever gullible souls they found within.

The mine's driver deposited Lucas and Amber into this melee, along with their security guard. Lucas and Amber's white faces exempted them from the worst of the shoving, as the chances of white folk being at the airport for reasons other than travel were slim. The people outside the terminal also knew that the fixers, pickpockets, chancers and outright thieves waiting in the terminal would not appreciate any impediment or delay to the white folks' progress into the building.

The security guard from the mine carried their bags as far as the terminal's doors. The guard ignored some noisy resentment among the locals, some of whom hoped to earn a few cedis from helping the travelers with their luggage. The guard did this because he knew there were plenty of others who hoped to make a lot of cedis from disappearing into the crowd with his guests' bags.

The guard deposited Lucas and Amber into the brief custody of the door's guard, and shook hands with them before departing. Their travel documents quickly afforded them entry into the building.

Once inside the terminal, Lucas and Amber were able to breathe a little easier. The offers of assistance with the luggage were still forthcoming, but they were considerably easier to resist. Lucas quickly spotted the United Airlines Business Class check-in desk, where the extensive security hurdles associated with travel to the U.S.A. would bring some level of familiarity to the otherwise foreign environment.

While crossing the room to join the check-in line, Lucas and Amber's attention was fully engaged in avoiding collisions with fast moving locals, so it was no surprise that they failed to notice Dirk and George moving smoothly through the terminal behind them. George's bulk created a flying wedge effect through the crowds, behind which Dirk was able to make quick progress. White faces were more common inside the terminal, and Dirk's clothing and general comfort with the environment allowed him to easily blend into the surrounding tapestry of color.

When they reached the check-in line, Lucas was pleased to note that there were two counters open and only three people ahead of them in the line. At the head of the line was a Ghanaian couple and behind them a white businessman.

The businessman turned and smiled at Lucas when he sensed a presence behind him. His eyes quickly scanned Lucas up and down, but lingered more luxuriantly on Amber, whose eyes were still anxiously jumping from face to face around her as she strived to come to terms with the confusing environment. The tension was yet to relax from her body.

'Congratulations, you made it,' said the businessman to Lucas with a smile. He was tall, a good four inches taller than Lucas with a friendly bronzed face and sandy hair. He was well dressed in a lightweight sports jacket, dark blue shirt and linen pants, and he gave the impression of someone who was very comfortable in such confusing environs. Lucas tried to place the accent he'd heard, but as it had been neutered by years of international travel Lucas failed to pick the businessmen's nationality as Australian.

Lucas nodded. 'Is it always like this?'

'No. The Haj pilgrimage just finished in Saudi. Those people outside are waiting for their relatives to come home. The chaos inside is pretty normal.'

Amber had calmed a little and became aware of a conversation taking place beside her. As she focused on the businessman, the Ghanaian couple at the front of the line moved up to one of the counters, allowing those remaining in line to take two paces forward.

'Must be a big plane,' Amber said.

'No, actually. There's only one plane provided by the Saudis for their Moslem brothers down here. It goes back and forth with whoever in Saudi was at the airport and was ready to come home.' The businessman smiled, happy to be able to educate some virgin Africa hands.

'So why all the people?' asked Amber.

'People don't know which flight their relatives are going to be on. So they come and meet every flight until their relatives show up.'

Lucas was fascinated by this. 'That's real devotion.'

'Getting to Mecca is a big deal for a Ghanaian.'

The businessman glanced over Lucas's shoulder and saw Dirk and George, standing a little way down the terminal in the Business class check-in line for the British Airways flight to London. Standing in a crowd of Ghanaians, Dirk's white skin stood out.

'Excuse me,' said the businessman. 'There's an old colleague of mine. Hey Klaus!'

With a wave and an elevated voice, his gesture apparently went unnoticed by Dirk. Indeed Dirk actually turned subtly away in response to the businessman's call. Lucas and Amber instinctively looked at the crowd of people gathered in the vicinity of the British Airways counters.

The businessman frowned as he turned back to face Lucas. 'That's odd. You'd think he'd remember me, given the project we worked on together. We bonded, as you'd say.'

Lucas turned back to the businessman, abandoning the search for the elusive Klaus. Amber continued to scan faces until her eyes were caught by George's. A thousand eyes were straining to make contact with Amber's but George's were the ones that connected. He returned her stare with intensity.

Amber flicked her eyes away and noticed a smaller white man standing beside the large black man. The white man stood side on to Amber, but as she observed him he furtively glanced over his shoulder in her direction, after which he appeared to be speaking to the black man. Amber shuddered. She was no stranger to being looked at, but the intensity of the stare from the large man blended with the furtive glance from the smaller man sent chills down her spine.

'What line of work are you in, exactly?' asked Lucas, unaware of the interaction taking place between Amber and George.

'We like to call it "Private Security",' the businessman replied with a wink.

The Ghanaian couple had quickly completed their formalities and vacated a check-in desk. They passed Lucas and the businessmen on the way to the departure gates examining their boarding passes with excitement.

'I don't want to know, do I?' asked Lucas with a smile, as the businessman turned, preparing to move up to the counter.

'On the contrary – I find most people are fascinated...' said the businessman enigmatically, before walking briskly up to the counter.

Lucas turned to Amber with a smile, but he quickly noticed that Amber appeared unsettled. George had held her gaze again for some moments, before turning and talking to his white travelling companion. Amber shook her head.

'Are you all right?' asked Lucas, with a concerned frown.

The second check-in desk had become free, and Lucas steered Amber forward.

'Sure – but I am *really* ready to leave this country now,' replied Amber.

The check-in attendant had overheard this, and her quizzical expression quickly made this obvious to Amber.

'Oh, I'm sorry. I didn't mean to...' Amber blustered, embarrassed to have slandered an entire country in front of one of its fine upstanding citizens.

The check-in attendant replied with a warm smile 'Don't worry – I hear it all the time. I'd leave too if I could find a nice cute westerner like yours. Hang on to him!'

Lucas and Amber looked at each other with a mix of embarrassment and amusement. After a short struggle, amusement won and they both dissolved into laughter, which they shared with the check-in attendant. The tension was released, George's ominous presence quickly forgotten.

Chapter Eleven

Detective First-Grade Charlie DiCarlo was tired. Very tired. He'd spent the last few months doing the tedious groundwork necessary to build a case. The seniority of his "First-Grade" title didn't exempt him from this tedium; indeed he'd achieved this elite ranking because he was so good at it. Too good at it, he sometimes thought.

He'd spent so little time in the precinct building recently that many of the cubicles he passed were occupied by faces he didn't recognize as he walked through the building to his office. That had become a normal experience for Charlie over the last few years, so he generally paid little attention to any newcomers and focused instead on getting to the haven of his office without delay. In turn, the newcomers paid little attention to him as he passed.

Charlie wasn't interested in making new acquaintances anyway, not at this delicate stage of an investigation. He was happy to remain anonymous, a ghost almost, he thought to himself. It helped that he worked hard to appear forgettable, and his physical appearance provided a perfect platform for him to achieve his goal. He was of average height and he worked hard to maintain an average weight. A six foot seven, three hundred and fifty pounder wouldn't get far in Charlie's world. Neither would a man who shared Charlie's five foot nine inches of height, but weighed one hundred and one pounds. Charlie kept himself fit, as was necessary for his job and his self-confidence, but the need to retain his averageness gave Charlie license to occasionally indulge in a pizza or burger to keep his weight up at his target of one hundred and sixty pounds.

He had brown hair, at a short but not too short length, which nicely complimented his brown eyes. A comparison of his appearance today to his driving license photo taken ten years earlier would reveal a slight thinning of the hair at the temples, but this was nothing unusual for a man in his mid-thirties and Charlie did not suffer from an excess of vanity in this regard. His skin wasn't pasty, but it also wasn't so tanned as to suggest any specific ethnicity. His clothing was bland, sourced from a mall rather than from a designer boutique. He had the knack of skillfully blending together items in muted colors to look somewhat stylish but at the same time not so stylish as to be memorable.

His appearance was so average he was almost invisible. If he hadn't chosen a career in law-enforcement, he often thought that he'd have made an excellent criminal as he'd be so difficult to pick out of a line-up.

He closed the door of his office and slipped off his jacket, hanging it on a hook behind the door. It was getting close to lunchtime, an important landmark for many of his colleagues in the cubicles outside, so although he knew he wasn't likely to be interrupted, he enjoyed the privacy he obtained by closing the door. Anyone who he wanted to see wouldn't be deterred by a closed door anyway, and closing the door had become a subtle way of communicating to others that he was actually in his office.

He looked around his office and saw that little had changed from when he'd last been there, a few days prior. A few additional files had appeared on his desk and an additional few push-pins had been added to a large map of the greater New York area that hung on a wall. Charlie's eyes, though tired, noted the new pins and he paused briefly at the board to ensure they'd been correctly positioned. After moving one pin a block south, he nodded approval and took a seat behind his desk.

After grabbing a Coke Zero from a small bar fridge that took up a large part of the foot well of his desk, he settled in to review the files that had been added to his stockpile.

Charlie had shown an affinity with large and complex cases from the very start of his career with the N.Y.P.D. He'd rapidly been promoted out of a uniform into an investigative role as his talents had been recognized by his superiors. Over the years he'd become a specialist at breaking up major crime operations in the city. Not your nickel-and-dime street corner drug dealers or dodgy pawn shops, but serious criminal enterprises with significant resources and sophistication. Building cases was a long, slow process but Charlie enjoyed it and was one of the N.Y.P.D.'s best at what he did.

The case he was working on was a complicated one, the most complicated one of his career. He'd gotten approval to open the investigation a little over nine months earlier, and he'd made respectable progress in that time, even if there was still a long way to go before they'd even think of requesting the flurry of warrants that he hoped would shut the criminals down. Charlie himself had written the proposal to open up the case and had worked hard to get approval.

The trigger for starting the investigation was a series of whispers received from various informers and other friends of the department that Charlie had accumulated over several years while working on other cases. Charlie's analytical mind had synthesized the information and had come up with a theory, which he'd eventually shared with his bosses.

Initially the theory was not taken seriously; indeed it was actually laughed at in some of the corner offices, although never in the presence of Charlie himself. The powers that be felt that it was incredible that the central plank of the theory could possibly be true, and besides, Charlie himself admitted that there were a number of assumptions in the hypothesis that required a leap of faith.

Charlie readily acknowledged that his theory was far from complete, and so was not disheartened by the initial skepticism. He continued to develop his hypothesis over the next few months while working on other cases. He knew that major criminal operations never were obvious by definition, and after a few months of lobbying, Charlie persuaded his bosses that the investment of a few weeks of his time would not be wasted. Shortly thereafter, he rotated off his other cases and started to develop his hypothesis full time.

Those first few weeks had produced a steady flow of solid information, which did nothing to undermine the central theory. Every time his case and its resourcing had come up for review, there had always been enough new material and enough increased suspicion that the powers that be granted an extension to Charlie on each occasion.

The weeks had turned into months. Charlie's bosses could see he was making good progress and after three months he had enough solid evidence in the books to take down a large number of individuals involved in the periphery of the crime ring. But they weren't the main protagonists, and the evidence gathered pointed to a criminal enterprise of a complexity and sophistication rarely, if ever, seen.

Certainly, taking a dozen or more fringe players off the streets would be a success that would validate the investment of Charlie's time and produce a healthy public relations victory for the department. The loss of that many bad guys, even peripheral ones, would certainly damage the wider operation, so several senior officers advocated banking the wins and closing down Charlie's operation. But the consensus was that Charlie was onto something really significant, even if the exact nature and scope of the wrongdoing was still unclear. So his authorization to operate was extended again and again.

After six months on the case, Charlie knew he was close to blowing the lid off of something monumental. The nature of his investigations meant he was rarely in the office, so his visit that day was going to be a brief one, to give some information he'd gathered directly to his superiors and to take the pulse of the department by spending an hour or two in its midst. Charlie didn't miss the politicking and associated bullshit when he was out of the office, but he recognized that he worked for a high profile organization that was innately political in its structure, so it was important to be seen to remain part of the department. Nevertheless, he was most interested in nailing the bad guys…

Charlie leaned back in his chair and opened the first file. As he read, he opened his mind to allow the information to soak in. His technique was to approach new data with a completely open mind, to file the information away without consciously processing it as he read it. This allowed his subconscious to make any connections that may exist with data already in his head. Often this often happened as soon as he closed the file. Occasionally it happened weeks after he first encountered the data. But Charlie knew it would happen.

Charlie knew the term "photographic memory", but had never bothered to take the time to investigate whether that was the explanation for the skill he had. It was just what he did, whatever it was called. Either way, he knew that this particular skill was his real asset, that it was the real explanation for his success as a detective, and was the real reason why his bosses allowed him to run his hunches. He also knew it would eventually allow him to crack the case wide open as soon as he'd gathered enough data for his subconscious to be able to join the dots. He hoped that would be sooner rather than later.

He took a sip from the can, and began to read.

Chapter Twelve

Davie Eason was having an interesting day. The day had started normally, as they usually did. He'd received the usual text which directed him to his posting for the day. Today this was mid-town Manhattan, on Second Street between Fifty-Fourth and Fifty-Fifth streets. This was a fairly regular posting so Davie knew the area well, and he knew there were a supermarket a block south and a McDonalds a block north, inside of which he could take periodic refuge from the unseasonably cold wind. The days passed more agreeably when there were convenient locations close by to use as a break room.

He'd already donned the regulation uniform – jeans, but not blue jeans, a dark hoodie jacket and Converse sneakers. He slipped a green wristband over the sleeve of his jacket, pushing it up his arm far enough for friction to hold it in place. He knew from his days as an entry-level Runner that the wristband was his signal to the world that he was open for business.

The process was simple. A Runner would approach – Davie never found them difficult to spot half a block or more away – they had a distinct look to them that made them stand out. They were always younger than Davie, they were usually nervous and would be dressed very similarly to him. If they were new, they'd be walking slowly, searching for their contact. Older hands moved more confidently. Davie knew almost everyone by now after fifty-plus shifts as a collector, but would still see a new face every week or so.

The Runner knew which block their collector was on, having received a text with the information at the start of their shift. Davie had no reason to believe the system had changed since his time as a Runner. They would approach when they positively identified their collector from his wristband. The collector, when he saw the Runner approaching, would use his other hand to twist the wristband around his arm which was the signal that he was available and the transaction could continue. Only then would they pretend to notice each other. They'd come together and would embrace like old friends.

Their interaction would follow a closely defined script. They'd clasp hands, right hand to right hand, the thumbs upturned with their fingers gripping the other's hand, as if preparing to arm-wrestle. This was a typical greeting among the youngsters they were pretending to be, but the grip would allow the Runner to palm the roll of cash into the collector's hand without exposing it to public display. They'd talk for a moment as if they were two old friends. They'd talk briefly about a sports game from the previous day, the Runner commiserating with the collector that his team lost. The Runner would joke that the collector needed to pay up from losing a wager they'd made on the game.

The collector would now have the cash secreted in his hand. He'd reach into his inside jacket pocket and would quickly pull his hand back out into the open, still palming the cash, in a movement which suggested to any onlooker that the cash had been in his pocket all along. Money deposited.

He'd then leaf through it, actually counting it but making it look to a passer-by as if he was searching for a specific note. Once happy with the total, the collector would verbally communicate it to the Runner, saying he only had that much on him. He'd then offer the Runner a bill chosen at random as if in settlement of their bet. If the total quoted by the collector was right, the Runner would refuse to take the note, making a show as if he wasn't interested in taking his friend's money. Money verified.

If the total was wrong, the Runner would take the bill, which would cause the collector to leaf through the roll again, recounting it, as if looking for a further note. A second bill would be offered along with a new verbal total. If the total was now correct, the Runner would return the original bill with a laugh and the count would be confirmed.

If the count still did not tally, the collector would make a show of passing the entire roll to the Runner with a huge laugh, as if his friend had cleaned him out with his betting acumen. The Runner would take the roll and would later go to a discrete location to recount it. The Runner would also receive a black mark on their record for not knowing the total they were depositing. The Runner would then repeat the process later that shift. Davie had never known a Runner miss his totals twice.

Once the total was agreed, as it usually was, the two men would talk for another few moments, shooting the shit about sports, clothes or women. Finally, the collector would start to wrap up the conversation, and would draw a business card from his pocket, and write a number on the back – perhaps the phone number of a girlfriend, perhaps another friend. The last digits of the telephone number would correspond to the amount deposited. This served as the receipt for the deposit that the Runner could take with them to return to the talent. Money confirmed.

With the transaction completed, the depositor would leave with the card and the collector would have the cash and an agreed, documented total. After a few minutes, the collector would take out his cell phone, the twenty-first Century's ideal cover for note taking. He'd clack away at the keys for a moment, as if updating his status on Facebook, Tweeting to his friends or any one of a hundred other telephonic diversions that would appear entirely normal to a passer-by. In reality he was recording the deposit into a notepad utility.

Davie had reflected on this process at length. All Runners went through the process in detail during their training and all collectors knew the process from having been a Runner. So by the time Runners and collectors met on the streets, the handover would be completely fluent and would look to a passer-by to be two friends catching up. Even if the collector was under surveillance and directional microphones had picked up the conversation, there was nothing said that was untoward or incriminating. Just two friends talking sports and girls. It was really a very clever way of processing large numbers of transactions in a secure way, or at least as secure a way as was realistic given the wider context of the transaction.

Before leaving home each morning, Davie would check he had a stack of the business cards in his pocket. The cards were for a gentleman's tailor in Greenwich Village. Davie had checked one day and the store was a real one - another example of the kind of attention to detail from his bosses that Davie respected and appreciated. He would check that he had three functioning pens in his pocket. Finally, he would unclip his fully charged cell phone from its charger. Only then was Davie good to go.

That day, he'd arrived at his post on Second Avenue five minutes before the start of his shift, giving him enough time to conduct a quick reconnaissance tour of his appointed block to make sure there were no red flags that might jeopardize his operations. He was looking for obvious things like parked cop cars, as well as less obvious issues, like the trivial kind of transgressions that might attract the attention of the authorities. Things like a car parked too close to a hydrant, that kind of thing. This pre-shift diligence wasn't in his job description, but Davie took it upon himself to add the step to his routine as it was his ass that was exposed on the streets, not Jorge's. He was sure Jorge's ass was hanging out in a dozen other ways, but Davie enjoyed his liberty and intended to retain it.

So far that shift, he'd taken two deposits totaling just over seven hundred dollars. Unusually high totals, he'd noted. It was too early to calculate his take as a meaningful percentage of the total collected. Nothing seemed amiss.

His day had taken a turn towards the unusual when he'd received a call from Jorge. Davie had been on post for a little under two hours. He'd only received one call from Jorge in his entire time with the organization, and that had been on the day he'd been promoted to collector.

On that occasion, he'd been summoned to a brief meeting with Jorge, in the back room of a pizzeria. Thirty minutes later he'd been standing on Ninth Avenue wearing the coveted green wristband, collecting cash from Runners. When he saw Jorge's name on his hone's called ID, Davie hoped today would be similar, and would bring another promotion. Davie was by no means clear on what the roles and responsibilities of the next position up the organization's hierarchy were, but he was keen to learn.

The next level up the organization was swathed in mystery. Davie doubted Jorge (or Juan, or Nigel) were the ones to take the cash to the next stop in its journey, which suggested there was another layer of "Super-Runner" above him. They'd probably have substantial amounts of cash in their custody at any one time, potentially tens of thousands of dollars. This suggested strongly that these roles needed to be filled with people who'd acquired a significant level of trust in the organization. Davie had thought a lot about this next role.

He knew Jorge wasn't a Super-Runner. Jorge operated as a co-coordinator. He was a trusted cog in the process, certainly, but he was someone whose job was simply to manage street teams, which didn't strike Davie as being a role integral to the success of the wider organization. Given the risks associated with frequently associating with the collectors, Davie doubted Jorge knew much detail about what happened upstream. So perhaps Jorge would be introducing him to someone further up the organization chart who'd then invite Davie into the narrower circle of trust and knowledge. Davie had been looking forward to that day since he'd begun working as a collector.

Jorge was extremely brief on the call, using the minimum words required to summon Davie to a location that they'd used a couple of times before for their Wednesday drop-offs and subsequent fireside chats. Jorge was terse on the phone, offering no clues as to the purpose of the meeting. Davie was simply told to come to the rendezvous as soon as possible. Davie was inclined to oblige.

Charlie DiCarlo was excited as he walked briskly down Sixth Avenue. The sidewalk was crowded, so his instinct and desire to run had to be suppressed. Instead, he walked as quickly as he could without crashing into too many of his fellow pedestrians.

The call had come out of the blue, but it represented the best chance he'd had so far to blow the lid off this case. It was still likely that he'd have to continue digging once he'd gathered all the information he was going to get from his contact, but he was excited that this could be the real thing.

The files he'd read earlier in his office had added little to his understanding of the operation under investigation. As was to often the case, they included a lot of speculation but very little concrete evidence. Which meant one of three things. Charlie could be chasing ghosts, pursuing a conspiracy that didn't actually exist. No proof could be found because there was nothing to prove. Everything he'd seen and heard was explained by something far more mundane than a major criminal conspiracy. Charlie knew this was unlikely, but was experienced enough to realize that it remained an option. A severely career limiting option for him, given the time he'd spent chasing his hunch and the energy he'd put into the investigation. He shuddered at the thought that he could have spent months on a wild goose chase, but his gut knew there was gold at the end of this rainbow.

The second option was that no-one had yet put in the hours or the legwork required to produce the kind of concrete evidence that was needed to break the case. Or if the legwork had been done, the person doing it hadn't connected the dots to develop a coherent theory. Charlie was prepared to put in that legwork himself.

The third, most worrying alternative was that his quarry was really, really good at covering their tracks. They'd built an infrastructure that segregated their operations so comprehensively that there was no single entry point to their organization. No single window through which you could see the entire operation.

This possibility was the one that excited Charlie the most. It would indicate a criminal organization of great sophistication and guile, an organization with real intelligence behind it. An organization that would be a real pleasure to crack open. Charlie knew from experience that the more sophisticated the criminals, the more serious or substantial the crimes were that were being concealed.

Charlie knew breaking a case like this would be a major fillip to his career, but that wasn't his primary concern. He was more interested in the intellectual challenge a complex case like this provided, and by the possibility of putting some really nasty people behind bars. Major criminal operations usually wouldn't flinch about perpetrating some of the heavier crimes, including murder. There was nothing Charlie liked more than taking a murderer off the streets.

Charlie hurried to his meeting, a mixture of excitement and apprehension coursing through his veins.

Chapter Thirteen

Three days had passed since Lucas and Amber had navigated their way through Accra's airport, leaving Ghana with a small sense of regret that they hadn't had the opportunity to explore the exciting and exotic country in more detail, but grateful to be getting back to the comforts of the west.

Those three days had flashed by. First, they'd endured a twelve hour flight to Washington, which had been followed by a lengthy wait in an understaffed immigration hall. Then a much shorter flight had brought them back to New York. The last forty-eight hours had been spent cycling between sleep, doing laundry and calling anxious friends and relatives to confirm their survival. At two o'clock in the afternoon of the Monday morning following their departure from Africa, Lucas and Amber found themselves sitting in the very same meeting room in GoldRock's New York offices that Carlos had conferred with ten days earlier.

They both found the meeting room to be eerily reminiscent of the one they'd spend so many hours in at the mine site in Africa. Key similarities included the furniture, which appeared identical to that which they'd experienced in Africa, and the wall decorations, which were the same type of topographical maps they'd grown to love in Africa. In the few minutes they'd had alone in the room before the meeting had started, they'd noted that the New York office displayed maps of some South American regions as well as the African ones they were already familiar with.

The major difference between the New York and Ghanaian meeting rooms was that in this first world location, the air-conditioner was able to maintain the temperature in the room at an acceptable level, without needing to sound like a jet engine at full thrust.

Another similarity was that they were alone in the room with a sole senior representative of the company under review. This time, however, it is John Showers, GoldRock's US Director of Operations.

The reporting relationship between John and Carlos had never been fully explained to them. Lucas and Amber were inclined to position John farther up the greasy pole than Carlos, as John appeared to have a supervisory role in a cushy office well away from the dangers and annoyances of a remote mine site. However, Carlos's demeanor and self-assuredness left one with the distinct impression that he was the one calling the shots. Either way, John was a senior member of the GoldRock management team, and an important player in the wider organization.

John was dressed in formal business attire, as were Lucas and Amber, who had the familiar pilot cases on the floor beside them. The familiar files and documents were spread liberally on the meeting table, as they reported back to the company's American management on their findings at the mine. John gave the appearance of being more engaged in the process than Carlos had been, in that he had brought several files with him to the meeting. He had also filled a number of sheets of his legal pad with notes during the discussions, which had been ongoing for some time.

Lucas, once again, was leading the discussion from his side of the desk. They'd been discussing the project for close to ninety minutes and all parties were growing a little tired.

'So, in conclusion, the fieldwork went very well,' he said. 'Cyanide is tricky stuff, but your team does a good job. You may be aware that we weren't able to observe the smelting because of security issues. This is the largest outstanding issue for us.'

Lucas immediately felt that John's response was too quick and too polished to not have been pre-prepared.

'Carlos mentioned that you were disappointed about this when we spoke a few days ago,' he said. 'I would add that I have been to the mine perhaps a half-dozen times and he's never allowed me to see the smelting process.'

Lucas considered John's statement. It did nothing to clear up his lingering question over the hierarchy between John and Carlos, neither did it move them any closer to a resolution of the smelting issue. John had accompanied the statement with a dismissive sweep of the arm, indicating that the subject was closed from his perspective. Time to move on…

Lucas has heard this more than enough. With a glance to Amber and a perceptible shake of the head, his body stiffened as he leaned closer to the table.

'Yes. Indeed. But there are some E.P.A. rules covering smelters and their emissions which we weren't able to test.'

As Lucas referred to a sheaf of notes he had in front of him, he noticed John shifting uncomfortably in his seat across the table. Amber looked on, silently noting that her irresistible force had encountered yet another immovable object. She wondered whether the force or the object was the favorite to win this particular tussle. After a moment of searching, Lucas found what he was looking for.

'Yes - here we are. Arsenic and cadmium oxides can be produced.' He lowered his notes and looked straight at John with a penetrating gaze designed to amplify the importance of the message being delivered. Something he'd practiced in a mirror many times but had rarely had to deploy.

'They're nasty contaminants.'

John was agitated that the conversation refused to end, despite his best efforts, yet his eyes betrayed a glimmer of amusement. Is this young kid trying to intimidate me? Does he have any idea how ridiculous he's making himself look? Time to be firm. Again.

'I think we've accommodated your requests fully and reasonably. It's time to draw a line under this process.'

Amber looked from John to Lucas. Lucas's face had adopted a slightly ruddier tone and his fingers were tightly balled into fists below the table out of John's sight, leaving a whiteness to his knuckles which betrayed his inner feelings. The immovable object was winning... Again...

'I understand,' Lucas responded. 'You'll appreciate that this may prevent us from providing a complete report to the E.P.A. That may prevent them from issuing you an operating certificate. That may prevent you from operating.'

Lucas looked pointedly at John, waiting for the magnitude of his threats to sink in. John appeared unruffled, and remained resolutely silent.

'We'll have to raise the issue with our boss,' Lucas said eventually. 'We'll see what he thinks.'

Capitulation. Again. Amber was disappointed to see her irresistible force surrender so easily. As Lucas shuffled his paperwork, she reflected that she couldn't realistically see how any other outcome could have been reached given the stubborn intransigence Lucas was consistently meeting across the table, both here and in Africa. Amber had real sympathy for Lucas but she felt the surrender had been too quick. Too total. Perhaps a little abject? Lucas reminded her of a dog who rolls onto his back for a tummy rub the second its owner comes through the door. Lucas was a good consultant and a pleasant guy to be around, but show some backbone, please, she thought.

John rose and extended his hand to Lucas. He didn't want the gloating over his victory to be too ostentatious, but it was clear to all that the victor was consoling the loser. Lucas nobly returned the handshake, conscious that having so recently balled his hands into fists, his palms were a little clammier than would be ideal. John also shook Amber's hand, holding her eye for a moment longer than was perhaps strictly necessary. Releasing her hand, he departed, leaving them alone in the meeting room.

Lucas sank back into his chair and sighed. He looked at Amber, shaking his head ruefully. He knew he'd looked weak, but there was only so far he could go. If the threat of not being able to operate didn't scare GoldRock, what the hell else could he say or do?

'They really don't want us to see their gold,' he said. 'Let's get the hell out of here. I'm about done with GoldRock mining for one day.'

Lucas and Amber crossed the lobby of the building GoldRock occupied, and emerged onto a busy sidewalk on Eighth Avenue. The cool, fluorescent lighting inside the building was a sharp contrast to the bright late afternoon sun that they encountered outside, and both of them were momentarily distracted as they blinked hard as their eyes accommodated to the abrupt change in lighting.

Lucas instinctively retrieved his cell phone from his pocket, looking down to check for new messages. Amber's attention had been drawn to a car parked illegally across the street.

The car was a burgundy Chevrolet, not one of Detroit's finest achievements but a vehicle that had been designed to offer an adequate number of features at a low enough price that would attract substantial orders from car rental companies. It was such an incredibly dull model to own and drive that very few civilians purchased it, and those factors combined in Amber's mind to make the car seem a little incongruous in downtown New York. She knew that very few tourists would attempt to navigate the confusing and congested streets of Manhattan when the public transport system was so convenient and efficient.

The car was parked in splendid isolation in a loading zone directly across the street from where Lucas and Amber stood. But it wasn't the car that most concerned Amber. Leaning against the car, chewing heroically on a hot-dog, was George Mensah.

Sparks of recognition flared through Amber's mind. She narrowed her eyes, looking more closely at the man standing across the street as her brain shuffled through her mental rolodex of faces to positively identify him. As she did so, she noticed that the driver appeared to still be in the car. Amber could see that he was holding a large map which obscured much of the windshield, which was presumably why he'd stopped the vehicle.

It would be easy to assume that the driver was trying to safely determine his location before moving on, even if doing so meant he was violating any number of traffic laws by stopping where he had. You could then conclude that his companion had taken the opportunity to sample one of New York's finest roadside snacks. What Amber noticed that led her to a different conclusion was that the driver had twisted the rear-view mirror through a forty-five degree arc. This had rendered the mirror useless for navigating the car through traffic, but made it very useful for monitoring the comings and goings of the building they'd just left.

Amber strained her eyes a little more and looked closely at the portion of the driver's face that she could see reflected in the mirror. The car was perhaps two hundred feet away so she wasn't able to clearly see his whole face, but she quickly saw that the driver was white. This was enough of a trigger to send a wave of recognition through her. With an audible gasp she realized she was looking at the two men who she'd seen passing through Accra airport just four days earlier.

George had been intently scanning the faces of those leaving the building, but Lucas and Amber had emerged during a moment when his attention was diverted towards getting the hot-dog from his hands to his mouth without smearing too much mustard on his face. Dirk's attention had been more complete, and he had seen Lucas and Amber emerge from the building. He had also seen Amber peering at their car, which he knew would prove to be a major inconvenience. Dirk curtly yelped at George, indicating it was time to move.

The plan that afternoon had been for Dirk and George to track them as far as possible, leaving the vehicle and progressing on foot if necessary. Back at the airport in Ghana, Dirk had successfully resisted the urge to react to the call from his former associate. He was now very pleased that he'd used one of his alternate identities for the project he'd shared with the Australian. He had listened to George's report of his prolonged eye-contact with Amber with great disappointment. A teachable moment had ensued when Dirk had pointed out to George that drawing attention to people you're trying to covertly follow by staring at them is not a great way to start a pursuit. Particularly when you're as memorable and recognizable as George.

The plan was to then listen to John's report on the outcome of their meeting before deciding whether to ramp up their operation. John had not wanted to bring other resources in unless absolutely necessary, but Dirk knew that was now inevitable as Amber had clearly recognized George. They'd have to leave the pursuit to others, which would be an inconvenience, but at least he and George had other tasks they could usefully undertake.

Amber broke her gaze from the car as George moved around the hood to climb back into the passenger seat. She fumbled in her shoulder bag while quietly addressing a distracted Lucas, who was still examining his phone.

'Don't look, but what are the odds that two people we saw in Accra airport are going to also be in New York four days later? And what are the odds that they'll be illegally parked outside the building we just left?'

Lucas's attention was firmly devoted to his phone, but by the end of the sentence he'd processed the detail of Amber's message. And he did the first thing most people do when told to *not* look? He looked.

Lucas scanned up and down the street but all he could see was that was in any way out of the ordinary was a bland rental car pulling out of a loading bay across the street. The profile of the driver held Lucas's attention for a split second, enough to engage a million of Lucas's neurons in a fruitless quest for a name to put to the face.

'I don't see anyone,' he said. 'Besides, I'm not a gambler,' he said. He looked at Amber who appeared to be shaking.

'Let's get a coffee,' she said gripping his arm firmly and steering him down the street.

Davie's phone rang for the fourth time that afternoon. Once again it was Jorge. This kind of frequent communication was unheard of and by now, Davie was certain that something was happening that was truly significant.

The third call had told him to hang out on Eighth Avenue around forty-seventh street, and to wait for further instructions.

Davie had thought hard about what might be happening while waiting for the next call. His greatest concern was that he was being set-up by Jorge and his mysterious bosses. Davie thought that this was unlikely, but it was still a concern that gnawed at him. Davie was certain he was a valued associate who was being given with these unusual tasks to perform because of his trustworthiness and his competence. But he'd asked a few questions, and been more inquisitive than was perhaps usual, which may have made him stand out.

Davie was not worried about the police. He'd had a lot of experience of the N.Y.P.D. and spending time in their care and custody didn't scare him. But this opportunity with the organization had been his big chance to make something of himself, to prove he could be successful in that kind of position and to finally make some decent money. He feared that this was being threatened by receiving these seemingly random tasks.

Think, Davie, think. There's got to be a pattern you can see here.

The fourth call had been a revelation. He'd been given two succinct but detailed descriptions of a man and a woman. From the language used, he knew that Jorge must be reading from a script he'd been given. "Petite" and "Attired" weren't words which would usually come from Jorge's mouth. So someone had given Jorge the descriptions to broadcast.

The only other information was that the two people were somewhere on Eighth Avenue, within a block or two of where Davie had been sent. If he saw them, he was to follow discretely and call in their location as soon as they stopped walking.

Showtime, Davie, he thought to himself. The chances he was being set-up had dropped off rapidly with this news. No, Davie was now certain that he was being trusted with something important. And that was excellent news. He pushed off from the wall he'd been leaning against and decided to head uptown.

Chapter Fourteen

Lucas and Amber stopped at the first humdrum coffee shop they saw, and were quickly huddled around a small table with cappuccinos in front of them. The atmosphere between them was tense, although Lucas was still not entirely certain why. Amber attempted to explain.

'The guys I saw with the car today were also at Accra airport last Thursday. That's just too much of a coincidence. I also think the white guy was the guy that "Private Security" guy was calling out to. Klaus, wasn't it?'

Lucas is listening intently. 'I didn't really see who the "Private Security" guy called out to in Accra. And I didn't clearly see anyone in the car today either.'

Amber continued eagerly, undeterred by Lucas's lack of input. 'Right. The big black guy was staring at me in the airport. Then he was staring at me again by the car.'

'But lots of guys stare at you.'

Amber was stopped short by this. She quickly recovered and flashed a smile at Lucas.

'No they don't,' she said exaggeratedly. 'And even if they do, this was different.'

'Yes they do,' insisted Lucas. He paused and cast his eye around the coffee shop. 'Hey, it must just be a coincidence.'

'An astronomical coincidence. Well, let's think about it. John wasn't himself this afternoon. And Carlos wasn't exactly welcoming when we were in Africa.'

'True. Then there's the whole thing about the smelting room. I get the need for security, I really do. And theirs is excellent. As we found out.'

Lucas looked at Amber with an expression that mixed embarrassment with guilt but Amber was intently staring at her coffee as she listened. Lucas realized that his companion was seriously concerned about the situation. He felt frustrated that he'd not got a better look at these two characters to be able to offer more support.

'They refused to accept that we have a legal right to observe the process,' Amber said without looking up.

'Right. But everything else about the mine seemed to be in good shape.'

They paused for a moment, thinking as they sipped on their coffees. Lucas leaned back to conduct a quick scan of the other patrons in the coffee shop. The store was quiet, with perhaps half the tables occupied. His eyes were held momentarily by a man in his twenties who was looking at Amber – nothing unusual so far. The man noticed that Lucas's gaze was on him and held Lucas's eye, for a moment longer than was comfortable. The man frowned as his attention was snapped back to his companion.

Lucas brought his attention back to the table and broke the silence.

'So the bottom line is that you saw two people in the airport in Ghana and you think you just saw them again in New York.'

'Almost right. I don't *think* I saw them, I *did* see them. But it's more than that. They were parked illegally right outside the GoldRock building that we came out of. And they took off the second they realized that I'd recognized them. It wasn't just that we bumped into them, which I could probably accept as a coincidence. They were definitely waiting for us and took off as soon as they knew we'd seen them.'

'That does sound odd. But they didn't run away at the airport?'

'No. But there was definitely something unusual about their body language there. I can't clearly explain it, but the black guy was staring while the white guy didn't seem to want to be seen. And that security guy thought he knew them, but they didn't acknowledge him.'

'So the rational conclusion is that they're following us,' Lucas offered, putting into words what they'd both been thinking.

'Do you really think we've been followed here from Africa?' Lucas continued. 'It's hard to believe, although it looks like the only explanation.'

Another silence engulfed them as they contemplated the consequences of this conclusion. Lucas's eyes again began to sweep the room, and they quickly fell upon an older lady, sitting alone at a table with tea and tea-making paraphernalia spread out around her. Making an espresso looked simple compared to the rigmarole of making a cup of tea the traditional English way, as was encouraged by this particular chain. She was reading what appeared to be a cross stitch pattern, which seemed to Lucas to be an odd choice of reading material. Was it her cover for a covert surveillance mission? Lucas snatched himself back into the present, wondering if he was experiencing the first symptom of paranoia.

Amber's eyes had moved to the window, through which she was looking at passers-by, checking for any familiar faces.

'Well let's think it through,' she said, after a moment. 'They were obviously sensitive about the smelting process. Nothing else looked out of place down in Ghana.'

'They were real explosions and they had real trucks moving real rubble. They use real cyanide, and lots of it.'

Lucas frowned in thought. His eyes were drawn to a guy sitting alone, at a table close to the counter. He was wearing the kind of street uniform Lucas would never have attempted to wear. Baggy jeans, a hoodie top and the kind of shoes kids thought they could play basketball in, until they actually tried to. He was drawing deeply from a large coffee cup. His eyes were active, darting from customer to customer, including Lucas's. Their eyes met but the gaze was broken as soon as it began. An honest guy topping off his caffeine tanks before starting his second (or third) job? Or a nervous scout tracking them?

Lucas's eye was momentarily held by a green wristband that looked a little out of place in the outfit. Lucas found his mind trawling through the range of wristbands he was aware of trying to identify it. Kabala? Livestrong? Aids? He realized he was getting distracted.

'So we have a major gold mine which won't allow us to see their gold,' Lucas said, trying to jolt the conversation back onto the rails.

'Yeah. And every time we mention the smelting process, they change the subject. Or ignore us.'

'Or set their guards on us,' Lucas added, cringing as he brought back the memory of them cowering on the ground before the aggressive guards.

As Lucas reflected on this for a moment, he looked to his right and his eyes met those of a lady sitting alone at a table close by. She was staring intently at Lucas, and was heavily made up for the time of day, complete with very fashionable clothing. Perhaps a little older than Lucas, she was not unattractive and seemed to be showing an interest in Lucas that he was unaccustomed to. A cougar, out on the prowl or an agent for the enemy?

Lucas shook his head again. His paranoia was becoming uncomfortable, although there was a very real chance that everyone was after him.

'This is getting to me,' he offered.

Silence fell again but both Lucas and Amber had realized where the conversation was taking them.

'Sometimes the obvious answer is the right answer,' Amber said, bringing their thoughts together. After another pause, they both said in unison:

'There is no gold.'

'And after God knows how many years,' added Amber, 'two gung-ho Americans turn up and start asking awkward questions.'

'Yeah,' Lucas agreed. 'There's one other thing that's been bothering me too. When we went to the smelting room and met those guards, Carlos got there really quickly. If he'd been in his office or even his accommodation unit, there's no way he could have got there so quickly.'

'You're right,' Amber responded thoughtfully. 'It suggests that they were monitoring us when we were at the mine. And we have to conclude that they're also monitoring us now we're back in the States.'

'So if it's true, and there is no gold, for whatever reason, they'd worry about us working it out. Sending people to keep an eye on us would then make sense.'

'Well we have worked it out.'

'But they don't know we have,' Lucas replied instantly.

'Well they haven't done anything to us yet.'

'Yes they have. They've scared the shit out of us by sending in the heavies.'

Amber reflected for a moment and concluded that Lucas had a point.

'But perhaps those heavies were supposed to just watch us, not scare us?' she reasoned.

'Perhaps. But God help us if they *do* decide to scare us.'

The thought hung in the air, ominously. Amber took her turn to break the silence.

'So let's assume we're right. What do we do? Carry on as if nothing has happened?'

'We *could*. But we *should* do something about it. Something's got to be badly wrong for them to be deploying resources to watch two people who are just doing their jobs. We're representatives of the U.S. government, after all. Kind of...' Lucas tailed off a little, unsure whether being a proxy of the government was enough of a reason to contemplate actions bordering on the heroic.

'But if we do something about it, and they find out. We risk getting, like, I don't know...' Amber is uncomfortable about finishing the sentence. 'Well perhaps we'd get really, really scared.'

Lucas understood Amber's hesitancy. 'But if we don't do something about it, things might unravel anyway. They'd assume it unraveled because of us so they'd probably, um, *scare* us anyway.'

That thought hung in the air for a moment.

'That's a lot of ifs...' Amber offered.

'It's a lot of scare,' Lucas replied, honestly. 'We should go talk to Ralph.'

Amber offered a quizzical face.

'Ralph West, the firm's senior partner. He'll know what to do,' Lucas offered in explanation.

They drained their cups and rose to leave.

'It's probably just a coincidence,' Amber offered, more in hope than in reality.

'Yeah. I am sure it is,' Lucas said reassuringly.

"I fucking hope it is,' Amber said emphatically.

Lucas recoiled at this. This was a strong word that he'd never heard from her before. He knew that it reflected the severity of their situation in her mind, which would inevitably lead to a realignment in their relationship. But where would that realignment take them?

Lucas allowed himself the luxury of a moment to think about some of the places he and Amber's relationship might end up. He found himself quite excited about some of the options that presented themselves.

Lucas and Amber moved towards the door to the street. As they passed the service counter, Davie Eason slipped easily from his chair, leaving the rest of his coffee on the table. He'd slipped his hoodie from his head when he'd entered as he'd figured he'd draw more attention to himself with it up – they may even have refused him service.

As he crossed the shop towards the exit door, he slipped his hood back up over his head and fell into step a cautious distance behind Lucas and Amber. At first he'd been annoyed that he'd allowed Lucas to catch his eye, but a vacancy in Lucas's eyes had given Davie the strong impression that he had been so distracted that it was unlikely that he would remember his face... Thinking it through, and given everything that might transpire, Davie realized that he wouldn't have minded too much if Lucas had remembered his face.

Chapter Fifteen

Lucas and Amber walked purposefully through their firm's offices on their way to a hastily arranged meeting with Ralph West. As they passed the cubicles and offices that they would normally consider to be their home turf, they were very conscious of the concerns hanging over them. The office was usually a refuge to be enjoyed after spending several uncomfortable weeks on the road, but on this occasion the sense of dread that prevailed made even their home turf fell foreign.

As was normal at this time of the year, the majority of the cubicles were empty, given that most staff members were out of the office on engagements, earning money for the firm. Clients felt that the fees they were charged were more acceptable when staff spent their time on their client's premises, even if it was more efficient for the work to be done back at the firm's office.

It was five in the afternoon, an hour where people would ordinarily be thinking about quitting time, but in the midst of the busy season there were still a number of familiar faces scattered around the office. Lucas and Amber were too focused on their destination to acknowledge any of the gestures of welcome that were extended to them as they passed.

They had called ahead, so Ralph was expecting them. His personal assistant showed them directly into his office. The office was small, and most visitors unfamiliar with the firm considered it to be surprisingly small for a man of Ralph's seniority and importance to the firm. Visitors didn't realize that the office simply reflected the corporate philosophy of thrift and minimalism.

The office was simply furnished with a desk and an adjoining cabinet. The cabinet was actually an integral part of the desk, and closer scrutiny revealed that the desk was designed to swing from horizontal to vertical, to be stored in the cabinet when the primary occupant was not using the space. This would free the room up to be used as a meeting room. Thrift and minimalism.

Ralph, however, had brought such a multitude of files into his office that any thought of converting the space to a meeting room could be instantly discarded, short of engaging a team of laborers to remove the room's contents. Whether this paperwork invasion was a deliberate strategy or not was a frequent topic of discussion amongst other partners, but Ralph chose to be enigmatically vague when asked directly. His thinking was that his seniority should bring some advantages, and besides, some of the files were of such a sensitive nature that Ralph preferred to be able to just lock his office door when he wasn't in residence, rather than having to stash certain files away each time he left the building.

Ralph looked up sharply when Lucas and Amber entered. He waved them to a small meeting table, and rolled his chair across the short distance to join them. Lifting a small pile of files from the table to create some elbow room for his visitors, he allowed them a moment to settle.

'Have a good time in Africa? How are the bowels?'

An English accent was one of the better clues to Ralph's origins. Born and raised in London, Ralph's father and his father before him had been accountants, and it had been no surprise to anyone when he showed an early aptitude for mathematics.

Excitement about Ralph's future diminished a little when he failed to secure a place at Cambridge, becoming the first West male to fail to go up to the University in over a century. Instead, Ralph spent three happy years in the southwest corner of England studying Accountancy at Exeter University. Ralph felt that the high quality and low price of the local cider more than made up for the reputational handicap he feared he would face with a degree from Exeter instead of Cambridge.

Ralph's early career back in London had been uninspiring, and he'd realized that reinventing himself as an Englishman in New York was his best path to success, so he sought and obtained a transfer.

Since crossing "the pond" his career had bloomed. His accent, his attitude and the mystery he was able to create around what a "lower second class degree" actually meant had allowed his career to blossom and in fifteen years he'd risen rapidly to become the senior partner of his firm's New York office.

Ralph accompanied his unwelcome enquiry as to Lucas and Amber's intestinal health with a broad welcoming smile. Lucas glanced briefly at Amber and once more, elected to take the lead in the conversation.

'Well as you ask, pretty disturbed actually,' he replied. 'It took about thirty-six hours after touching down for the fun and games to really began.'

Lucas's reply was greeted with riotous laughter by Ralph. Even Amber cracked a smile at his disproportionate response. Ralph had always prided himself on the ease with which he was able to bond with his subordinates and this exchange would further prove the point, in his mind at least.

'Excellent! Look, I've started to review the files. Nothing seems, um, amiss. Nothing at all. A good job, by the looks... To what do I owe this pleasure?' Ralph's speech patterns were usually staccato in nature, but this offering struck Lucas as being unusually choppy. Lucas's defenses began to rise.

'There is one outstanding issue. We were prevented from accessing the smelting room. Physically prevented, by armed guards on one occasion. Their attitude seemed very defensive.'

'I'm sure there's nothing to be, er, to worry about,' Ralph replied. 'They obviously have security issues. Valuable stuff, gold!'

Ralph paused, looking from Lucas to Amber, hoping for a reaction from this penetrating joke. None was forthcoming;

indeed Lucas and Amber were beginning to shift a little uncomfortably in their seats.

Ralph continued, undeterred. 'I actually just got off the phone with John and he mentioned you'd raised the issue. Absolutely nothing to worry about, I'm sure. Safer, even. Your work is, er, your professionalism is to be commended.'

Ralph's enthusiasm visibly faded through the course of this short speech and, at the end of it, feeling somewhat deflated, Ralph forced a smile that he shared first with Lucas, then with Amber.

'Surely we can't sign off to the E.P.A. on GoldRock's certification without reviewing such a large area of their operations?' asked Amber. She was anxious to contribute and was not certain that Lucas was prepared to make that particular point.

'You don't, sorry we don't have any reason to believe their processes are, well, any less adequate for the smelting process than they are elsewhere in the operation? Do we? I don't think it's a material problem.'

Lucas reflected on Ralph's answer. As his boss, it was ultimately Ralph's call as to what was material and what wasn't. But his overwhelming sense was that the discussion was being shut down, yet again. The only difference was that as the person responsible for the project, Ralph actually had the power to end the discussion for good. It was his call and his neck on the line. There was only one conclusion Lucas could draw from that…

The room remained silent, as Ralph looked from Amber to Lucas, silently questioning whether either person was prepared to challenge his ruling. Human nature yearns to fill silences. Ralph, despite his failings, was an experienced interrogator and he knew to remain resolutely silent and wait for someone else to speak with what might be a poorly timed comment. Lucas's mind was churning on the implications of Ralph's comments, so he wasn't in a position to speak. Amber was not able to resist.

'We also think we're being followed.'

Lucas shot Amber an angry glance as Ralph's eyes fell to his hands, which were clasped together in his lap. Amber immediately realized she'd made a mistake by sharing her suspicions without Lucas's approval.

Ralph's demeanor instantly changed. When he raised his eyes to his guests from his hands, his face portrayed a calm iciness. His speech also became measured and precise.

'I can't believe that is the case. You must be mistaken. Given the excellent work you've done, I'll clear your schedules for the next week. Take some leave. I am sure you'd both enjoy a break after the rigors of Africa.'

Lucas and Amber were both rendered momentarily speechless at this abrupt change in Ralph's demeanor. Ralph rose and with a broad sweep of the arm indicated that their meeting was over. Lucas and Amber also rose and with mumbled thanks and nods, quickly left the office. Ralph firmly shut the door firmly behind them, causing Amber to flinch. He did not set out to slam it shut, but found he'd used more force than was appropriate to such a professional environment.

Lucas and Amber retraced their steps towards the exit, leaving at a somewhat faster pace than they'd arrived.

'What did you make of that?' enquired Amber, gently attempting to bridge the ground between them after her faux pas and Lucas's stern visual reprimand.

'We went in scared, we came out fucked,' was Lucas's curt response.

Amber's step faltered as she processed Lucas's strong language. She understood that she'd introduced the word into their relationship, but was still shocking that he'd chosen to echo it now. With a stutter step she caught Lucas back up and fell back into step alongside him.

'You're not suggesting he's in on it?' she asked gently.

'Up to his eyeballs. You saw how his body-language changed when you mentioned us being followed. He'd spoken to John... That materiality speech was bullshit. The smelting process has to be material. He's covering something up. And besides, have you ever heard of a partner ordering people to take leave?'

'So what do we do now?' enquired Amber after she took a moment to absorb Lucas's comments. Apologizing for her mistake was pointless, and besides, Lucas should be thanking her as her outburst appeared to have revealed some very valuable information that might not otherwise have emerged.

'We get the hell out of Dodge. Then go to the authorities. Where do you live?'

Despite the shock and confusion coursing through Amber's soul, she was surprised to find herself a little buoyed by the question.

'Jersey City. About twenty minutes on the subway.'

'Let's go there. We can grab some supplies. Regroup. Decide.'

Lucas wrenched open the door to their firm's offices and waited politely for Amber to exit.

Chapter Sixteen

When the call came in, John Showers was sitting at his desk thinking through some of the more exotic contingency plans that had been developed. Of the three men who'd been on the call with Carlos from Africa after Lucas and Amber's ill-advised excursion to the smelting room, Ralph West had been the second.

From the outset John had been concerned about Ralph's position in the "inner circle". Ralph had insisted that access be a central condition of his participation, but he would always remain an amateur in John's eyes. This demand had been easier to accept as John knew that he would still easily control the extent of Ralph's access, so the information shared could still be rationed if necessary.

John recognized Ralph's number when it appeared on his cell phone's display – he'd been expecting the call. He had also been expecting the key headlines of Ralph's report, not that he'd admit it to anyone, least of all Carlos. He'd met with Lucas and Amber several times now and they were not the dumb, compliant fools that Ralph had promised to supply.

The conversation with Ralph had been short, on John's part at least. Ralph had blustered on for a while, until John cut him short. Much better to receive Ralph's detailed report in person. Much better, for several reasons.

John pressed the intercom button that connected him to his personal assistant, sitting far enough outside of his office so as to not be able to overhear John's conversations, even those conducted at high volume as was occasionally required.

'Jane? Clear my schedule for the next few days. A situation has arisen I must handle personally. Thanks.'

John looked out of the window at the panoramic view of the New York skyline. It was a view he'd been able to enjoy for several years while anticipating a day like today. He'd rehearsed just about every scenario that could arise, including this one.

With a small sigh of resignation he turned back to his desk and hit speed dial button number one on his desk phone. There was a moment's hesitation as numerous telephone circuits aligned themselves before a ringing tone came through the phone's speaker. John only had to wait a short moment before the call was answered by a gruff and somewhat irritated voice.

'Si?'

John picked up the handset and held it to his ear, not wanting the call to be broadcast even though the room was empty.

'Carlos. Yes, I realize it's the middle of the night. We have a situation.'

John briefly explained the developments that had taken place in Ralph's office. John knew that Ralph wouldn't add anything that Carlos needed to know when he reached John's office, so was confident to make the call in advance of Ralph's arrival. He listened in silence as Carlos recounted his instructions.

'I understand completely,' John replied. 'As we discussed. It will be done. Tonight.'

John disconnected the call. Taking a scrap of paper from his desk drawer he quickly dialed another number that he'd scribbled down the day before. It was one he didn't want to commit to his or his phone's memory. He waited another moment until his second call was connected.

'Yes, it's John. Be here in ten minutes. And bring your equipment. All of it.'

Lucas and Amber only had to wait a few minutes on the 33rd Street Station platform before the New Jersey Path train arrived that would take them under the Hudson to the Grove Street Station in Jersey City. Amber's apartment was a five minute walk from the station, located in a converted mill that was home to a number of young professionals who commuted to Manhattan each day.

Davie Eason was easily able to follow them, as they'd made no effort to confuse or distract any follower. Davie had called Jorge just the once, as he descended into the subway system, to say he had them in his sights and they were taking the subway. His instructions were to keep following them, to call in when they reached their next destination and to keep a low profile. This he did throughout the short subway ride and subsequent walk.

As Lucas and Amber entered her apartment building, Davie found a bench close to the main entry door and made himself comfortable as he called Jorge again with their new location.

As Davie and Jorge were speaking, Amber was unlocking the door to her apartment. She pushed the door open, stepping back to allow Lucas to enter. Lucas, ever the gentleman, deferred and allowed Amber to bustle in ahead of him. She quickly cast her eye around for any embarrassing items she may have left on display, but was pleased to see that the room's tidiness was broadly in order.

Lucas followed Amber into her studio apartment. Pausing respectfully at the door as Amber completed a quick lap, he noted immediately that her small studio apartment was immaculate. A small kitchenette sat off to one side, sparkling clean with no dirty dishes in the sink or on the draining board. A sitting area was adjacent to the kitchenette, comprising a sofa and a coffee table, on which sat a small display of home and garden magazines, perfectly organized as one might find in a show-home.

A queen sized bed was the largest piece of furniture in the room, upon which were arranged a large number of scatter cushions in an intricate and complex pattern that no male could ever hope to replicate.

The only item that obviously not a permanent feature of the décor was a large clothes airer, located adjacent to the kitchenette. On it was arranged a number of Amber's clothes, many of which Lucas recognized from their African trip. Lucas currently had a similar display on show in his apartment, but he was surprised to find his attention momentarily held by the items of intimate wear that filled the top two rails of the airer, none of which he'd had the opportunity to see in Africa.

Lucas chastised himself for invading Amber's privacy, and turned to close the door behind him. As he turned back towards the center of the room, he saw that Amber was momentarily on her knees retrieving something from under the bed.

'You live alone?' he asked, largely rhetorically.

Amber emerged from under the bed holding an overnight bag.

'Yes. I shared with all sorts of filth freaks at college. That was enough for me.'

Lucas nodded in understanding. That explains a lot, he thought.

'I have a friend from college who I'm sure can help us,' Lucas said, returning their attention to the serious issues at hand. 'He lives in Chelsea, back over in Manhattan. His dad is in the F.B.I. Grab enough clothes and stuff for a couple of nights. I can borrow some of his stuff.'

Amber nodded, turning to her wardrobe that stood on the far side of the bed. As she took a pace towards the wardrobe, she suddenly froze and stuck a finger up in the air.

Lucas also froze, unsure as to what Amber was communicating. Amber turned her upper body towards

Lucas and slowly moved her finger to her lips, motioning for silence. Lucas mouthed the single word 'What?'

Amber theatrically pointed towards the wardrobe. Lucas peered at the piece of furniture, but nothing looked amiss to him. Once again he mouthed 'What?'

Amber moved back across the room towards Lucas, almost painfully slowly and quietly. When she was close enough, she leaned towards Lucas's ear.

'Someone's been in here,' she whispered. 'The cushions on the bed have been moved and there's something on top of the wardrobe.'

Lucas looked disbelievingly at the bed.

'The cushions have moved?' he whispered back. 'How the hell can you tell?'

Amber looked at him the way a wife might look at a husband, who after twenty years of marriage still asks how she'd like her coffee.

'I just know, OK?' Amber replied testily. 'Act normally, OK?'

Amber turned away from Lucas and repeated the egg-shell walk back towards the wardrobe. Lucas found himself hopping from foot to foot, anxious to fully understand the latest development in the surreal adventure they'd found themselves on. He found it just as hard to "act normal" as he did to "don't look".

The wheels of his brain span furiously as he tried to decide what to do. Act normally, he thought. What does that mean? What does normal mean? What is normal? In the end of his deliberations he decided he needed to break the silence. Talking was normal, right?

'So where did you go to college?' Lucas asked.

Amber stopped, turned and looked at him, mouthing "What?" Lucas shrugged – just acting normally.

'I studied environmental science at Vanderbilt.'

Amber had reached the wardrobe and was standing on tip-toe, investigating what she believed was a foreign object.

'So why did you move to New York?' Lucas continued, persevering valiantly, or at least so he thought.

Amber heard the question but was distracted by what she had found. After a beat, she remembered to answer.

'I was a big fan of Gary Sinise in C.S.I New York and there's a fucking camera here!'

Amber realized that the device she'd seen was a camera, not merely a microphone. This meant that they were busted, and had been since the moment they stepped into her apartment. Acting normally wasn't going to work.

Lucas moved quickly across the room and, standing beside Amber, looked closely at the object Amber had found on the wardrobe. He saw a small pinhole camera with an even smaller transmitting antenna protruding an inch from the unit. A battery pack was tucked under a bag resting on the top of the wardrobe.

'Fuck it!' whispered Lucas.

'You said it. And I don't think we need to whisper any more. We're busted,' Amber responded.

'Come on. Fill your bag and let's go. Bring your passport,' Lucas directs.

Despite the adrenaline coursing through her veins, Amber found herself pausing at this request. She frowned at Lucas, but he was emphatic.

'Who knows how deep the rabbit hole goes?' was his simple response.

Amber nodded and moved quickly across the room to a small desk built into the wall adjacent to her sitting area. As she threw her passport into the bag, Lucas took the camera unit from the top of the wardrobe and decided to depreciate it to a zero net book value with the assistance of one of Amber's more sensible shoes, which he grabbed from a shoe rack adjacent to the wardrobe.

Amber moved from the desk to the clothes airer, and paused when she noticed that Lucas's attention was still occupied by his task of senseless destruction. Amber's hand paused momentarily over the rail of more sensible, substantial panties, but instead she grabbed a selection of the more exotic, skimpier panties and popped them into her bag. Who knows how deep the rabbit hole goes? Besides, the skimpier items were much lighter to carry...

Lucas looked across the room at Amber with the tattered remains of the camera unit in his hands. He gave her a huge grin, which simultaneously sought her approval and conveyed pride at his recently discovered prowess at destroying small electrical devices. Amber forced a smile back at Lucas and pointed anxiously towards the door.

Lucas nodded, and without a backward glance, he and Amber left the apartment.

Davie was a little surprised to see his targets leaving the apartment building so quickly, and he noted that the girl now had a bag with her. Silently, he rose and slipped into step behind them, following Jorge's guidance to stick with them. This is turning out to be a very interesting day, he thought to himself as he followed them back towards the Grove Street station.

Chapter Seventeen

The burgundy rental car was being driven aggressively through the streets of mid-town New York by George Mensah. The sun was low in the sky, but the streets were not noticeably emptier than they'd been earlier in the day. George was somewhat perplexed that every other car on the road appeared to be a taxi.

Dirk Bekker was sitting in the passenger seat, holding a small monitor in his hands, from which a large antenna and a small wire protruded. The wire ran all the way up Dirk's body to an earpiece lodged in his left ear. Dirk was peering at the small screen, his attention fully devoted to the reality show being played out in front of him.

He'd watched with interest as the melodrama in Amber's apartment had played out. Lucas and Amber had entered, after which Amber had retrieved a bag from under the bed. Dirk smiled as he was able to hear every word clearly, but his smile faltered when he saw that Amber had spotted the camera transmitter. He thought he'd hidden the camera well, but she must have some significant powers of observation to have detected it so quickly. It was clear to Dirk that Amber had noticed the device, and he looked on in mild amusement as Lucas and Amber imitated an Abbot and Costello sketch as Amber crept up on the device. Only then did Dirk realize that they hadn't initially identified the device as a camera, and all meaningful intelligence ceased to flow as soon as the device was identified for what it was. Dirk's last image of his quarries was of both of them peering into the lens, noses and foreheads grotesquely overemphasized by the physics of the fisheye lens.

He flinched slightly as Lucas removed the camera from the top of the wardrobe, which threw the orientation and focus of the picture into spasm. Seconds later, the audio died and the picture dissolved to static, from what Dirk correctly assumed was a violent assault on his equipment. Dirk switched off the unit, removed the earpiece from his ear and carefully retracted the antenna.

'They found the camera,' he reported. 'I hate clean freaks.'

His speech revealed a definite southern African accent. George had always assumed Dirk was South African, but knew enough history about the white man's penetration of southern Africa to know that Dirk's accent could easily be from Zimbabwe or even as far north as Zambia. George also knew Dirk and his reputation well enough to not ask unnecessary personal questions.

'He mentioned something about a friend in Chelsea, father in the F.B.I.,' Dirk reported.

The car pulled up to a security barrier guarding the entrance to the downtown skyscraper housing GoldRock's

US office. The guard had gone for the night, so Dirk dialed a number into the keypad to connect with the tenancy.

'I think Chelsea is a district, south of here and north of Greenwich Village,' George added helpfully, having spent quite some time studying maps in recent days.

'Good. It looks like that's our next stop,' Dirk added. 'Once I've taken care of this chore.'

As Dirk and George were arriving at Mike's building, Lucas and Amber were standing on the busy platform of the Grove Street station in Jersey City. The train indicators showed that the next eastbound train was headed for Manhattan's 33rd street.

A large group was standing at the edge of the platform, waiting for the next Manhattan train. Lucas encouraged Amber to try and subtly merge into the group with him, in a way that provided them with some cover without infringing on the group's existing dynamic. Lucas had overheard them excitedly discussing the latest musical which was playing in Manhattan and had assumed they were heading to the Theatre District to see a show.

A distant rumbling heralded the arrival of a Path train. As Lucas saw the train's lights slowly illuminating the tunnel to his right, he was suddenly struck by a thought.

'Back in your apartment, can you remember if I explicitly said "New York"?' he said. 'Or for that matter "Chelsea"?'

'I can't remember – I was distracted by that camera at the time but I think you probably did,' Amber replied. 'We should assume you did.'

The train emerged from the tunnel and began slowing to a halt beside them. The tour group began to prepare for action, closing any gaps that may have existed between them, anxious to get onto the train as quickly as possible. An onlooker would conclude that they were not regular patrons of the subway.

'Did I mention Eric's name – my friend in New York?' Lucas continued anxiously.

'I'm pretty sure you didn't. I remember something about the F.B.I., though.' Amber replied, taking a step towards the train.

The train was now at a full stop with the doors open. The tour group had begun to board, politely jostling amongst themselves to get aboard as if there was a real risk that only the first ten passengers would be accepted.

'So they probably know New York and they probably know my buddy's father is in the F.B.I.,' Lucas continued. 'Well that should slow them down a little. But we also think they've been following us since Africa so they obviously have access to significant resources.'

The tourists in front of Lucas and Amber were gradually being accepted into the carriage as Lucas spoke. He kept his voice low so the conversation would remain private.

'That's what we concluded,' Amber replied.

Lucas and Amber moved to board, still conspicuously trying to blend into the larger group. Lucas waited politely as Amber climbed onto the train ahead of him, and with a last quick look up and down the platform, he followed her quickly onboard. He had no idea what he was looking for, but felt compelled to look nevertheless.

As Amber moved to shuffle down the carriage's aisle, he grabbed her arm and gently restrained her beside the doors.

'So it's not out of the question that they're following us right now,' he said.

As he spoke, Amber froze. Lucas's words seemed incredible, yet they held a truthfulness that she struggled to deny. Involuntarily she looked around her at her fellow passengers, who were a blend of tired commuters and the group of theatre-goers who had boarded before her.

'It's possible,' she said eventually.

Lucas was also looking around him, turning every few seconds to look out of the carriage's open door. He could hear a growing noise from another train which would shortly occupy the other platform. He could see a number of passengers on the platform reacting to the approaching train. In that moment, he decided what they needed to do.

As Lucas heard the beeping which heralded the imminent closure of the train's doors, he firmly planted a foot in the path of the left hand door. As the door hit Lucas's foot, he was thrilled to see its motion was arrested, as planned. He'd expected some pain as the door hit his foot, but the distance of travel had been so short that the door had not had the opportunity to achieve a pain-inflicting velocity.

Seeing that he had succeeded in holding the door open, he delicately steered Amber back out of the carriage onto the platform. She stepped onto the platform, immediately understanding Lucas's intent. She looked around anxiously when she reached the platform.

Lucas quickly followed her, but as he passed through the door frame the right sliding door, which he had not been able to impede, slammed into a closed position, connecting firmly with Lucas's shoulder as he passed through the rapidly narrowing gap.

This collision jolted Lucas's foot free from its position restraining the left door, and he spun though ninety degrees, falling heavily onto the platform with a grunt. Amber gasped as she saw Lucas's ungraceful arrival on the platform.

The left door slid quickly closed, and as Lucas sat up on the platform, he saw that his dramatic exit did not appear to have caused any great commotion among other passengers on the platform. Their attention was mostly focused on the train drawing to a halt at the other platform, and its noise had obscured the sound of his grunt.

He realized they'd be able to jump onto the westbound train, which would surely throw off any pursuers, who must be stuck on the eastbound train he'd just exited. A wave of elation surged through him as he realized his plan had worked! He'd done it…

He found himself almost hoping that they were being followed as their shadows would now know who they were dealing with – smart people capable of looking after themselves. His subconscious politely pointed out anyone following them would now know for sure that Lucas and Amber knew they were being followed, which may trigger the next level of interference in their progress. But Lucas's conscious elation discounted the wiser counsel of his subconscious.

Lucas's elation was only momentary. As the train on the opposite platform beeped its warning that its doors were about to open, he was shocked to hear the train behind him emitting the same noise. Lucas's interference with the door's closure had tripped a safety system which automatically reopened the doors in the event that a passenger had become trapped. From his seated position, Lucas looked in horror as the doors to the eastbound train re-opened, allowing anyone who had been tailing them and had seen Lucas's antics ample time to exit the train and resume their pursuit.

Lucas looked up and down the platform, but new passengers arriving on the platform were taking the opportunity to board the eastbound train as its doors had reopened. From his seated position these passengers obscured his view of anyone else exiting the train.

He quickly rose, and steered Amber across the platform where boarding for the westbound train was underway. His only hope was that any followers would have moved deeper into their carriage when they'd seen the doors closing, not expecting such an advanced maneuver from amateurs. They quickly boarded the westbound train and pressed themselves deep into the carriage, attempting to conceal themselves from anyone who might still be tracking them.

Davie slipped into the carriage behind the one now occupied by Lucas and Amber, his heart beating a little faster as a result of Lucas's attempt at deception. His fascination with what he was involved with had grown. That hadn't been an amateur move and if the door's safety mechanism hadn't tripped, Davie would have certainly lost them. He'd been lucky that the guy had fallen on his way out of the train, as that this had allowed him leave the train and duck behind other passengers on the platform without being seen. The girl had just stood looking at the guy with her mouth flapping. Davie didn't think she'd have noticed a marching band passing her. So they were really heading for Newark. Jorge would be real interested to hear that.

Chapter Eighteen

Seventeen floors above George Mensah's parked rental car, John Showers paced around his office waiting for Dirk Bekker to arrive. The task ahead did not fill him with enthusiasm, but he knew it was a key requirement of one of the contingency plans that had been developed when this whole process had become inevitable three months earlier. Carlos had assured him that Dirk was the right man for this kind of job.

Dirk eventually entered the office, carrying a small canvas bag. He was alone, as George had remained with the car and the equipment it contained. Dirk trusted George, but John had made it clear that he didn't need to participate in this meeting.

Dirk and John did not shake hands or exchange pleasantries. The exchange of glances on Dirk's arrival communicated that they were there for business, not pleasure.

'We have a guy following them,' John reported. 'They went straight from their offices to the girl's apartment.'

'We saw them at the apartment. Our surveillance operation paid off,' Dirk added. 'We overheard them saying that they'll be coming back to Manhattan, to Chelsea. A friend's father is in the F.B.I.'

'OK,' John responded enthusiastically. 'Did you get a name?'

'No.' Dirk decided not to share the irrelevant detail that his surveillance device had been so easily spotted and destroyed.

'OK,' John continued, undeterred. 'This we can contain. Actually, it's just about perfect.'

He smiled hopefully at Dirk, who had moved to the window and was lowering and closing the blinds. As he did so, he used a handkerchief to wipe down any of the cords he had touched.

'Yes. Good thinking,' said John.

The intercom buzzed. John connected to his assistant.

'Yes?'

"Ralph West is also here to see you,' reported his assistant, her voice electronically distorted by the intercom.

'Show him in. Then you can go. Thank you.'

John smiled again at Dirk, who had taken a seat at the meeting table with his canvas bag inconspicuously resting on his lap. Game faces on, time to rock and roll.

Ralph entered, extending his hand to John, who did not take it, instead indicating that Ralph should take a seat at the meeting table. Ralph was a little disconcerted by this, and was further perturbed when he saw a stranger already sitting at the table. A stranger who had obviously been invited to this meeting, a meeting which Ralph had assumed would be a private gathering just between himself and John. As a condition of his participation, Ralph had negotiated that there would be full consultation before any newcomers joined any sensitive discussions. He'd have to raise this with Carlos.

Ralph paused, expecting to be introduced to the stranger according the antiquated English protocol that had been beaten into him throughout his schooling. It's not that Americans are unable to maintain a mental matrix of which of their acquaintances had previously met each other. Americans just assumed that if you hadn't met someone before, you would get on with introducing yourself rather than waiting for some elaborate ritual to be completed before you were allowed to communicate directly.

'Speak,' commanded John.

Ralph looked back to John, and took a seat with a further quick glance to Dirk. He realized he was not going to be as in control of this meeting as he'd hoped.

'They may be on to something,' Ralph reported. 'I'm not sure. I think I handled it pretty well, but they are smart people.'

Ralph immediately knew he'd made a mistake. Admitting that Lucas and Amber were smart was a major error. He'd promised John idiots, automatons that would go through the motions without causing any ripples or shaking any trees. He'd picked Lucas carefully, as he was one of the weaker associates on his staff, based on the performance reviews he'd read in Lucas's personnel file. Amber had been picked largely at random, being a more junior resource who had completed relatively few projects in her short time with the firm so had accumulated few meaningful ratings. But how dangerous could a twenty-six year old female be?

Ralph's problem had been that even his firm's weakest resources were still intelligent, educated people who wouldn't easily be snowballed or bamboozled. He'd not appreciated this, and even if he had he'd have been reluctant to share such a detail with John.

John recognized the error, and saw Ralph's cheeks flush a little. Ralph had given him more information than he'd expected, not that John would be immediately sharing it with Carlos. He stared at Ralph in silence; he was perhaps an even better exponent of giving the silent treatment than Ralph was himself. Ralph become even more uncomfortable as each second passed, and could not help himself from adding more fuel to the fire.

'I mean there was nothing definite, but they did talk about being followed.'

Ralph was now visibly uncomfortable, shifting his eyes rapidly from John to Dirk, both of whom caught and returned his gaze with an unrelentingly intensity.

Ralph paused, reminding himself that he was the senior partner of a major consulting firm, and was also part of the inner circle of the leadership team of GoldRock mining. He shouldn't be intimidated by a hired hand and some random thug. Carlos would smooth over any misunderstandings. They needed him.

'I told them to take some time off,' he added more confidently. 'I was against the visit, remember, but times are changing.'

John seized the initiative. 'They know everything. Carlos is coming to contain the situation.'

'Oh. God. That's, well that's...' Ralph's self-assuredness evaporated as he processed this information. He looked down at the table for a moment, gathering his thoughts.

'It's not my fault,' he continued boldly, plumping himself up in indignation. 'I said all along that we should be very careful. The guys you tasked with following them have really fucked up. If they'd done their jobs properly and kept a low profile I could have smoothed over any issues the kids raised. I could easily have overruled their concerns and sent a clean report on up to the E.P.A. You're paying me well, and I'd have done a good job, if these clowns had let me. Whoever those guys are, there are going to be in real big trouble.'

'Maybe,' John replied. 'But so are you. This is Dirk. He's one of the "clowns" who's been following them since Africa. He will now kill you.'

Without a word, Dirk smoothly lifted his hand above the level of the desk. In it was a small handgun, sporting a large silencer. Ralph looked in turn at Dirk, his hand and the gun with a combination of amazement and interest. Ralph's last thought was to ask himself whether the silencer could actually have been larger than the gun it was attached to.

Dirk fired four shots in very quick succession, moving the barrel marginally between each shot so that four distinct wounds were created, all within a sixteen square inch area of

Ralph's chest. One bullet per ventricle. Ralph was dead by the time the third bullet left the gun.

Dirk rose silently from the table, and slipped the gun back into the canvas bag, from which he then removed a plastic sheet. He carefully unfolded the sheet beside Ralph's chair, and pulling gently on Ralph's suit lapels, he used Ralph's dead weight to topple the body out of the chair and onto the sheet.

John looked on appreciatively. 'Nice work. No exit wounds.'

'Thank you,' replied Dirk as he folded Ralph's arms in so they were contained within the footprint of the sheeting. 'For this kind of job I like to use a low velocity bullet. You need a few hits to be sure, but it produces minimal splatter. I find the set-up is perfectly suited for use in a professional environment like this.'

'It's good to be working with a pro, unlike this *clown*,' John added. He smiled at the word. Who is the clown now, he thought.

He looked at his watch. 'The disposal team will be here in five minutes, so you'd better get scarce. I'll call Mike at the bureau, get him up to speed. Good luck with the kids.'

'It will be a pleasure,' Dirk replied without emotion. He quickly looked around the office, carrying out a quick inventory on his movements, what he had touched and what traces of his presence he had left behind. When he was confident that his attendance in the office that evening would be invisible to any forensic tests that might realistically be deployed, he nodded to John and departed.

* * *

Lucas had jumped onto the westbound Path train without having the first clue as to where the train was heading. Amber was able to explain that the train terminated at Newark station, where they'd be able to double back to Manhattan on either the Path or Amtrak services. Lucas thought the Amtrak was the smartest option, as this would quickly take them to Penn Station, which was only about ten blocks from his friend's apartment in Chelsea.

As their train arrived at Newark station and pulled to a gentle halt at its terminus, Lucas evaluated his options. If there was a 50% chance they'd been followed to and from Amber's apartment, Lucas thought it was at least 90% certain he'd given their follower the slip through switching trains so cleverly at Grove Street. He'd temporarily edited the part where he'd been left sprawling on the platform out of his mental highlight reel.

So he calculated that left only a 5% chance that there was someone following them on the train they were on. On the other hand, if someone *was* still with them after the Grove Street maneuver, that would make them extremely competent trackers who were skilled at avoiding detection. That would make them real pros, a thought which brought its own family of concerns to Lucas's mind. On balance, Lucas thought they would be unlikely to outsmart anyone that had the competence to still be on their tail.

So all things considered, Lucas thought they should just behave normally, or as normally as they could under the circumstances. After all, the bad guys probably knew they would be heading back to Manhattan anyway from their discussions in Amber's apartment.

Amber agreed with Lucas's analysis, quietly relieved that the worst might be over, for now at least. They agreed that Amber would shout out if she saw the big black guy or the smaller white guy, although they both doubted they'd appear as they'd be recognized instantly. Lucas would also keep his wits about him for familiar faces.

They exited the train looking around them for faces they recognized, but saw none. On the station's concourse, they saw that the Amtrak service to New York was very frequent, but as it was coming up on seven o'clock in the evening, the station traffic was at its heaviest. They realized they were both hungry, so after buying a ticket for the 8:32 train to New York's Penn station, they took a seat at the pizza restaurant on the concourse and shared a surprisingly good meal, making a point of talking about anything other than gold.

Davie was finding this too easy. He'd had a stroke of luck at Grove Street, but the guy and the girl did not appear to suspect he was still behind them so he was able to track them with ease. Each time he thought there was a chance that they'd got a clean look at him, he'd subtly altered his outfit. He'd rotated through three looks: wearing his hoodie with the hood up; wearing it with the hood down and taking it off completely. The simple subterfuge appeared to have been very effective in concealing his presence behind them.

The greatest risk he'd taken had been to get close enough to Lucas when he was at the Amtrak ticket counter to hear which specific train he'd bought the ticket for. That had brought him within four feet of Amber, but she'd been unaware of his presence and he'd clearly heard Lucas purchasing tickets for the 8:32 train.

Once Davie had called this information in to Jorge, he'd been told to stand down, as others would pick up the trail back in Manhattan. Jorge had promised Davie a considerable bonus, and had been very grateful to Davie for having kept so doggedly on the guys' trail.

Davie was a little uncomfortable about handing the guys off to persons unknown, but he had no real choice. He bought a ticket for the 7:10 train and decided he'd use the short travel time to walk through everything he'd seen and heard today to see what additional information he had gleaned on the organization.

As Lucas and Amber boarded their train back to Manhattan, Davie's message passed through three sets of ears before finally being delivered to Dirk. The daisy chain of calls had taken as long as to be completed as it had taken Lucas and Amber to share a large pizza, which annoyed Dirk a little as he and George would now have to hustle to reach the station before the train. But Dirk realized the importance of segregating information, and besides, it was fortunate that the kids had stopped to eat as this gave them a fighting chance to reach the station first.

George was again driving the rental car with Dirk in the passenger seat. Dirk's canvas bag sat largely out of sight in the passenger foot well, with Dirk unconsciously pressing his foot against it, as a dog likes to maintain contact with its master at all times.

Chapter Nineteen

Penn station in the waning hours of a New York day was a busy place. The more dedicated elements of the commuter population were dragging their tired and occasionally inebriated bodies back home for a nap before turning around and coming back to do it all again the following day. Theatre goers were starting to make their way home, babbling about whatever show had taken their fancy that night. Large numbers of tourists were arriving or departing, having not paid close attention to timing of their reservations when making their bookings. Many were silently regretting having to pass through a hectic railway station after nightfall, when the pan-handlers, touts and other detritus of New York's under belly were at their most tenacious.

Lucas and Amber's train had contrived to lose ten minutes against its schedule during the nine mile journey from Newark's Penn Station, and so pulled into the station at exactly nine pm. Lucas and Amber were eagerly standing by the door awaiting their arrival, striving to be first off the train and first into the New York night.

As the train stopped, every door flew open and six hundred passengers began to disgorge onto the platform, quickly turning it from a quiet nocturnal cave into a seething mass of humanity.

Lucas and Amber were indeed the first out of their carriage, but they were so quickly swept into the mass of alighting humanity that any tactical advantage was instantly lost. Progress towards the exit was slow, and they looked around nervously.

'Can you see anyone?' asked Lucas.

'No, but it's hard to see through the crowd,' Amber replied. 'How far is your friend's place?'

'It's about ten blocks. I'll call him from a pay-phone on the concourse. I can't believe they'd be tracking our cell phones, but let's take no chances.'

'Jeez – there's so much to think about. Will your friend be home?'

'Oh yes.'

Suddenly, Amber felt a strong hand gripping her arm, just above the elbow. The pressure on her arm suggested that her assailant was behind her and to her right, and she spun to see who was holding her.

She instantly saw that the hand belonged to Dirk, and her heart leapt into her throat. Dirk's face was intense with concentration, but his eyes are flicking around him as the bustle of humanity was everywhere. Their eyes met briefly and Dirk's expression told her all she needed to know.

Amber gasped, forcing her heart back into her chest, then inhaled and released a piercing scream. A natural reaction to the moment, and as she would reflect later, not a bad tactical move given the peril she faced.

Disappointingly, but as New Yorkers would tell you, unsurprisingly, no-one responded. No-one leapt to her defense, no-one reached for their cell to dial 9-1-1. Few people so much as flinched.

Lucas had continued his progress down the platform and had opened up a two-step gap while Amber's progress had been constrained by Dirk's grasp. He heard the scream, and fearing its likely origin he turned instinctively to confirm its source. His eyes scanned the crowd for a millisecond before settling on Amber, and a millisecond later, Amber's captor.

Dirk and Lucas's eyes locked. The oblique glimpses Lucas had had of Dirk's face at the airport in Accra and outside GoldRock's offices in New York combined to form a positive identification. Klaus. Dammit!

A second seemed to pass into an eternity, during which time a throng of passengers intervened, filling in the gap between Lucas and Amber that had been created.

Dirk quickly broke Lucas's gaze and began to steer Amber laterally across the flood of passengers. The platform was designed to handle just the one train, so other side of the platform away from the emptying train was a wall, against which pillars supporting the ceiling created a number of eddies in the flow of humanity, one of which Dirk was targeting. Amber wriggled in Dirk's grip, twisting to try and break his hold, but his other hand had slipped around her waist and he was easily able to steer her in his desired direction.

After taking barely a pace towards the wall, a commuter collided into Dirk's back, jolting his arm and releasing his grip on Amber's wrist. Sensing a degree of freedom, Amber spun her body and was able to slip out of the grip Dirk held around her waist. In an instant she sensed freedom...

'Hey, watch out fella,' said the commuter, angry to have had his progress impeded by some weedy fellow out with his wriggly girlfriend.

Dirk regained his balance, and on instinct, span to face the new threat, with his hands balled into fists, Amber momentarily forgotten. His eyes met the commuters, and the intensity and animal passion in the eyes put the commuter instantly on the defensive. The impression that had been formed of a weedy commuter was instantaneously dispelled.

'Hey, take it easy fella,' the commuter said, anxious to save face in the confrontation. 'Watch your step there, OK?'

Amber flexed the arm that had been in Dirk's grip and sensed that the unwelcome arm around her waist had also disappeared. With agonizing slowness, her brain deduced that she was free and could flee.

Using the motion of the people around her as a guide, she reoriented her body towards the exit, and took off, easily dodging around the other passengers. With two balletic leaps, she quickly bridged the two pace gap that had opened up between herself and Lucas, reaching him in an instant.

Lucas had watched Dirk's collision with the commuter, and had seen Amber achieve freedom. As he saw Amber begin to dance towards him, he swiveled his head, appraising the situation. He wanted to increase their separation from Dirk while he was still turned away from them, tackling his new adversary.

As Lucas turned back towards the exit, Dirk had completed his confrontation with the commuter and was also spinning back around, his eyes searching the crowd to reacquire his targets. His hand slipped inside his jacket, reaching for the steel enforcer he'd selected for this engagement, which he had secreted in a shoulder holster. His cursed under his breath as he concluded the same as he had when he'd first stepped onto the platform – there were just too many people around to justify deploying his weapon. A screaming woman could be ignored, a drawn gun not so much.

In the heartbeat it took for Dirk to review his strategy, the gap between him and his prey had been completely filled by commuters, spotting an opportunity to gain an additional step on their competition as they raced for the platform exit.

Lucas looked down at Amber who, sensing his movement looked back deep into his eyes. Lucas saw her eyes were wet with tears from the stress of the confrontation with Dirk. He sensed dependence in her eyes, a need for him to take control. To save the day. His heart raced, already overloaded with the stress of handling the adrenaline his body had created, but was also now burdened with the responsibility of navigating them out of the confrontation Dirk had initiated.

'Follow me,' he said firmly. 'I know my way around this place.'

Amber was in no position to argue, and she nodded. Hand in hand, they made for the exit. Paces behind them, separated by just a handful of passengers, Dirk followed.

The platform was still packed with passengers and the exit was still twenty paces away. Lucas and Amber dodged and weaved their way through the throng as quickly as they could, overtaking the occasional passenger but just as often being baulked by another.

Now four passengers behind, Dirk had the advantage of being alone, and so was able to nip into smaller gaps than Lucas and Amber could. But Dirk was frustrated that the gap was narrowing too slowly, and he soon realized that Lucas and Amber would reach the exit first, a mere two passengers ahead of him.

The exit was designed in an earlier age when ticket inspections were a key revenue protection device. As passenger numbers had grown over the years, the staff tasked with this goal found that already testy passengers rarely thanked them for further impeding their progress through the crowded station. So now guards checked tickets on the trains and the barriers had been removed, although the narrowing of the platform exits was an inbuild feature that could not be changed. Staff now manned the exits mainly to ensure the health and safety of passengers as they crammed through the narrow exit.

This relaxation of policy was what had allowed Dirk onto the platform without a ticket in the first place. His thinking had been that a confined platform, even one where everyone was moving at just above walking pace in one direction towards an exit, was a better venue to detain two people than the open concourse, where passengers fanned out rapidly and could easily disappear up any number of escalators or into any number of stores and restaurants.

As Dirk realized he would fail in his goal of sidelining the girl before they reached the barriers, he subdued his aggression and fell into step with those around him. He figured there was no point in making himself memorable to the employees notionally monitoring the exit.

As Lucas slowed and passed through the exit, he realized that the crowds fanned out rapidly on the far side. This would allow them to increase their pace considerably, but the downside would be that the mass of humanity was less dense, allowing quicker or more nimble pursuers to catch up with greater ease.

Lucas's trump card was that he had been to this station before, when he worked on a project with the local railroad to evaluate the environmental consequences of digging an additional tunnel under the Hudson. He'd spent two weeks on-site, working in the administration offices and so he had a very good grasp of the geography of the station, which he hoped would give him and Amber the edge they needed.

As Amber slowed and passed through the barrier, she couldn't resist the opportunity to glance over her shoulder. She gasped as she saw Dirk barely two passengers behind them. His eyes burned with the same fire, but his body language was calmer, blending in more innocently with the crowd. Her grip tightened on Lucas's arm, which conveyed to him everything he needed to know. They passed the barrier and began to run.

As Dirk slowed and passed through the barrier, his eyes scanned the concourse ahead, looking for George who had been left with the thankless task of parking their rental car slap bang in the center of New York City. Plan A, to sideline the girl on the platform, had failed but he knew that Plan B, a pincer movement on the concourse, was certain to succeed.

Chapter Twenty

George had succeeded in parking the car, having found a lot with vacancies just seconds before he ran out of patience and time. His alternative would have been to dump the car in the streets outside the station, which would have been a major inconvenience in the medium term even if it provided a short term benefit.

George jogged down an escalator onto the concourse, thrusting the car keys and the parking receipt into his jacket pocket. Pausing for a moment to scope out the platform layout, he quickly spotted the platform Dirk had called him to communicate three minutes earlier. As he started to jog towards the entrance to that platform, he quickly spotted Lucas and Amber running almost directly towards him. Behind them was Dirk, getting up to running speed and noticeably gaining on them.

Amber held tightly to Lucas's hand as they dashed across the concourse. Her eyes closely monitored the ground for obstructions as she ran, but she looked up briefly to try and deduce the target Lucas was heading for. All she could see was a wall with an unmarked door, and as she began to question what Lucas was planning, she saw George. Heading straight for them, around seventy feet away. Amber gasped and gripped Lucas's hand even tighter.

Lucas heard the gasp and felt the increased pressure on his hand, which was followed by a tug as Amber veered sharply to their right. Lucas looked ahead of them and saw a large black man running towards them. The neurons in Lucas's brain very quickly realized that this could only be their other foe, the large black man who was Klaus's companion. In that flash of recognition Lucas learned all he needed to know. Large. Mean. Approaching, rapidly. Lucas veered right, re-evaluating his exit strategy.

'That's the other guy?' gasped Lucas. He heard a shriek of acknowledgement from Amber and a new plan flashed into his mind.

Modifying their path slightly farther to the right, he headed for another unmarked door. George was now perhaps sixty feet behind them over their left shoulders, closing quickly. Dirk was somewhere over their right shoulders, but Lucas had neither the time nor inclination to look to estimate the gap. He figured it was probably less than fifty feet, and Dirk would be closing the gap more rapidly than George as Dirk was the more nimble pursuer. The brain's ability to perform complex differential calculus quickly enough to catch a speeding baseball gave Lucas the confidence that they'd reach the door before their pursuers. Lucas breathed a little easier realizing this. Once through the door, Lucas was on home territory and their chances of escape would increase significantly.

Lucas did indeed reach the door first, which he wrenched open and shoved Amber through. They burst into a surprisingly large administration room, which was filled mostly with cubicles housing the accounting function of the company running the station. Theoretically deserted at that time of night, Lucas was immediately irritated to notice that the lights were still burning, contravening his recommendation that motion sensors be installed to minimize energy consumption. A consultant's brain rarely switches off...

The door they entered from was unmarked from the concourse as railway management did not want to advertise what lay beyond. To further discourage rubberneckers who may glance in when the door was opened, it was equipped with a spring loaded closing mechanism, set to full power, which rapidly pulled the door closed behind Lucas with a clang. Several other doors led from this room.

Lucas jolted Amber to their left, towards a door when a head popped up from behind a cubical wall.

'Hey, the restrooms are on the platform,' shouted Theresa, a clerk engaged overnight to balance the previous day's ledgers. This was not the first time she'd given this information to lost souls, but she quickly realized that tonight was different.

'Is that you, Lucas?' she added in recognition.

Lucas initially flinched to hear a voice, then relaxed as he heard his name coming from a female. Looking over his shoulder as he dashed to the door, he recognized Theresa, who he'd worked with briefly during his stint at the station.

Three thoughts began to fight between themselves in his mind. "Don't stop". "That's why the lights are on". "Must be polite". He reached their target door, just as the door from the concourse was being wrenched open.

'Hi! Theresa, isn't it? Can't stop,' shouted Lucas.

Theresa raised a hand to wave, perplexed as to why Lucas and a stranger would be running through her office so late at night. Before she could complete the gesture, her attention was drawn to the hulking shape of George coming at speed through the first door.

Her struggle between "discretion" and "valor" was brief. George's large and animated state meant that discretion easily triumphed, and she ducked back into the relative safety of her cubical, fairly confident that George had not seen her.

George moved into the room, allowing Dirk space to enter behind him. Their eyes scanned the room, looking for clues as to where their quarries had gone. A moment passed and the door behind them clanged shut before they noticed the door swinging silently closed behind Amber, over to their left. Silently, they set off again in pursuit. In her cubicle, Theresa held her breath until she heard the large guy moving, at which time she silently picked up her phone.

Lucas and Amber burst into a long, narrow corridor. Amber looked up at Lucas with a quizzical face.

'Did some work here,' breathed Lucas, as his eyes scanned the corridor for the correct exit door. 'Come on.'

As the door swung shut behind them, they quickly covered the ten paces that took them to the second door of four down the right hand side of the corridor. As Lucas held it open for Amber to enter, he watched as the door behind him continued to lazily swing closed, dreading the inevitable moment when it re-opened. A wave of relief surged through his body when he was able to break his gaze and follow Amber without seeing the door re-open. His relief was misplaced as George wrenched the door open a millisecond after Lucas turned away.

Lucas and Amber entered a kitchen area which supplied the station's staff canteen. Lucas led Amber sharply to their right as he headed for a yet another door. The kitchen was very well lit, filled with stainless steel surfaces and little else, as the support for staff working the late shift was very limited. A serving window stretched the length of the kitchen, revealing a larger seating area beyond, which was deserted at this late hour. An overweight chef sat slumped on a chair beside a large range, comfortably warmed by the heat emitting from the oven, but sound asleep. Lucas and Amber's entry did not disturb his slumber.

In the corridor behind them, George and Dirk paused momentarily to determine the next door they needed to reach in the warren of offices and corridors that made up the back of house facilities of the station. They quickly noted the second door swinging closed but Dirk was becoming aware that each time they paused, the gap between them and their prey stretched. Not good. Following them into unfamiliar territory might have been a tactical error.

Lucas and Amber burst through the yet another door and Amber was surprised to find herself emerging into the cool of the New York night. Lucas knew this sidewalk well, as it was notionally a fire exit from the kitchen, but was better known as the closest area to the kitchens that the chefs could use to smoke.

In one smooth motion Lucas flagged down a passing taxi and flung open the door for Amber, looking anxiously behind him at the door to the kitchen.

George ripped open the door to the kitchen and threw himself through the gap as soon as it was wide enough to take his frame. His mistake was to pause when he saw the sleeping chef, a mistake he compounded when he paused for Dirk to enter the kitchen and gestured to him to indicate the chef's presence. This delay was enough to allow the door to the street to close fully before Dirk and George were able to scan the new room for telltales as to their prey's next destination. Dirk immediately realized the game was up. He motioned George into the dining area, away from the chef's earshot.

'Enough,' he commanded. George stood with his hands on his hips, breathing heavily. Dirk was barely breathing. 'We've drawn too much attention to ourselves. Let them run. They'll make mistakes. John will know where they're going by now. We'll get them there.'

A smile slowly built across George's face.

Lucas anxiously looked over his shoulder out of the back window of the taxi as the street door to the kitchen receded into the distance. The door remained resolutely closed until his view was broken by traffic moving into the lane behind them.

Lucas sighed. 'Thank God for that project,' he said after calming his breathing.

'Good job through that maze,' Amber replied, genuinely appreciative of Lucas's efforts. 'I think the rabbit hole is pretty deep.'

'No kidding,' Lucas replied, paternally patting Amber on the knee. 'How are you doing?'

'I've been better. They don't teach this stuff at college.'

Lucas smiled. He looked at their driver, largely hidden behind a large Perspex screen. Lucas's conclusion was that English was not the driver's first language which allowed him to relax a little more.

'This is getting serious,' Lucas added.

'So we can assume that *they* know that *we* know. And we can assume that they know that we're scared.'

'Yeah. Let me call Eric. He'll know what to do. I'll risk the cell.'

Lucas paused, looking for some signal of consent from Amber. He'd saved the day at the station but it had been more responsibility he didn't particularly enjoy and hadn't really sought.

Amber frowned, but was smart enough to know that what you see in the movies is not reality, and a cruise missile was unlikely to hit their cab within seconds of Lucas's call connecting. The bad guys knew they were in New York, and they were still within a few blocks of the station, where they'd been chased moments earlier. Making a call couldn't do any harm, even if the bad guys were monitoring the calls. She nodded and Lucas pulled his cell from his pocket.

Chapter Twenty-one

Eric Crick was sitting in his apartment, staring intently into one of a number of computer monitors in front of him. His apartment was an unusual blend of cutting edge technology and bleeding edge domestic chaos.

One side of his apartment comprised a large, unmade bed, a sofa covered in a throw that was pockmarked with holes and splattered in stains and a La-Z-Boy, which was currently pulling double duty as a laundry basket. Dishes lay unwashed in the sink, takeaway food cartons overflowed the trash can and soda cans were liberally scattered throughout the apartment. The overwhelming perception was of untidiness, although Eric would never recognize it as such – he simply didn't see the mess in his apartment. To Eric, his apartment was merely a support mechanism for his real passion in life.

The other side of his apartment comprised a wall of computer racking, which would not have looked out of place in a data center. Innumerable servers, switches and other high-tech pieces of equipment sat securely on the rack's shelving, connected by what seemed like miles of cabling, all of which was corralled and restrained by tags, ties and clips. Many of the larger boxes had L.E.D. light panels which blinked their mysterious signals with a beautiful and hypnotic rhythm. The overwhelming perception was hi-tech efficiency. People who criticized the tidiness of Eric's apartment would be directed to the computer wall, which was a model of organization and order.

Eric himself mirrored the union of chaos and order of his apartment. He was scruffily dressed in a gray long sleeved undershirt, over which he wore a black t-shirt bearing the slogan "Rehab is for Quitters". The outfit was finished with jogging bottoms and white socks. His choice of clothing sharply contrasted with his hi-tech watch and the futuristic spectacles he wore.

Eric spent a solitary life, interacting with others mostly via electronic means, yet was hugely in demand for the very specific skills he possessed and offered for sale. Talking to himself was a habit he'd fallen into over the years, and it only bothered him when others pointed it out to him.

'That's not good. Not good at all,' he said, as he paged through a report he'd pulled up on his screen from a system to which he regularly gained illicit access.

The intercom buzzed, which broke Eric's concentration. Eric, being an electronics hobbyist as well as a world class computer hacker, had routed his apartment building's intercom system through his computer. When the intercom buzzed, a window popped open on his screen, streaming the image captured by the building's security camera, mounted over the front door. Eric smiled as he saw Lucas's face looking earnestly up into the lens. Eric's attention was quickly drawn to a very attractive companion standing beside Lucas. The full extent of this companion's attractiveness was hard to measure as the camera lens had focused on Lucas, who was filling the majority of the screen as he peered eagerly into the lens. This left his companion alluringly blurry beside him.

Eric picked up a headset which contained an integrated microphone and spoke a simple word of welcome as he typed a password into his computer to relax the entry door's electronic lock. He watched as Lucas and his companion passed beneath the camera and entered the building.

Knowing that it would take a few minutes for his guests to reach his apartment door, Eric took the opportunity to page through another dozen sheets of the online report he was "borrowing".

'Not good at all,' he said to himself. 'What have you two been up to?'

His concentration was interrupted again by a sharp knock on the door. Eric keyed a password into another security window that he kept permanently open on his desktop, and the locking mechanisms securing his front door responded by retracting on command. The door clicked open. It never failed to amuse Eric that he could even control the locks on his front door from his computer.

He rose to greet Lucas as he and Amber entered the room. Amber, seeing Lucas embracing Eric, turned to close the door and instinctively looked to re-apply some of the locks she'd heard opening on the way in. She recoiled a little in surprise when she saw a number of complex mechanisms kicking into action as soon as the door closed, automatically returning the locks to their closed position. She frowned – what exactly did this Eric friend specialize in? She turned her attention back to the male embrace, which was coming to an end.

'Man, good to see you,' said Eric. 'What the hell have you been up to?'

'Hi Eric,' replied Lucas, ignoring the question, for the moment at least. 'This is Amber, a colleague from the firm.'

Eric was not renowned for his success with the ladies, and his awkwardness was illustrated when he screwed his face into a ball and delivered his best Joey Tribbiani impersonation.

'How you doin'?' Eric asked, in a passable imitation, his right eyebrow rising suggestively on the middle syllable. He turned to Lucas and gave an exaggerated wink.

'She's a colleague, dumbass,' Lucas replied.

Amber thought Lucas's response was a little quick and a little exaggerated, but decided to let it pass. She stepped forward to shake Eric's hand.

'Pleased to meet you,' she said.

'Indeed,' Eric replied. 'I say again, what the hell have you two been up to?'

'Were having an interesting day, to say the least,' Lucas responded. Where did you start with a story like theirs?

'I think I know what you mean,' said Eric. 'Take a look at this.'

Eric motioned for them both to look at a screen he had opened on his computer. Lucas and Amber leaned in, to see photos of themselves on a page prominently headed by a banner labeled "F.B.I.".

'This is the F.B.I. "hot-sheet",' Eric continued. 'As of an hour ago you are both wanted for the murder of Ralph West.'

Lucas and Amber both recoiled from the screen, momentarily unable to process the incredible information they had just learned. Lucas's mouth flapped open as he repeatedly attempted to form a coherent sentence, failing each time.

Amber continued to back away from the screen until her calves hit the edge of Eric's bed. She crumbled back and sat sharply on the bed, but quickly realized that sitting did not fully reflect the depth of her despair, so she collapsed backwards, ending up lying fully horizontal on the bed.

Eric watched her topple with another raised eyebrow. He leaned towards Lucas.

'Not the way I hoped to get a girl that cute onto my bed!' he whispered.

This jolted Lucas out of his stupor, enough to shoot Eric what he hoped was a withering look. I shouldn't protest too much, he thought. Gathering his senses, he realized his brain would now co-operate with his mouth so he nudged Eric and pointed back to the screen.

'That's impossible,' he said evenly.

'Obviously,' replied Eric. 'How long have I known you? Ten years? You couldn't kill a chicken, let alone another human being. It says you "shot West in a parking lot after a dispute over a performance rating". It goes on to say that you were both seen earlier that afternoon "leaving his office in an agitated state".'

Amber remained prone on Eric's bed.

'Fuck!' she exclaimed at the ceiling.

"Feisty,' Eric quietly said to Lucas. 'Not your usual type, buddy.'

'This can't be happening,' said Lucas, ignoring Eric's barbs. 'The rabbit hole's deeper than that damn mine.'

'You'd better go back to the beginning,' said Eric, realizing that his comedic talents were not being embraced by his visitors.

Chapter Twenty-two

Back in the GoldRock offices, John paced anxiously around his office, desperate for news of any developments in the manhunt. The blinds were still drawn but Ralph's corpse had long since been removed. John was confident that his disposal crew had left no incriminating traces.

Several hours had passed since Dirk had reported the near miss at the station. Dirk and George had left the scene and laid low for an hour or so, in case their activities had been reported and the authorities were involved. None of the conspirators knew that Theresa, the station's night auditor, had indeed called the transportation police when she'd seen Dirk and George lurching through her offices. They also couldn't know that her glimpse had been so brief that the police had decided to take no action when learning that her descriptions of the intruders extended little beyond "big and black" and "small and white".

John's hopes of achieving a rapid interception were fading as the hours passed. Their best lead was this friend in Chelsea with a father in the F.B.I., but tracking him down was proving to be harder than they might have anticipated as for some reason the guy seemed to be unusually hard to trace.

John took a deep breath and began to replay the sequence of events in his mind that had brought about the growing crisis he was facing. He found it useful to regularly do this, for two reasons. Firstly, the process often provided him with the perspective to project the time line forward, which often produced some clue as to what to do next. Secondly, and John thought most importantly, regularly refreshing his memory with precisely what had happened allowed him to clearly apportion blame.

He dwelt at length on the phone conference he and his collaborators had had with Carlos in this very office, during which Carlos had used the fatalistic words "no cause for concern'. Yes there was cause for concern, Carlos. Lots of fucking concern.

John was sure that the three men present for that call had all taken Carlos's assurances to heart. After all, Carlos was not a man to be doubted when making assertions like that. John instinctively looked at the conference table when he thought of Ralph West, who had been the second man at that meeting. John had reluctantly accepted Ralph's participation as a necessary consequence of complying with that damned law that Congress had passed, something that was now looking like a catastrophic mistake. John was sure Carlos would remember his protestations.

It seemed simple. GoldRock would already have to pay a significant amount of money to a consulting firm for the pleasure of being reported on. So they would just need to pay a little more, directly to the chosen firm's managing partner, to guarantee a positive report. Actually, pay quite a lot more, John thought, wondering briefly if there was any way of getting his money back given the beneficiary was now dead.

Finding a cooperative firm had been surprisingly easy. There were very few to choose from anyway, as the law was still fresh on the statute books and only five firms had gained the accreditation from the Environmental Protection Agency needed to conduct the required reviews.

Ralph and his firm had been an easy choice, as Ralph was known to have taken on some morally ambiguous clients in the past, including one in particular who'd had been slaughtered in the press for allegedly employing child labor at a diamond mine in western Africa.

Ralph's firm had been engaged to review these questionable operations as the firm in question believed that an independent report which found nothing of concern would be a significant step in to process of rebuilding public confidence. Sure enough, after what was described as a thorough review, Ralph's firm had indeed reported that nothing was, or had been, amiss.

The problems reappeared when an investigation by a particularly militant human rights group had found the exact opposite a few months later. The undercover footage was so damning that the credibility of Ralph's entire firm was called into question. Fortunately for Ralph, the mining company in question owned up to having deceived its consultants and Ralph's firm was exonerated in the court of public opinion.

Despite the exoneration, there was some lingering speculation in the industry that illicit payments had been made to Ralph West prior to the original project. The rumors were that these payments had been substantial, payments which John's sources were able to confirm had indeed been made to a Mr. R. H. West.

The trick had been to persuade Ralph to participate in GoldRock's scheme without overtly threatening him. Money was obviously the key factor in the negotiations, but they needed a partner who was fully engaged, not someone fearful of being turned in the moment he was no longer required. The clinching factor in the negotiation had been access. Ralph would get to sit at the top table throughout the process, building a mutual complicity between all participants that reduced the degree to which Ralph was an outsider. John had reservations about this arrangement but eventually had been persuaded.

From this participation, Ralph had learned facts about the wider organization that John was not at all comfortable sharing, but Congress's law was a game-changing development. No-one in the GoldRock organization had foreseen the law, although they'd agreed that it was not reasonable for them to have anticipated the development. They'd also been surprised by the speed of the law's passage. An evaporating majority in the Senate combined with a faltering Presidential re-election campaign had taken the process from concept to fully fledged law in less than a year. GoldRock had needed to scramble.

John's thoughts returned to the payments Ralph had negotiated. Half a million dollars had already been paid to an offshore account in Labuan, of all places, with another half million due when Ralph lodged the unqualified report. John had planned to ask Ralph why he'd chosen Labuan, which John had needed to look up on a map. John was always on the look-out for interesting financial centers with particularly opaque banking regulations, and that specific Malaysian island seemed like an interesting place to investigate.

Not that it mattered now that Ralph was dead. In fact, John thought, Ralph was likely to be more valuable to GoldRock dead than he had been alive, as he could be used to provide a cast-iron motive for taking down the kids.

The third man who'd been on that conference call from Carlos several weeks earlier had been Mike Pointer. Mike was another expensive investment for GoldRock, but unlike Ralph, this particular investment had been repaid at least a hundred times over the five years of their relationship. It was Mike that John was waiting for. On cue, Mike walked briskly into the room.

Mike was tall, six foot three to be specific, but he was solidly built with height proportionate to his weight, which did not make him appear lanky as many tall people so often did. He wore a dark blue suit, tailored to be baggy around the armpits where he carried his service issue gun, his particular service being the Federal Bureau of Investigations, where he was a twelve year veteran.

'How did we miss them at the station?' Mike asked.

'It was a tough break,' John replied. 'We got close, but there were too many people around.'

Mike's shoulders sagged at the news was confirmed. He inhaled, holding the breath for a long moment before exhaling and opening a new chapter in their pursuit.

'OK. Well, the news is on the wires. Every police officer in the country will be looking for them.'

'We have evidence that will make the charges stick?' asked John.

'Sure. I'll get physical evidence on the gun if I have to,' Mike replied. 'We picked up some good stuff from their apartments that should more than cover it. There's enough circumstantial evidence out there right now to keep people motivated.'

'You've assumed jurisdiction over the case?' John asked.

'Yeah. There was a helpful clause in the original law that created this mess. It extended federal protection to employees of firms accredited by the E.P.A. So the murder of West is technically a federal crime, so the F.B.I. was able to take over jurisdiction of the case.'

'Good,' John said quietly, reflecting that the federal status of the felony might one day be as relevant to John and Mike as it was now to Lucas and Amber. This was already obvious to Mike, so the thought hung in the air between them for a moment.

'Do we know where they're heading?' John eventually asked.

'Yeah. It took some cross-referencing but we've got an address. I had to do it myself. I've missed a lot of computer courses over the years.'

Mike drew a scrap of paper from his pocket and handed it to John. John looked at it and smiled. He picked up the phone.

Chapter Twenty-three

Back in Eric's apartment, an hour had passed which had allowed Lucas and Amber to take showers and to change clothes. Both now wore jeans and t-shirts, Amber's very well-tailored to her figure, Lucas's not so much, as he and Eric's body shapes weren't a close match.

Eric was sitting at his computer station.

'I think you're right,' he said. 'There is no gold. But there must be drugs. It's the only explanation that makes any sense. Only drugs could generate that volume of cash.'

Lucas and Amber exchanged glances. That sounded reasonable. Eric leaned back in his chair, reflecting. After a moment he leaned forward.

'So a gold mine with no gold is being used to launder drug money,' he said. 'There's supposed to be lots of gold, so they can launder lots of money. The only question is how?'

Lucas had moved across the room and was crouching beside Eric's chair.

'That would be a pretty sophisticated operation,' he said respectfully.

'Yes,' Eric replied. 'And then you geniuses turn up and figure it out. Or figure enough of it out to scare the shit out of them. I hope you didn't leave any clues as to where you were going...'

Lucas and Amber instinctively looked at each other. Their guilt could not be more obvious. Lucas looked back at Eric with a strained smile.

'You left some clues,' concluded Eric, his head sagging forward in dejection.

The burgundy rental car was slowly being navigated through the confusing streets of New York. George was driving, but the G.P.S. system was struggling to get a clear sightline to its satellites given the canyon-like nature of the streets. To counter this, Dirk was in the passenger seat struggling to orient a large street map of Manhattan to remain in synch with the frequent turns George was taking.

Dirk peered out of the window as George slowed the car to a crawl. It was close to midnight so the traffic was much lighter than it had been earlier, although there was still enough activity on the streets of the city that never sleeps to prevent them from gaining any real momentum.

'Yes. Here we are,' said Dirk.

George spotted a parking spot and eased the car in.

In Eric's apartment, the energy level was high. Lucas and Amber were in confessional mode.

'We may have left a clue,' Lucas said. 'Amber's apartment was bugged. Some microscopic camera unit they'd hidden on top of the wardrobe. There was no recording capability on it so it must have been broadcasting a picture in real time.'

'Do you have it with you?' asked Eric. 'I could probably tell a lot about who is after you from looking at it.'

'We destroyed it,' Lucas replied, regretting his decision to be violent.

'Good job,' said Eric sarcastically. 'So what makes you think you left clues?'

'We might have mentioned coming to see you before we noticed the bug,' replied Lucas, studiously avoiding eye contact with Eric. He recounted the details of the conversation he'd had in Amber's apartment.

'We're pretty certain we didn't mention you by name though,' added Amber, hopefully.

'Well that's something,' said Eric sarcastically. 'So they know "friend", "New York", "father in the F.B.I.". Thanks guys. It would take *me* about two minutes to find me. We should assume it'll take *them* a few hours.'

Seven stories below, Dirk and George stood before the security panel outside Eric's apartment building. Dirk was carrying his familiar canvas bag. George was carrying a large sledgehammer, trying hard to make the object appear like a normal accessory for an urban New Yorker out and about in the late evening.

Dirk retrieved a roll of masking tape from his bag, and deftly stuck a piece of tape over the lens of the camera. Turning his attention to the lock, he swapped the tape for a small device with a number of protruding prongs. Looking from the lock to the prongs, he selected one and inserted it into the lock. He pressed a button on the device and seemed perplexed when the lock did not open. He withdrew the prong, reinserted it and pressed the button again. George looked on with interest.

Back upstairs, Lucas was reflecting on Eric's last statement. The room had fallen silent as the implications of Eric's pronouncement were thought through.

'Yeah – I've been meaning to ask,' said Lucas, deflecting the subject away from his shortcomings in Amber's apartment. 'I thought you were a network administrator.'

'Yeah, kind of. Smile!' Eric had grabbed a very compact digital camera from the shelving above his monitor and proceeded to snap photos of Lucas and then Amber. He swung his chair back to his desk and deftly connected the camera to a cable that snaked into one of the servers located in the racking.

'I tend to administer other people's networks,' he added, talking over his shoulder while he pounded away on his keyboard. 'I try to administer them in a way their owners don't know about. I do a lot of freelance stuff for my Dad these days. The Patriot Act was fantastic for those in my line of work.'

'Hence the access to the F.B.I. hot-sheets,' Amber said.

'Exactamundo,' Eric replied. 'You guys had better hit the road. Probably best to get out of the country. I'll get my old man on the case. He'll believe me so he'll believe you. And he met you at our graduation. He won't believe for one second that you're a cold blooded murderer.'

Eric's fingers positively flew across his keyboard.

Dirk continued to wrestle with the lock, becoming increasingly frustrated that his hi-tech gizmo was not working. The very brief research Mike had been able to conduct had told Dirk that Eric was a bit of an electronics whizz, and Dirk was beginning to think that the lock's resistance to his persuasion might be an indication of the kid's talent.

George stood by, patiently waiting for his turn, which he knew would be coming soon. After another moment, he tapped Dirk politely on the shoulder. Dirk hated to be defeated, but time was not their friend so he nodded before putting the electronic device back into his canvas bag. He retired dejectedly to a safe distance.

George looked quickly around him to make sure there was enough clearance for the maneuver he'd been planning, then, gripping the sledgehammer firmly in both hands, he wound himself up to deliver a massive blow to the door. The head of the sledgehammer easily gained speed in George's massive hands as it flew through a graceful arc, a precision instrument in the hands of an expert.

* * *

Upstairs, a machine on Eric's rack wall emitted a gentle beep, indicating that its task was complete. A plastic card dropped into a tray beneath the machine, followed seconds later by another.

'We've got our passports with us,' said Lucas, swelling a little at his foresight. 'But won't they be looking for us?'

'You're thinking the right way,' Eric replied, encouragingly. 'I can help with that. Passports might be a problem, though. They're easily tagged. Don't use your credit cards either, as they'll also be tagged. There's some cash in the drawer. By the bed.'

He pointed towards the far side of the room and Amber quickly moved across the room in response.

Opening the drawer, she removed a significant roll of cash, held together with a sturdy elastic band. Her face betrayed surprise at the size of the roll, along with a measure of confusion as to its origins. She held it delicately, as if it carried some disease she might contract from physical contact. Eric glanced across at her, interrupting the furious typing on his keyboard.

'My deal with my Dad is not exclusive,' he said by way of explanation. 'And the IRS has some of the best systems of any government department. I kinda leave them out of some things... Take it – bring me back what you don't use, there's plenty more under the bed.'

'Thanks man,' Lucas said as Amber began peeling hundred dollar bills from the roll. 'We appreciate it.'

He paused for a while thinking.

'Won't buying a ticket with cash set off a whole other set of alarms?'

Eric reflected for a minute. 'Good thinking – good catch. Go somewhere where people have a lot of cash, so you won't stand out so much. Like Las Vegas.'

'Or Atlantic City. Its closer,' said Amber, pleased to be contributing something constructive to the discussion. Her pleasure grew as Eric gave her a radiant, supportive smile.

Chapter Twenty-four

Downstairs, the bulky entrance door had comprehensively and quickly yielded to George's persuasion. George and Dirk looked up and down the street, concerned that their dispute with the door may have been overheard. After a moment, they were able to relax as no-one seemed to have been disturbed by the brief but noisy altercation.

Silently, they entered the building.

Eric stood, allowing the keyboard to slip from his lap to his floor. He looked at Amber, who was putting a roll of cash into her bag, and Lucas, who was hopping excitedly from foot to foot.

'Atlantic City is a great idea,' he said. 'Not the biggest airport in America, but no-one would expect you to head there. I'll go shack up with my old man until this blows over. They won't take him on. Better use the fire escape – they may already be staking the place out.'

Lucas and Amber straightened at this, sensing that the threat was real and any sense of security they'd felt from being in Eric's apartment was likely to be over.

In the lobby of the apartment building, Dirk and George's next battle was with the elevator, which steadfastly refused to obey their command to elevate. These commands became increasingly emphatic, but the elevator would not budge. As part of the building's security system, the lift was constrained to operate only if a tenant had authorized access through the front door. As Dirk and George's access had been unauthorized to the extreme, the elevator wasn't moving.

Dirk had no electronic gizmo in his bag that would help. George was tempted to use the sledgehammer, but he realized his desire grew from frustration, rather than a belief that beating the snot out of an elevator would make it obey their commands.

Dejectedly, they left the elevator and headed to the stairwell.

Lucas's moment of tension passed, and he resumed his nervous jiggling.

'Wait,' he said. 'You haven't told us how to get through the border if we can't use our passports.'

Eric moved rapidly around his apartment, throwing clothing into two backpacks, one for him and one for Lucas.

'Just use your passports as normal,' he said. 'There's a flaw in the border security system, which I actually found. The fix is blocked in committee for some bullshit reason. I just accessed the US passport database and swapped two digits of your passport number. I also added a space character to the name field.'

Lucas looked at Eric, shaking his head gently as if the preceding sentence had been delivered in a foreign language.

Downstairs, Dirk and George quickly found the stairwell and easily defeated the security door which momentarily blocked their access. Fire doors at ground level open outwards, and can always be opened from the inside, but are rarely have handles on the outside.

Once inside the stairwell, George and Dirk looked at the stairwell spiraling upwards and exchanged glances. A silent question, easily answered.

'Seven,' said Dirk.

George shrugged. 'Could be worse.'

'They swipe your passport and your name shows up, matching with the reservation and everything,' Eric continued as he threw clothing into the bags. 'The extra space is enough to stop the name from hitting the alert list.

'Computers are really, really smart, but only in a really linear way – they see differences that the human eye wouldn't discern. So "Lucas space space Steadman" doesn't match the "Lucas space Steadman" they're looking for, so no alarms go off. Computers can be really dumb at times, so dumb that people like me can be made to look brilliant. Once the name checks out and no alarms start ringing, no-one's going to check the number that flashes up on their system. It's human nature. Name? Check. Face? Check. Nine digit number? Too hard. So they'll let you through.'

Lucas nodded appreciatively. Eric was one smart guy.

'So you just hacked into the government's system and changed our passport records?' he asked.

'Yeah. It's pretty simple actually,' Eric said modestly, standing by the wardrobe, choosing to observe his guests as the depth of his genius sank in. 'I think the money for the fix is blocked because the Homeland Security wonks don't want to admit that there's such an easy way to circumvent their controls.'

Eric stretched a little, basking in his own glory for an indulgent moment.

'My trick's not completely foolproof though.' he continued, returning his attention to filling his and Lucas's bags. 'A super observant clerk might spot the number issue, but passport controls are done by the airline agents these days and they're rarely super-observant people. The Border Protection people can obviously also manually cross reference names and numbers after the fact. But by then you'll be far, far away.'

Dirk and George reached a landing marked four. Dirk noted the number and pressed on, not noticing the small gap that had opened up between himself and George, who was lumbering up the stairs behind him.

George reached the fourth landing, paused, looked at the number and inhaled deeply. He held the precious oxygen in his lungs for a luxurious second, before turning the corner and continuing to climb. He was a little embarrassed to notice the size of the gap that was opening up between himself and Dirk.

Eric's dance around the room was just about complete, and he'd filled both bags with what he thought would be enough clothing for a few days. This crisis wouldn't last much longer than that, he thought. He tossed one of the bags to Lucas, who caught it at the second attempt.

Amber had been thinking while Eric had been packing.

'Perhaps we should go as far as we can before we use our passports?' she said. 'If the trick isn't foolproof? They're going to be less alert in San Diego than they'd be in New York, surely? Besides, that would give you and your dad more time to get this all squared away.'

'Yeah,' Lucas added. 'Good thinking. We should go somewhere like, Hawaii?'

'Sure,' Eric replied. 'My trick *will* work, thank you very much for the confidence. But I understand your caution. It's not my ass. Perhaps you should go even further. Somewhere like Guam. Or Saipan. They're US territories, so it's still considered a domestic flight from Hawaii. So no passports are required. From there it's like three hours flying time to the Philippines or Japan. The T.S.A. still runs the airports out there so you'll still need to be on alert, but it's a long way from the mainland.'

Lucas and Amber nodded enthusiastically.

'Don't use your driving licenses either,' Eric continued. 'They'd be real easy for the bad guys to catch.'

Dirk opened the fire door to the seventh landing and waited patiently for George to catch him up. Dirk had a lot of time and respect for George, but had quickly realized that his skill set did not include running great distances or climbing stairs in a hurry. In fact, it excluded any activity that raised the pulse rate above ambient levels. He sure knew how to swing a sledgehammer, though.

George appeared beside him. Dirk and George exchanged glances and a George nodded that he was good to go. Small beads of perspiration had formed on George's temples but his breathing was silent and Dirk judged that they were ready. Silently, they moved down the corridor looking for Eric's apartment.

Eric pulled the two cards from his printer's dump tray and handed one each to Lucas and Amber. Lucas looked at the object and saw a Texas State driving license with his picture on it. He looked at Eric with a smile.

Eric nodded and tapped the card printer appreciatively. 'I love Ebay almost as much as the Patriot Act,' he said.

Lucas turned to Amber. "Hello, I'm Larry Shelton,' he said. 'Pleased to meet you!'

Amber looked down at her card and replied: 'Hi. I'm Abigail McNally.'

'LS and AM,' Eric nodded, smiling at his friend's amusement. 'I tried to give you some hope of remembering your own names.'

'I haven't had a fake id for years...' Amber offered to no-one in particular.

Lucas raised his eyebrows, a reaction that Eric saw. Amber used to have a fake id? Maybe he had been underestimating her... Eric smiled knowingly. He could tell that he was out of the hunt but perhaps his friend wasn't entirely without hope...

Dirk was standing in the hallway outside Eric's apartment with his ear to the door. He frowned as the door seemed to be unusually thick, and he found he could hear nothing with his naked ear. He quickly reached into his canvas bag and withdrew another small device, this time a metal box with two long cables snaking from it. Dirk easily slipped the end of one of the cables through the crack under the door – this was a sensitive microphone. The other cable ended in an earpiece, which he slipped into his ear.

After tuning the device, he was able to clearly hear the occupants. They were talking about college parties, something Dirk had no knowledge of and no interest in. As Lucas, Eric and Amber joked, he raised one, then two and finally three fingers as he heard each voice. Hearing enough, he pulled the microphone smartly out from under the door. He turned to George, who was standing with his sledgehammer primed in both hands, ready for more action.

'Bingo,' whispered Dirk with a crooked smile. 'A full set.'

George swung the hammer.

Chapter Twenty-five

Inside the apartment, the sense of amusement died instantly as the door to Eric's apartment bowed in under the pressure of the attack from George.

Lucas gasped, Amber emitted a small squeak of shock and both froze. Eric was the first to react.

'Showtime,' he said. 'Out the window, down the fire escape. Go right at the bottom and head through the comic book store at the end. It's open twenty-four hours.'

The door bowed inwards again under the impact of the hammer. Eric noticed with interest that the blows were being aimed at the door's hinges, which benefitted from considerably less protection from Eric's locking devices than did the side of the door with the handle. Eric chastised himself briefly, and took a mental note to remedy that shortcoming when he got back to his apartment.

The window was an old fashioned sash window with two panels, the lower of which slid up behind the upper. Amber easily wrenched the lower window open and quickly looked outside, seeing a landing with a precarious iron ladder leading down to the ground via landings on each intermediate floor. She quickly climbed out of the window as the third blow hit the front door. The wood began to splinter as the door inevitably yielded under the assault.

Lucas swung one leg through the window. Amber had quickly descended to the sixth floor landing, where she paused to look up and was pleased to see Lucas emerging onto the seventh floor landing.

Another blow from George fractured the integrity of the door, and created a small channel through which light could be seen.

Eric had one foot out of the window but paused when he remembered his system. His assumption had to be that the bad guys would destroy the set-up, or at the very least would compromise it irreparably. He did not pause because of the cost or inconvenience of rebuilding the set-up elsewhere, or for any sentimental attachment he had to his apartment. He paused because he'd left the printer window open, showing the names he'd used on the fake driving licenses. Within seconds, any competent computer user would have been able to review what had been printed and would see the names he'd used. Then any hope of escape for his friends would be snuffed out.

Chastising himself again for making such a stupid mistake, Eric resigned himself to having to re-enter the apartment.

As was the case with everyone employed in Eric's specialist profession, he'd anticipated the need to power down his equipment quickly and discretely under circumstances such as these. He had installed a kill switch under his desk which would superficially shut down the system in an instant, blanking all monitors and extinguishing the lights on the servers. The shut-down was only superficial, as enough system resource remained active to covertly conduct an orderly power down within the guts of the machine, saving all data and purging histories.

It would take an expert to realize that the seemingly dormant machines were still active, and it would take a real expert to be able to interrupt the power down process in the few minutes it took to complete. Real computer experts tended not to be also highly skilled with sledgehammers. If the shutdown process was allowed to complete, it would take an expert several hours if not days, to crack the system back open. Which should buy Eric and his friends enough time to get scarce.

Eric quickly pulled his leg back into the apartment and danced across his apartment. He was able to hit the kill switch which he'd cunningly concealed in the racking frame at the same moment that the door fractured more comprehensively from another blow from George's sledgehammer.

The break in the door was now large enough to comfortably see through, and a panicked glance from Eric saw a huge black man in the corridor with a sledgehammer. Behind him, Eric caught a glimpse of another man, smaller, whiter, and holding something metallic and shiny, which Eric quickly concluded was a gun. This really was serious…

* * *

In the hallway, Dirk was becoming concerned at the time it was taking to get through the door, and the noise that George was making in achieving his goal. The die was cast though, so he bobbed and weaved in an attempt to see past George, through the break in the door. He caught a glimpse of a scrawny fellow fiddling with the computers. He raised the gun to take a shot, but his target disappeared before he could get the bullet away, having being obscured by the head of the hammer as it disappeared once more into the door.

George was tiring from the exertion, but he could sense that victory was close so redoubled his efforts. He could feel Dirk's eagerness to get into the room, but the door was reinforced with some kind of rebar system that George had not encountered before. A few more blows, he thought.

Eric paused for barely a second to ensure the system did indeed go to black in response to his hitting the kill switch. His knowledgeable ear could hear the master server gently continuing to whirr as it covertly stepped through the background shut-down processes it had been tasked with, but the various displays and L.E.D. panels went instantly dark. He allowed himself a small smile as the process worked exactly as he'd designed, but another blow to the door from George quickly snapped him back into action.

He turned back to the window and covered the four paces in less than two seconds, but was alarmed to hear that George's latest blow had caused the door to emit a significant groan as it continued to succumb. Eric glanced down the fire escape through the window, but both Lucas and Amber were obscured by the solid metal landings. Eric smiled when he heard distinct metal clangs as they descended. Great, he thought, they're going to make it. Now to make sure I do as well.

As Eric swung a leg back out of the window, he glanced behind him to see the door was now in two pieces. The left half with the handle was still secured by the bulk of Eric's locking mechanism, but the other half with the hinges had yielded and was lying on the floor. Eric saw George stepping back into the hallway as Dirk dodged through the gap, gun raised, pointing at Eric. Shit. Eric froze.

'How you doing, this morning?' asked Eric with a smile.

Eric's brain went through an unusual arc in the second that followed. He assumed that the "enemy" presented before him had killed before, so they were more than capable of doing so again. Lucas and Amber certainly hadn't killed Ralph West, who was certainly dead. But was this the guy who'd actually done the killing? He certainly had a gun, which was bad news. But the guy they'd murdered had almost certainly been part of the conspiracy, a conspiracy they were frantically trying to cover up. Eric was just a friend, a nobody. Might that be good news? Might they be less willing to murder an innocent? How exactly was this going to pan out?

Eric was mentally phrasing an answer his own question as Dirk crossed the room with his gun pointed unwaveringly at Eric. Dirk hesitated for a split second, as he surveyed the tactical situation. He could see that the room was empty, save for this Eric guy, frozen half in and half out of the window. The other two could be safely assumed to be already some way down the fire escape. If they'd hidden in a bathroom or somewhere else in the apartment, and Eric's window ploy was a decoy, they would be trapped – they wouldn't get past George through the front door and it was unlikely that there'd be a second exit as the fire escape was obviously blocked by Eric. No Eric was the issue and his current positioning, half in and half out of the window was Dirk's primary impediment to completing the mission. Decision taken.

Dirk steadied himself to make sure of a clean aim, then fired two shots at close range. He killed Eric instantly.

The gun used to kill Ralph was in Mike's hands, waiting to have physical evidence from Lucas and Amber applied to it if required. The gun Dirk used here was larger and did not benefit from a silencer, as gunfire in the early hours of a New York morning was not uncommon. Dirk had also decided that splatter was also not a concern.

In the alleyway below the window, Amber had just reached the ground and had taken two steps out of the lee of the metal landings. She'd just looked to her right to locate the door to the comic book store that Eric had promised would represent safety, when she heard the gunfire. She flinched and ducked, both instinctive movements she could not control. The next natural reaction was to find the source of the noise, so she slowed, turned, and looked up towards the origin of the noise.

She saw two things. First, she saw Lucas, midway between the first landing and the ground, frozen in place with one hand holding onto a rung, the other wrapped around his head.

Secondly, as she'd taken a few paces away from the fire escape, she could see up past the landings. She saw Eric, slumped half out of the same window she'd exited moments before. His body was wedged between the frame and the raised lower window panel, but was oddly slumped forward. She struggled to find the words to describe Eric's positioning. It then dawned on her that the word she was seeking was lifeless.

A foul taste of bile rose in her throat as she realized the gunshot must have come from the apartment, and that in all probability Eric had been killed.

Dirk lowered the gun and reappraised the tactical situation. Eric was obviously dead, but his body had inconveniently wedged in the window. Dirk had expected the force of the bullets to have pushed Eric's body back and out of the window, and was irritated to see that this had not happened.

He covered the four paces from his firing position to the window in seconds, skirting the bed, and tried to look past Eric's body to see his primary targets. He could see nothing through the open lower panel as Eric's body was filling ninety percent of the space. Dirk had to jump to achieve enough of a downward angle to see his targets through the upper portion of the window. On his second jump he caught a fleeting glimpse of Amber standing frozen in place at the foot of the fire escape.

Dirk evaluated his options again. Firing through a double pane of glass was never a great option as the bullet's path would almost certainly be deviated by the obstructions, resulting in an almost certain miss. As there was no chair or other piece of furniture immediately at hand for him to climb on, he'd struggle to get enough elevation on his arm to achieve the downward angle he'd need to be able to target the girl. He quickly realized his only option was to enlist George.

He stepped to one side and flicked a finger between George, who had entered the room behind Dirk, and the lifeless form of Eric in the window. George immediately understood, rested the sledgehammer against the remaining portion of the door, and began to run towards the window, lowering his shoulder.

He connected squarely with Eric's body and successfully expelled his lifeless form from the window. The force of George's impact was such that Eric's body actually flew beyond the limit of the landing outside the window and began to freefall into the alley below.

Chapter Twenty-six

'What the fuck was that?' asked Lucas to no-one in particular, in response to the gunshots.

Lucas removed his head from his hand and craned his neck upwards. The landing above his head obscured his view. He looked down and saw Amber turn and run towards a door at the end of the alleyway, which was twenty paces away.

'Come on,' he heard her yell.

Lucas needed no further encouragement, and jumped off the steps to the ground. He stumbled forward a little on contact and quickly picked up his feet and began to run in pursuit of Amber.

He'd taken barely two steps when the irresistible force of gravity brought Eric's silent seven story journey to an end. A body's center of gravity is just above the waist, and the seven story fall provided enough time for the body to have tipped head-down during the fall.

Eric's body hit the ground headfirst with a loud whoomp, as the surface tension of his skin failed to constrain the momentum of his internal soft tissue. The result was ugly, as Eric's body split open on impact with the ground. Blood, tissue and organs crashed out of his broken body, bouncing off the concrete and creating a ten foot circle of bodily matter around the central core of his body.

Lucas and Amber both froze as they heard the impact. They span to see the source of the noise and could scarcely believe that the shattered form on the alleyway behind them had very recently been their friend Eric. Their eyes met, Lucas's wet with tears as their brains processed the horror before them.

Seven stories above them, it took George a second to bring his momentum under control after colliding with Eric, after which another second was taken up by him stepping aside to allow Dirk access to the window.

As a result of Eric's ejection, the friction holding the lower panel of the window in its raised position had been disturbed, causing the panel to slide back down into a closed position. As George stepped back, Dirk used the handle of his gun to shatter the window, pushing the fragments of glass out onto the iron landing outside the window.

Dirk was momentarily inconvenienced by a shard of glass from the shattered window that had embedded in the lower portion of the window frame, at the exact point Dirk would need to lean to allow him to get his shots away at the guys below.

As he elbowed the shard out of the window, he was pleased to see Lucas and Amber, both now visible through the window, having left the shelter of the landings. He was even more pleased to note that they were both frozen in place in the alleyway below; he assumed they were looking at the body. His own view of Eric's body was obscured by the fire escape but he'd seen bodies after similar falls before and he knew that the sight took some getting used to, so he wasn't surprised to see his targets had frozen.

He braced himself against the frame and took aim at Amber, who was the furthest target and therefore the more difficult shot. His finger gently increased its pressure on the trigger, as he'd done countless times before.

In the alleyway below, Amber stood transfixed by the distorted body that had recently been Eric. The adrenaline continued to course around her body, and lactic acid continued to build in her muscles, forcing her body to move. Her subconscious knew the threat was still real even if her conscious self was momentarily distracted.

She turned just as Dirk fired, a stationary target unexpectedly on the move. The bullet missed her by less than an inch. Amber's confused senses picked up the whistle from the passing bullet even if her brain failed to recognize the sound over the thumping of her heartbeat.

Her senses did pick up a puff of dust that was kicked up by the bullet four feet in front of her and slightly to her left. As her brain reacted and tried to process the sight and diagnose its origin, her ears clearly made out the bang of a gun.

She flinched and ducked involuntarily, which was enough for Dirk's second bullet to miss her head, this time by less than an inch. As with the first bullet, the puff of dust was visible before the sound could be heard, but by now Amber knew she was under attack. She had covered almost half of the distance to the door so she flung herself forwards to reach her goal.

Behind her, Lucas was jolted back into life by the second volley of gunfire. Looking up, he could make out Dirk's form in the window where his friend had so recently been, with a gun pointed slightly farther down the alley. To Lucas's horror, the gun swung through a short arc until it was pointed at him.

Seven stories above, Dirk cursed to himself that he'd twice missed his target, something he couldn't remember doing since he'd been a boy. Sometimes dumb luck is just not on your side.

Dirk cursed again when he realized that he only had two bullets left in his magazine. With two having been used up in removing the Eric obstruction, his plan had been to take two bullets to clean up each of Lucas and Amber.

Having fired four shots in total, he had a difficult choice to make. Should he risk another bullet on Amber, who by now was very close to the door she was obviously expecting to find unlocked at one end of the alleyway? Had she not been certain that the door was unlocked, she would doubtless have run in the other direction, towards the cross street that provided the alley's only natural outlet.

Hit or miss with his fifth bullet, this would only leave him one bullet for Lucas, which may not be enough for a kill.

Dirk knew he had additional magazines available in his pocket, but he knew he would take perhaps four and maybe five seconds to withdraw from the window, eject the magazine, load a new one, and reposition himself back in the window to take any further shots. Such a delay could only hand the tactical advantage to his foes below.

In this instant of calculation, Dirk decided to redirect his attention to Lucas with his remaining two bullets. It was a much simpler shot and it would certainly immobilize one of his targets. This was inferior to his original goal of eliminating both, but Dirk realized that stopping one was better than the zero he might be looking at if he fired at Amber again. He swung his gun through the short arc from Amber to Lucas.

In the alley below, Lucas panicked. Seeing the gun pointing at him, he knew he had to move. In that instant, all that was left for Lucas to decide was which direction to move in. Three paces to his left was the relative safety of the lee of the fire escape. That would give him seven solid iron platforms between him and the gun, which surely would be enough to stop a bullet? But he'd be unarmed and trapped. All the killer would have to do would be to climb down the ladders and pick him off at his leisure.

Twenty-five paces to his right lay the door to the comic book store. Amber was virtually there, and as the gun was now pointing at him, Lucas knew she was going to make it. A greater distance to cover but, greater safety if he made it. Infinite safety, perhaps. Decision taken.

As Dirk's eye picked up his new target, he was not surprised to sense movement. Few people in Lucas's position accept death without trying to avoid it. For Dirk, a moving target at this distance would not be a problem.

A frown formed on Dirk's forehead as he sensed Lucas moving towards the fire escape. Which, tactically, Dirk recognized as the wrong choice. The fire escape represented temporary safety, rather than the permanent safety of whatever was through the door at the end of the alley. I am dealing with amateurs, thought Dirk.

Dirk's brain took a nanosecond to conduct the calculus required to adjust his aim for Lucas's expected position in the few milliseconds it would take the bullet to reach him. He fired. One bullet left.

Dirk did not fire his last bullet at Lucas. Dirk's training had been so thorough that his brain kicked in to override his muscles in response to the unexpected movement from Lucas. Dirk realized that with Lucas trapped under the fire escape, unarmed, he would be a sitting duck, whether or not the first shot had been a kill shot. That would give Dirk plenty of time to reload his gun and finish the job. What Dirk realized in that split second of reaction to Lucas's unexpected movement was that he could afford to take his last shot at Amber, before she reached the door and escaped. It was effectively a free shot.

Dirk's muscles reacted to his brain's command and he started to swing the gun back through the short arc towards Amber.

Down below, Lucas had made his decision to run towards the comic book store.

In a flashback to countless playground games of chase, his body decided to throw in a fake movement towards the fire escape, before the earnest movement towards the door began. That childhood memory saved his life.

The blur of movement towards the fire escape caused Dirk to aim two inches to Lucas's left, where Dirk expected him to be when the bullet reached him, based on the movement Lucas had telegraphed from his head fake. Instead, Lucas was two inches to the right, picking up speed in his ultimate direction.

Lucas sensed the bullet impact the ground by his feet, quickly followed by the sound of the gun firing. Lucas flinched and braced himself for the pain that would inevitably follow. Pain which never came.

……*

Dirk's eye followed his gun sight towards Amber. One last bullet, one target winged and cornered if not killed outright. Amber had reached the door and was momentarily stationary as she pulled on the handle. The door was heavy, and she needed to put some effort into opening the door.

He fixed his sight on her back and exhaled, preparing for the shot. But as his finger squeezed on the trigger, he detected an unexpected movement out of the corner of his eye.

As his finger continued to squeeze the trigger, Dirk realized that not only was Lucas somehow alive, but he was also running towards Amber. How could that happen?

Dirk's finger completed the action of depressing the trigger, but his concentration had been jolted by this impossible development. His aim had moved around four tenths of a degree to the left, which over the seventy-eight feet to the target was enough for his shot to miss by seven inches. His last bullet slammed into the door beside Amber's head.

Amber heard the impact of the bullet and shrieked. The door was open and the safety of the comic book store was beaconing. She had no choice but to move, and as she did she looked over her shoulder and was thrilled to see Lucas tearing down the alleyway towards her, a crazed look in his eyes, his mouth open in a silent scream.

......*

Seven stories above, with his gun empty, Dirk relaxed his arm and inhaled. What the fuck had just happened? Four shots, moving targets certainly, but not over any great range, and he'd somehow managed to miss them all.

George stood beside him, unable to see the result of the shooting as Dirk's body had virtually filled the window when firing. As Dirk climbed fully back into the apartment, George moved to look out of the window.

'No,' said Dirk. 'Don't ask.'

Dirk scanned the room, his eye lingering with interest on the computer bank.

'Let's go. They won't get far, when we pin Crick's murder on them as well.'

Lucas and Amber flung open the front door of the comic book store and ran onto the street, panting and perspiring. Lucas looked down the street for a taxi, and was delighted to see a vacant vehicle barely fifty feet behind them. He anxiously flagged it down.

He wrenched open the door, shoved Amber in and jumped in behind her.

The driver had seen their exit from the store, and spun to watch their entry into his cab with amusement. His eyes passed from his new passengers to the comic book store.

'Such a rush!' he said. 'Get scared by that Manga stuff?'

Lucas had tears streaming down his cheeks as he tried to focus his attention on the cab driver.

'Forty-second street bus station please,' he said.

'Hey c'mon,' replied the driver. 'That's only a few blocks. I'm trying to earn a living here, buddy.'

Amber looked anxiously over Lucas's shoulder at the front of the store, expecting their adversaries to exit in pursuit of them at any moment.

Lucas tried again. 'What the hell. Take us to Atlantic City.'

'Do I look like a bus? My shift ends in an hour and that's a two-hundred-and-fifty-mile round trip. No way, buddy.'

Amber was beside herself with anxiety, looking between the comic book store door and the driver. Lucas sagged into his seat in dejection. He turned to look at the store, a look of defeat in his eyes. The cab had not moved.

'Well take us wherever you fucking like you fucking moron!' Amber exclaimed. 'Just MOVE THIS FUCKING CAB. NOW!!!!!'

'You're the boss, lady,' replied the cabbie.

Chapter Twenty-seven

The New York skyline was at its darkest at three in the morning. John stood at the window of his office watching as the city that never sleeps endured its most somnolent few hours.

It was proving to be a long night. News had been scarce and progress scarcer. Every hour that passed had brought Carlos's plane an hour closer. John had easily been persuaded to trust Dirk, and that trust had been rewarded by his impressive handling of Ralph West. Dirk was a professional, and while John had no interest in personally getting involved in the dirty work, he wished there was more he could do personally to resolve the situation. Delegating certain responsibilities was an absolute necessity for John, particularly when the skills involved were so specialized.

Mike was also in the office, dozing doubled over the meeting table, head resting on his forearms. John observed Mike and perversely admired the man's ability to sleep at such a challenging time. Deep down, John knew that a few hours restorative sleep could only help him navigate the day ahead, but the ability to shut down one's mind and induce sleep when that mind was so burdened with stress was a skill John had never developed. So while Mike slept he'd spent the small hours pacing his office and making calls to equally frustrated associates.

John's mind snapped back into focus when his phone rang. On the second ring, Mike jolted awake and upright. John had crossed his office and snatched the handset from the cradle before the third ring.

'OK...,' he said, pausing as information was passed to him. 'I understand... I'm sure you did your best... Stay scarce and await instructions.'

He hung up the phone and paused, collecting his thoughts, framing his next words carefully. His eyes drifted across his desk to the framed photograph of his wife and kids. With a heavy heart, John picked up the photograph and gently fingered the silver frame, which had been an anniversary gift from his wife. Mike waited patiently for John to report.

After a moment John spoke. 'We missed them. Again.'

Mike looked at his hands, dejectedly. John tensed his muscles and exploded in fury, throwing the photograph across the room, smashing it against the far wall. Mike flinched at the sudden movement and noise.

John breathed deeply and regained his composure.

'OK,' he said. 'There's another victim. That Eric Crick fellow. We need to repeat the Ralph trick and pin his death on the kids as well. Get everyone in a uniform looking for those bastards.'

Mike nodded and pulled his cell phone from his jacket pocket.

'Sure,' he said, dialing a number. 'I'll get our guys on it. Don't sweat it, John. This isn't over.'

'Don't sweat it?' John said, his voice rising in anger. 'Carlos lands here in six hours. I want them snuffed by then, otherwise this will get real ugly.'

'I'm on your side John, remember. It's not over. We have flares on their credit cards, cell phones, passports and driving licenses. They're amateurs, up against the most advanced law enforcement technology on the planet. The only way we'd get them quicker would be if they were Arabs.'

Mike looked directly at John and allowed a gentle smile to form around the edge of his mouth. Mike knew that John needed to keep his focus, but a little gallows humor was Mike's way of showing John that they were still a team. He was pleased to see John's spirits lift as the joke sank in, culminating in John shaking his head with a slight smile on his face.

Charlie DiCarlo hadn't planned to be in the office so early that morning, but he'd had difficulty sleeping so had decided to stop in and review some files before his later commitments took him from the office.

Within ten minutes of his arrival in the office, Detective Julie Tang noticed that Charlie's door was closed and realized that he must be in. She knocked gently on the door and was immediately summoned to enter.

Charlie had his feet on his desk and was leaning far back in his chair reading a preliminary investigation file concerning GoldRock prepared by the I.R.S. three years earlier. The report revealed that some unspecified source had tipped the revenue service off about suspicious transactions passing through one of GoldRock's subsidiaries. An investigation had been opened, but nothing untoward had been found. The IRS had closed the file in less than a week classifying the tip-off as spurious, coming from a disgruntled employee. The file told Charlie nothing he didn't already know.

He looked up as Julie entered. She had been on the force for five years, having just come out of the uniformed branch into the detectives' office. She was yet to be given her own case to run, and was used as a gopher for the more established detectives in the unit. She didn't seem to mind being a lackey, and Charlie had heard nothing but compliments about her work.

He'd brought her into the circle of knowledge as regards his investigation several weeks earlier, and had asked her to keep her eyes open about anything untoward concerning GoldRock that crossed her desk. Seeing her enter so soon after his arrival aroused his interest.

'Morning, Detective DiCarlo,' she said formally, as she always did. She'll go far, Charlie thought.

'Hi,' Charlie replied. 'Want a Coke?'

He lifted his feet from the desk and opened the bar refrigerator under his desk, pulling out two cans.

'Sure,' Julie replied. 'Something interesting came in about an hour ago.'

Charlie nodded his enthusiasm for Julie to continue.

'Remember that murder yesterday we talked about on the phone? The partner supervising the E.P.A. review of GoldRock was shot dead in the parking structure of his office? The two guys that had been in Ghana at GoldRock's mine doing the fieldwork were pegged with responsibility by the F.B.I.?'

'That's right,' Charlie replied. 'A guy and a girl, if I recall. We had some questions about the jurisdictional basis for the F.B.I. to leap all over the case.'

'We did, and the guys in the corner offices have been scratching their heads about it too, I hear. But if the F.B.I. wants to take on a murder investigation, its one less for us, eh?'

Charlie smiled in acknowledgement. He'd planned to follow the investigation closely, as any unusual activity linked to GoldRock was cause for interest in his book. He'd been irritated that the F.B.I. had taken over the case as it meant he'd have to requisition their files through channels, rather than having unfettered access to any files created by an N.Y.P.D. investigation.

'So what's new today?' Charlie asked, nudging Julie along.

'Well there's been another murder,' Julie continued. 'A guy was shot in his apartment early this morning, and his body was thrown out of a seventh story window. It's quite a mess, apparently.'

'Let me guess,' Charlie interjected. 'He's linked to GoldRock.'

'Not directly, as far as anyone can tell. But the F.B.I. was onto the murder in a flash. They've linked it to the first murder. They're convinced it was the same perpetrators.' Julie referred to a sheet of paper she'd been holding. 'Lucas Steadman and Amber Marshall.'

'F.B.I. onto it in a flash? Doesn't sound like them,' Charlie added thoughtfully.

'Word is they had some information, an informant perhaps. Anyhoo, we've got a crime scene set-up. Thought you might want to take a look.' She handed Charlie the sheet of paper.

Charlie wouldn't ordinarily have been interested in trampling through a crime scene. He'd seen enough mangled and mutilated bodies during his time in uniform that these days he went out of his way to avoid crime scenes. He looked at the address and realized he'd be passing within a block of the location en route to his next meeting.

'Sure. I might stop in and take a look. It's hard to imagine what could be so bad about the environmental standards of a gold mine's operation that set these guys off on a killing spree. Thanks Julie.'

Charlie rose from his desk and grabbed his jacket from the back of the door.

Chapter Twenty-eight

Charlie got to the crime scene within twenty minutes. It was a circus. Dawn had just broken, which had brought the house lights up on the dramatic scene. Bodies were rarely found in such a public location, and bodies that had been subjected to the degree of disintegration that Eric's had experienced were a real rarity. Charlie's uniformed colleagues had taped off all of the alleyway and part of the outlet street, which had the unfortunate effect of seriously interfering with the traffic flow. An unfortunate consequence was that the gently fluttering "Crime Scene, Do Not Cross" tape served to advertise the tragedy so efficiently to passers-by that a large crowd had gathered.

All the rubberneckers could see was a gaggle of crime scene techs receiving a briefing, and a heaped tarpaulin that could only be concealing a body. The distance of the tarpaulin from the spectators and the angle they were looking at it from would make it difficult for them to see how much of the alleyway it covered, and therefore how mangled the body must have been that it was concealing.

204

Charlie could hear news choppers circling overhead, but he could immediately tell that the narrowness of the alley in and the height of the buildings would make it very difficult for them to get a good, steady shot of the scene.

Charlie showed his badge and as usual, the "First-class" designation which followed his "Detective" title drew a pleasing level of respect from the uniformed officers controlling the bystanders. As the officer quickly allowed Charlie to duck under the tape, he pointed out the senior investigator, requesting that Charlie check-in with him first.

Charlie approached the crowd gathered around the body and attracted the attention of the senior officer. He was finishing up a briefing with the C.S.I team, but noticed Charlie and acknowledged his presence. Charlie recognized the face and quickly placed the fellow officer. Enrique Riojas had been an undercover agent working a big prostitution case Charlie had also helped out on a few years earlier. Charlie was pleased to note that successful undercover agents could get good jobs back on the streets once their time in the bowels of the enemy was over.

The group receiving the briefing broke up and Enrique came over the greet Charlie, they shook hands enthusiastically.

'To what do I owe the honor?' asked Enrique.

'Heard about this and there's a possible link to something I've been sniffing around for a while now. I was passing so I thought I'd check it out.'

'You're more than welcome. What happened seems to be fairly straightforward. Preliminary findings are that the victim is an Eric Crick, resident of an apartment seven stories up. He had two G.S.W.s to the chest prior to taking a seven story swan-dive. The degree of disintegration of the body indicates he was dead before he hit the ground. There's also a few cuts and abrasions on the body, or at least on the parts of the body that didn't break up on landing. The theory is that the guy died up top, then was ejected through the window.'

'Which suggests a desire to make a point above and beyond just killing this guy,' Charlie added.

'Possibly,' agreed Enrique. 'D'ya wanna see the body?'

'Quite a mess, right? You know, I just ate so I'll wait for the report. I hear the F.B.I. is up your ass?'

'Yeah. They quickly linked this to another case they're on. There's a guy upstairs taking a look around called Mike Pointer. He said something about a surveillance operation tipping them off about something going down at this location. That pissed me off, as you'd imagine. If they knew there was likely to be a crime perpetrated here, why didn't they bother to tell anyone? And I told him as much. Time will tell if their info could have spared this guy's life.'

'I bet he appreciated that input,' Charlie added wryly.

'He seems a straight-up guy. We'll do the clean-up and hand them the files. Keeps this case off my statistics as I think it's more complicated than the simple domestic dispute. The guy lived alone.'

'Well thanks buddy,' Charlie added.

A tech wearing a white plastic coverall came up to Enrique, who stepped aside to confer. Charlie took the opportunity to look up at the seventh story window that had been Eric's departure gate for his short flight. He could see crime scene tape gently fluttering on the railings surrounding the fire escape. Enrique's summary seemed to be about right.

After a moment Enrique turned back to Charlie as the tech departed.

'Dammit,' Enrique reported dejectedly, colleague to colleague. 'Things just got more complicated. The tech thinks there's a bullet hole in a wall farther down the alley. Could be old, but the tech thinks it's new, and they're usually right. We'll quickly be able to tell whether it came from the window or the alley from the angle of penetration in the wall. I could be here all damn day… Why would someone fire into a wall forty feet from an already dead body?'

They both knew the answer, and neither had to express it. Having additional parties involved beyond the killer and the victim exponentially increased the paperwork Enrique would have to complete before he could hand the case over to the F.B.I.

'Sorry brother,' Charlie commiserated. 'I'll leave you to it.' He turned towards the large crowd and made to depart.

'Hey. Take a look upstairs before you go,' Enrique added. 'It's not a normal apartment. You won't get the full picture from the report. Not even from the photographs. Apartment 704.'

* * *

Charlie was irritated to find himself puffing gently after the seven story climb to Eric's apartment. His busy schedule had relegated the gym to a once weekly treat in recent months. He took a mental note to get himself back into shape. It would make that occasional pizza or burger all the more satisfying.

The corridor outside the apartment was crowded. Crime scene techs were jostling with each other as they worked to unpack their equipment prior to starting work in the apartment. Several uniformed officers were patrolling the corridor, taking statements from neighbors and escorting residents along the corridor if they needed to travel past the open door to Eric's apartment.

Charlie slowly weaved his way down the corridor and showed his badge to the officer posted outside the apartment's shattered door. He explained Enrique's suggestion that he take a look. The officer had been in the apartment himself, so he understood Enrique's request and allowed Charlie to pass.

Before Charlie could cross the threshold, a crime scene tech intervened, requesting that Charlie to pull some plastic booties over his shoes and slip on a pair of latex gloves. As he did so, he gave a cursory examination to the door.

He could see that someone with an anger management issue had inflicted some serious damage to the woodwork. Jagged, inconsistent rips to the portion of the door that remained vertical indicated to Charlie that a heavy metal instrument had been used, perhaps an axe. That wouldn't have been much quieter than using a chainsaw, thought

Charlie as he looked up and down the corridor. It was impossible to count exactly, but Charlie estimated that the door must have received over a dozen blows before yielding. That's quite some door, thought Charlie. His apartment door wouldn't have withstood two decent blows, he thought, beginning to understand why Enrique had recommended he make the climb.

Charlie entered the apartment and looked at the interior door frame. He was surprised to see a network of locks which seemed to be controlled by a series of small motors bolted to the frame. Odd…

He turned his attention to the wider apartment, which had been brightly illuminated by two large lights installed either side of the door by the crime scene techs. He immediately noticed another occupant, clad in the same boots and gloves as he was. The other visitor was examining a mound of dirty clothing on the recliner.

'Hi,' said Charlie. 'Charlie DiCarlo, N.Y.P.D.'

The other man spun quickly to acknowledge Charlie's presence. Charlie's suspicious mind questioned whether the man had spun a little too quickly, but the thought died as quickly as it was born.

'Mike Pointer. F.B.I.' the man said authoritatively.

They took a pace towards each other before both men realized that shaking hands was out of the question given the gloves they were wearing and the need to preserve the integrity of the crime scene. Both men stopped and gave an abbreviated wave to each other.

'I'd heard the F.B.I. was interested in this case,' Charlie continued. 'You guys were onto it real quick.'

Charlie couldn't resist giving the man a gentle nudge himself on behalf of the entire N.Y.P.D. An ounce of prevention is worth a pound of cure, particularly when you have to do the curing.

'We'd been tracking the perpetrators for twenty-four hours. They murdered someone working under federal protection yesterday evening. They gave us the slip and came here to murder this guy. We think he had information about them they didn't want to get out.'

With this comment Mike pointed at the wall containing Eric's computer equipment. Charlie spun and exhaled at the scale of the installation he saw.

'Good God,' he said. 'What was this guy into?'

'More than just playing Halo by the looks of it,' Mike replied. 'We need to get some specialists over here to crack this open so we can work out what was so important that this guy had to die. It looks like the perpetrators shut things down before leaving. My guess is that it'll be a real challenge to get things back online. People with this kind of kit are usually fairly paranoid about it.'

Charlie looked closer at the wall and saw several monitors, servers and printers. All were a mystery to him.

'Not my specialty,' he said. 'There is a guy in the Computer Crimes team of my precinct who's good at interpreting this kind of stuff. Really good, actually. The guy's kind of tough to deal with interpersonally, but he's the best I've ever seen at this kind of work. D'ya want me to give him a call?'

'Sure,' Mike said enthusiastically. 'The quicker we can crack this open the quicker we'll know what was going down. Get him to call me.'

As Mike closed the gap between him and Charlie, he slipped off a glove and drew a card from his pocket. Both men were old hands at crime scenes so Charlie knew to let Mike slip it directly into his jacket pocket.

A crime scene tech appeared at the door.

'Gentlemen,' he said. 'Please finish up; we've got work to do here.'

Mike acknowledged the tech, who disappeared back into the corridor. Mike looked quickly at the recliner, then to Charlie, who missed the glance as he was still looking at the computer equipment. Mike thought quickly.

'Hey, take a look at the window before you go,' Mike said.

Charlie nodded and padded delicately across the room and looked through the window, cautious not to tread on anything that might produce any meaningful evidence.

Through the window he could see the fire escape which he realized would block his view of the body. Down and to his right he could see the end of the alley, which was a dead-end with only a sturdy door to break up the monotony of the brickwork. In the other direction he could see the opening of the alleyway into the cross street, roped off with Police tape. The crowd beyond the tape only seemed to be growing.

'They shot the guy, then dumped him out of the window,' Mike said by way of commentary.

Charlie took a half step back to look at the window frame. The pane of shattered glass appeared not to have been safety glass, so there were a number of large shards still held in place by the frame. Must be a violation of some building regulation somewhere thought Charlie, sympathizing with Enrique as that would be another citation he'd have to write. He leaned closer to the frame to look at one of the larger shards of glass that remained embedded in the frame to the right of the window. There appeared to be a thread of clothing caught on the glass. No doubt the crime scene techs would catch it.

As he looked closer, a curious thing happened. The glass had no backlighting, as there was only the relative darkness of the alleyway outside. The high contrast provided by the crime scene lights behind him reflected off the shard of glass, creating a clear mirror reflection of the room behind him.

Charlie eye was drawn to the reflection, and as he was about to refocus his eyes onto the thread attached to the fragment of glass, his attention was grabbed by what he saw behind him. Mike was standing back by the recliner, side on to both the front door to the apartment and the window. He saw Mike glance quickly to his right and left, in a way Charlie's instincts told him was designed to check whether the coast was clear. He then leaned towards the recliner and Charlie was convinced he saw him snatch something out of the pile and quickly put it in his pocket. Something small and white. Charlie's immediate instinct was that Mike had pocketed a sock.

Charlie was immediately conflicted. He wanted to spin and confront Mike, but he hesitated. He'd worked on enough investigations and been in enough delicate situations to know that your immediate instinct was rarely the best course of action. Knowledge gathering was his primary objective as an investigator, and once a case was built he'd have more than enough time to confront the F.B.I. agent. Was he building a case though, he thought? Why would Mike want to take something like a sock from a crime scene?

Perhaps it was his, and he'd dropped it before Charlie had entered the room? It was unlikely that a professional investigator could be so clumsy. And why would he be carrying a sock? Perhaps it had been an optical illusion? No, Charlie was certain of what he'd seen.

Charlie quickly developed a plausible theory. Perhaps Mike wanted to send the sock to an F.B.I. lab to get a DNA sample? By doing so, he'd not have to wait for the N.Y.P.D. lab to do the analysis, and hand the info over, which would take several days. Yes, that was more likely. In fact that was quite likely. If Charlie had been working a case where he'd been dependent on another agency, it was something he could see himself doing. Especially if that other agency had been as antagonistic as he and Enrique had been. Yes, that was the most likely explanation. Especially as Charlie couldn't rule out the possibility that he'd do the same thing if the situation was reversed.

It bothered Charlie a little that the sock was presumably the victim's, rather than the perpetrators'. So any DNA would be from the victim. Getting a DNA sample wasn't difficult when you had a disemboweled body splattered over a sidewalk close to hand. But Charlie was not privy to the details of the F.B.I.'s case, so he quickly shelved his concerns. Perhaps placing the victim's DNA at some other location was critical to solving another crime?

He watched as Mike again glanced from the front door to the window. Charlie could understand why he didn't want his actions to be seen. Mike could have no way of knowing his pilfering had been noticed, so Charlie continued to scan the window frame.

He turned back to the room as the technician reappeared in the doorway, looking pointedly at his watch. Mike was already by the door, acceding to the tech's remonstrations.

Charlie walked gingerly back across the room, and was surprised when one of his cell phones rang. From the ringtone, Charlie immediately knew it was the phone he had equipped with an untraceable pay-as-you-go SIM card, so his informants could be confident to use it to communicate with him without fear of eavesdropping.

He looked apologetically at the tech and pulled the phone from his jacket pocket, looking at the number. It was a number he couldn't ignore, and it was a caller with whom he couldn't allow his conversation to be overheard. He gestured apologetically to the tech and quickly stepped back to the window before answering the phone.

Chapter Twenty-nine

Lucas and Amber had switched cabs an appropriate distance from the comic book store. They'd generously tipped the driver, hoping in vain that financial lubrication would help him forget his two crazy pre-dawn passengers. In fact their over-payment only served to guarantee he'd remember them. Not only that, their largesse meant he would be sure to tell all of his friends at the dispatch center about the couple of crazies at the end of his shift.

After a brief stop in a twenty-four hour pharmacy, which offered a surprisingly wide range of items suitable for building a disguise, a second taxi driver had been more than happy to drive them to Atlantic City. Lucas had negotiated a decent price, cash payable in advance. Their calm and measured entry into the cab and the ensuing negotiation was in marked contrast to their first cab of the day, and had failed to raise any alarms from the driver.

They'd agreed that they would make themselves too memorable if they'd asked to be driven directly from Manhattan to Atlantic City's small airport, so they'd asked to be driven to the only hotel in the city that either of them could name unprompted, neither of them being regular casino patrons.

The cab dropped Lucas and Amber under the porte-cochere of the Harrah's hotel on the boardwalk of Atlantic City. They'd waited just inside the door of the casino for ten minutes expecting at any moment to see people jumping from taxis or cars in pursuit of them, but after that time had passed without incident they had concluded with relief that they weren't being followed.

They realized that they were both hungry, so embracing the luxury of not being threatened with imminent death, they grabbed a hearty breakfast at the buffet. With full bellies, they hailed a third cab to take them the ten or so miles to the airport. By seven thirty in the morning they were standing in front of a rather vacant and overly made-up ticketing agent at Atlantic City's small airport.

They were standing arm in arm, having agreed to pose as a couple for the immediate future. The new found closeness was not providing either of them with any difficulty, given the horrors they had so recently faced together.

As regards disguises, Botox and collagen injections had not been on offer at the Lexington avenue pharmacy, but hats and sunglasses had been. Lucas wore a Jim Beam trucker-style baseball cap, drawn low over eyes concealed behind aviator style sunglasses. Amber sported a large floppy straw sunhat, and similarly dark sunglasses. They had agreed to present an image of tired elation to anyone they encountered, which they'd agreed would be the easiest set of emotions for them to display.

The check-in agent who greeted them that morning was herself no stranger to Botox and collagen.

'How you doing this morning?' she asked in a pre-programmed, over-familiar manner that served mainly to irritate the customer rather than engage them.

'Just dandy thanks!' Lucas replied, working a little too hard on the "tired but elated" shtick. 'It's been a long night, but a profitable one!'

Lucas pulled Eric's roll of cash from his pocket and flashed it at the agent, winking at her in a conspiratorial way. His other arm squeezed Amber tighter still to emphasis his point, eliciting a short squeak of surprise from Amber.

'Well good for you there!' the agent replied happily. 'How can I help you?'

'We want to go to Guam!' Amber replied, in a southern accent she'd worked for years to suppress but at that moment was exceedingly helpful to the development of the character she was portraying. She squeezed Lucas right back. No yelp, but Lucas smiled as their eyes met. Hell, let's roll with this!

'Guam?' enquired the agent with what on a Botox free face would be a frown but for her looked like a small child passing gas. 'I'll have to look that one up, honey!'

She started clacking hopefully at her keyboard, first attempting to spell Guam, then trying to work out where the hell it was. Lucas noticed that the agent sported wildly overelaborate fingernails, eminently suitable for an Asian dictator's wife, but hopeless for someone who had to actually use their hands in a professional capacity. He noted that the keyboard's decal marking the backspace key had been rubbed clean off from frequent use.

The momentary silence between them once again yearned to be filled. Lucas was unable to resist.

'We're going to have our honeymoon,' he said, creating a confusion of tense and grammar that caused Amber to visibly finch.

The agent looked up from her struggles, once again giving a gassy frown. Her senses alerted her to the oddness of the statement, but her training was telling her to be polite at all times.

'Well congratulations!' she said, having no reason to suspect anything beyond Lucas being a moron. 'OK, for the island of Guam, Agana is the airport. Looks like you're going to have a chance to catch up on your sleep! Atlantic City to Detroit to San Francisco to Honolulu to Guam.'

Everyone grinned. Lucas squeezed Amber, and Amber squeezed Lucas right back. The agent showed some serious teeth in realization that there would be quite some commission coming to her for selling such an elaborate itinerary.

Lucas reached into his pocket and withdrew the fake ids, handing them to the agent with the biggest grin yet. He leaned in and adopted a look of conspiratorial fraternity.

'Hey honey, as it's our honeymoon, perhaps you can help us out with an upgrade?' he asked hopefully.

The almost smiley face returned, albeit slightly more forced this time. The agent internally winced as the widespread fantasy resurfaced that airlines give a shit about your honeymoon / birthday / anniversary. Platinum frequent flyer? Certainly sir, here's your upgrade. Trailer trash going on your umpteenth honeymoon? Not so fast…

'Let's take a look,' she said, setting up the tried and tested method of blaming the inevitable rejection on the computer system.

Amber pulled Lucas gently to one side as the agent resumed the battle of the backspace.

'There's twenty-seven thousand dollars in that roll of cash,' she whispered supportively. 'You've just seen your friend die in front of you and God knows who is chasing us. Let's just splash for first class. We can have some food, perhaps take a shower in a lounge somewhere and we can get some sleep on the plane. None of that will happen in coach.'

Lucas's eyes glazed over a little as the significance of Amber's comments sank in, but he could see her point and so he nodded dejectedly. Amber turned back to the agent, and as her arm was still intertwined with Lucas's, she spun him back with her.

'Hey honey,' she said, back in the cutesy country voice. 'Just book us up the front of the bus right off the bat there, OK?'

The agent nodded enthusiastically, figuring that her commission had probably just trebled. Smiles all round. Amber leaned in to Lucas once more.

'From Ghana to Agana, eh?' she whispered.

'Funny,' he said. 'Look, I'd really like to call my mom. Don't you have family you want to call?'

Amber's smile faded as her game face returned. She turned their backs to the agent to ensure she didn't detect the change in their attitudes.

'No. My mother died from cancer when I was young,' she said. 'She didn't have any other children. My father was always distant, even before my mother died. We last spoke when he transferred control of my college fund to me. I guess he figured he completed his parental duty when I turned eighteen.'

As Lucas listened, he realized that Amber was giving him a glimpse into what must have been a difficult upbringing. As he listened to her talking, he felt closer to her than ever.

Amber stiffened as she realized she'd revealed more to Lucas than she'd intended. Her personal life was none of anyone's business, and she was proud to have achieved success in life without the parental support network her peers took for granted.

She turned quickly to the agent and was relieved to see that she was still engaged in preparing their tickets. Looking back at Lucas, she could see his was distracted in his thoughts.

'I've always been close to my parents,' he said, attempting to continue the personal conversation Amber had started, without realizing that she'd become uncomfortable with the intimacy. 'I want to call them. Let them know we're safe. Let them know we didn't do it!'

'I understand,' she replied gently, steering Lucas back towards pressing matters at hand. 'But we shouldn't use our phones. In fact we should probably discard them completely in case they're traceable when they're switched off.'

'Sure,' said Lucas, snapping out of his emotional reverie. 'But using a pay-phone should be all right?'

Amber considered this for a moment. She was not immediately comfortable with being deferred to by Lucas on a question like this. He was her superior and ought to be in charge, but she understood that this experience had been more traumatic for him than it had been for her. Eric was Lucas's friend and he'd been closer to the falling body than she'd been.

'I tell you what,' she answered. 'Why don't we wait until they call us for boarding? Even if they can trace a public phone or they're monitoring your mom's phone, we'll be moving before they can react?'

Amber replied authoritatively, confident that her response was a good one, but she still felt the need to couch her response in the form of a question to maintain Lucas's self-esteem. Lucas nodded enthusiastically. Amber wasn't comfortable with the thought that she was becoming the leader, but she knew someone had to be.

After leaving Eric Crick's apartment, Charlie DiCarlo spent an intense ten minutes in a coffee shop reflecting on what he'd seen at the crime scene. As a result of his deliberations, Charlie made two calls before heading to meet the informant who had called him in Crick's apartment with an urgent message.

The first was to his associate on the N.Y.P.D. computer crimes unit. Charlie had worked with the guy on a couple of cases and in his experience, there was no-one better in the city. The F.B.I. may have smarter geeks squirreled away in Washington but there was no way they'd parachute them into New York for a simple murder case like this.

What Charlie's guy lacked in interpersonal skills and, towards the end of a day, personal hygiene, he more than made up for with a mind that Charlie swore operated just like a computer. He needed to be managed, because just like a computer he operated solely in terms of black and white. He did not understand the concept of gray, which was where investigations often hovered while the grunt work was being completed.

Charlie quickly explained the situation, lingering a little on the high-tech apparatus he'd seen in Eric's apartment. Charlie passed on Mike Pointer's phone number and his associate was more than happy to help out. Charlie noted that he actually sounded quite excited.

Charlie's second call was to Enrique Riojas, who was still striving to control the combined annoyances of C.S.I. teams, over-excited civilian onlookers, and increasingly, media crews. Enrique reported that it did indeed look as if the bullet holes found in the wall had come from the apartment window on the seventh floor. They'd found another indentation on the floor and one in the door at the end of the alleyway. He expected to find more.

Enrique reported that the door led into a comic book store. The clerk reported that he had not seen or heard anything suspicious around the time of the incident. Based on the pervasive smell of marijuana he'd detected in the store's office, Enrique suspected that this was because the clerk had been stoned at the time and had probably been sound asleep. The store had an ancient video-surveillance system but it was on a two hour loop and by the time anyone had figured out that something was wrong, the tape had been overwritten.

Charlie listened, mostly out of politeness and courtesy. He knew that it was always helpful to have a peer to vent to when you're running an investigation. You have to maintain a façade of professionalism to your subordinates in the team, no matter how frustrated and irritated you may be personally.

Charlie asked two things of Enrique. Firstly, keep a close eye on the F.B.I. guy if he showed his face again. Charlie did not elaborate further, and Enrique did not ask him to, but both understood the undertone.

His second request was a little more unusual. He knew he couldn't ask it of the computer tech directly, as it was a decidedly gray request, but he knew Enrique would honor his wishes as a colleague, even more so as a former undercover agent.

Charlie asked Enrique to give him at least a thirty minute head-start on anything interesting that the computer geek dug up before Enrique passed it upstream to the F.B.I. A full hour if at all possible. Enrique had willingly agreed, which pleased Charlie greatly.

Charlie knew he was onto something, and he was realizing that the two kids who were the subject of such intense F.B.I. interest were the key to unlocking the whole GoldRock case. He was sure the evidence at the crime scene would indicate that shots had been fired from the window down into the alley. The Crick guy was dead before he left the seventh floor, so there must have been someone else at the scene apart from the two kids.

Either the kids had shot Crick, and had then fired at someone or something in the alley. Or someone else had shot Crick, then had tried their hardest to shoot the kids as they were escaping down the alley. Charlie's instinct was that the latter scenario would prove to be the truth. It would also help explain why that sock had left the apartment in Mike Pointer's pocket.

All of which meant someone wanted the kids dead. Possibly the F.B.I., although Charlie thought that was unlikely. More likely it was someone being helped by the F.B.I., and specifically by Mike Pointer. Which meant the kids knew something. And Charlie needed to know what they knew. But where had they run to?

Chapter Thirty

John Showers had collected Mike Pointer a discrete few blocks from the crime scene, and together they had driven to Teterboro airport, seven miles west of GoldRock's offices across the state line in New Jersey. They watched from the tarmac as Carlos's Cessna pulled to a precise stop having conveyed him from the Ghanaian mine's airstrip via a refueling stop in the Azores. Mike's presence had obviated the usual need to screen the airplane through the usual customs and immigration formalities.

A few seconds after pulling to halt, the engines fell silent and seconds thereafter the door opened, triggering an integrated stairway which hydraulically descended to the ground. Carlos emerged from the plane and climbed the short distance to the tarmac. No handshakes or other signs of welcome were exchanged. John and Mike remained silent, knowing Carlos would take the initiative.

'I will have no opinion as to blame until the situation is under control,' said Carlos, not disappointing them. 'There has been no contact for four hours now, correct?'

'Correct,' said John, recognizing that the question was directed largely at him as the direct subordinate. 'In the Chelsea area of New York City.'

'And we have all of their options covered?' Carlos continued.

Mike recognized this question as being his.

'The entire F.B.I. is looking for them,' he said, 'and the N.Y.P.D. Every electronic aide is pointing at them. And believe me, we have a lot these days. If they fart, we'll find them.'

Carlos nodded, impressed by the definitive nature of the assurances. John looked on and frowned, realizing that Mike had left himself, and by extension, John, very little wriggle-room with his comment. It was what Carlos needed to hear right now, but it would be difficult to back Carlos away from such an absolute statement if they needed to later.

'Good,' Carlos added. 'Resources?'

Back to John. 'As you requested, we have brought in everyone available from the other wing of the business.'

'So we wait?'

'We wait,' replied John and Mike in harmony.

Davie Eason had been excited to receive a call from Jorge that morning. Davie had expected things to be quiet as he'd been given the day off following his success at tracking Lucas and Amber the day before. Davie thought he detected a deferential tone in Jorge's voice when he started the call by apologizing for bothering Davie on his day off. Davie could only conclude that his share price within the organization was rising, given Jorge's atypical show of respect.

As the call developed, Davie knew things were definitely changing. Jorge asked if Davie would be available to fill in for one of his Buyers, who Jorge explained was otherwise engaged in hunting for the guys Davie had followed the day before.

This simple question told Davie a lot. Firstly, Jorge was confiding in Davie, which amplified the sense of respect Davie had detected at the start of the call. Secondly, there was a role called a "Buyer" in the organization which Davie assumed was the next position up the ladder. This was the position he'd been craving to be promoted to.

Finally, the kids had not been picked up back in Manhattan after his hand-off yesterday. Either that or they had been picked up and had been subsequently lost again. Davie was very interested to learn that the organization did not appear to know where the kids were. That was very, very interesting.

Davie was already close to Jorge in central Manhattan, but had limited time before his next commitment. Jorge understood, and asked for an hour, an hour Davie was very happy to commit. Jorge promised Davie one hundred dollars for the hour, which was well over an entire day's wages for a Collector. Buyers must be important cogs in the process, Davie thought.

Jorge was with the pasty guy Davie recognized as Nigel when he arrived for the meeting. Nigel didn't appear to recognize Davie, but Davie had filed Nigel's face away when he'd deposited his collections with him on the one occasion they'd met before. Nigel seemed distracted, and appeared to be as keen as Davie was for the meeting to be a short one.

What followed was enlightening. Nigel started what was a very one-way conversation by expressing real gratitude for what Davie had done for the organization the day before. He went on say how Davie had been identified as a real talent that would go far, not just because of his previous day's contribution, but also from the accurate and diligent execution of his duties over previous months.

Davie listened closely, trying to remember every word as it represented huge validation for the hours of tedium he'd had to endure to get this far. From Nigel's speech patterns, Davie could tell he was an educated man and so was likely to be a real player in the wider organization.

Nigel moved on to explain how they needed Davie to perform the role of Buyer that day. Indeed, that hour. He may need to still take occasional shifts as a Collector while the organization was reacting to the issues raised by the two kids he'd followed, but once that was settled he'd be permanently promoted to a Buyer.

This was music to Davie's ears.

Nigel then quickly but efficiently explained the mechanics of the Buyers role. Davie's neurons were in overdrive as he absorbed the specifics of the new role. Just as was the case with operating as a Collector, there were a number of details and rituals that needed to be observed, some of which seemed convoluted but which Nigel emphasized were essential.

Nigel asked Davie to repeat back the process, step by step. Davie did so, and was corrected by Nigel when he'd missed or misunderstood a step. Davie had fully grasped the process from Nigel's initial walk through, but instinctively considered it prudent to throw in a few errors to mask quite how easily he'd absorbed Nigel's descriptions.

After running through the process one last time with no mistakes, Davie found himself back on Seventh Avenue with around six thousand dollars in his pocket and an address scribbled onto a scrap of paper. Davie had been instructed to destroy the note at the end of his brief shift.

Lucas and Amber had traversed the Atlantic City airport without incident. Although it was a small airport, it still offered the full range of T.S.A. indignities and inconveniences, but at such an early hour of the morning, during what the airport regarded as its "rush hour", the service was delivered with as much good humor as possible. The fast track aisle available to first class passengers had helped considerably.

An alert for Lucas and Amber's detention had indeed been received by the airport that morning, and the airport's administration manager had indeed noted that the adjectives supporting the warning were unusually severe, specifically with regard to Lucas and Amber's propensity for violence. However, the alert had arrived along with twenty-seven other warnings of lesser or equal importance, nineteen of which had emanated from authorities up and down the northeastern crime corridor from Washington DC to Boston. These represented people likely to attempt travel *from* airports such as Atlantic City, rather than *to* the airport, and so were most likely to be encountered by that airport's T.S.A. team.

If the manager had counted, that would have brought the total number of criminals actively being sought to over two thousand, in addition to the roughly eight and a half thousand names and faces on the no-fly list maintained by the government. The terrorist list maintained by the Terrorist Screening Center contained a further million names.

The sheer volume of people passing through the T.S.A. checkpoints made the task of intercepting specific passengers on the basis of their appearance all but impossible. Osama Bin Laden would probably have been stopped, but the entire system had to rely on electronic flags and alarms, which Eric Crick had effortlessly defeated. Accordingly, the paper-based alert that the airport had received remained in an in-tray on the manager's desk.

So Lucas and Amber had smiled and stripped their way through the last T.S.A. checkpoint they would encounter before Guam. When they heard the final boarding call for their flight, Lucas quickly called his mother, after which he and Amber climbed nervously onto the plane.

Charlie received his first call from Enrique roughly ninety minutes after his computer geek had been set lose in Eric Crick's apartment. The call arrived just ten minutes after the meeting with his informant had ended. The call had contained two crucial pieces of information.

Firstly, the computer geek's quick walkthrough of the apartment had recognized one of the items on Eric Crick's racking as being a specialist printer, which had the ability to burn images into plastic cards. The tech knew it was possible to adapt the machine to produce credit cards, and he had read that some States used very similar machines for the production of driving licenses. The tech wouldn't be certain as to what specifically the machine had been used for until he could access the printer drivers, but Enrique felt there was a strong possibility that the perpetrators were equipped with fake identities.

Charlie wanted to correct his friend about his assumption that the kids were the perpetrators of anything, but he restrained himself.

The second piece of information was equally interesting. The computer tech was still wrestling with the security over the main servers in Eric's set-up, but he had been easily able to defeat the web server's security, from which he had been able to pull up a list of the websites visited by Eric in the hours before the system had been shut down. Along with a variety of news site, the ones that provoked the most interest was the website for Atlantic City's airport, and a tourist information site covering Guam.

Charlie received this news with gratitude, and Enrique promised him at least one hour's grace before he passed the information on to Mike Pointer at the F.B.I.

Charlie pushed his luck by requesting that Enrique omit to report the part about the Guam website, and Enrique was able to accept Charlie's argument that it was pure speculation that the site had any relevance. Even if it did, everyone was interested in where they were right now, not where they might be going. Besides, Eric had visited several dozen other websites in those hours, and it wasn't realistic to pass every single one across to the F.B.I.

Enrique concluded the call by noting that he hadn't had lunch yet, which may get in the way of him achieving the one hour goal…

Charlie thanked Enrique profusely. To Charlie, it was obvious. They would somehow travel to Atlantic City's small, touristy airport and try and slip past the T.S.A. using fake id's manufactured by Eric. Their ultimate goal was to get to Guam. Charlie had no idea what was so appealing about Guam, but that didn't matter. All Charlie needed to do was figure out their likely routing, which he planned to do using his N.Y.P.D. issue smart phone in the back of a taxi as he travelled to La Guardia airport. He really needed to talk to the kids.

Chapter Thirty-one

Mike had driven John and Carlos back to the office in downtown New York, conscious that his phone had not rung during the journey and equally conscious that Carlos's calmness had seemed to erode a little with every passing moment.

They were sitting around the meeting table in John's office, in a heavy silence. Small talk was not an option, and they all had concluded during the drive from the airport that any detailed contingency planning was pointless until new information was received. The array of possible developments was so broad that working in detail on any one contingency would almost certainly be a waste of time and resources.

Carlos looked at his watch.

'It has now been eight hours since the confrontation at the apartment,' he said, snapping the room to attention. 'No-one under this kind of stress sleeps for that long. They have to be moving.'

The room was silent, as neither Mike nor John had an immediate response. After a moment, Mike felt compelled to dispute one of Carlos's assumptions.

'They probably aren't moving, which is why we've not captured them,' Mike offered. 'They'll be lying low, evaluating their options. I'm certain they're holed up at some hotel within a short cab ride of that Eric's place. We'll get them when they re-appear. Certainly when they reach a transportation hub.'

With perfect timing, Mike's phone rang. His phone recognized the number as being one used by the National Security Agency. Mike didn't realize it, but that particular morning the N.S.A. was far more disposed to help the F.B.I. than was the N.Y.P.D.

Mike looked from John to Carlos with a look that blended a smile with a smirk, but which only ended up looking smug. He quickly answered the phone and listened intently for a moment.

'Yeah,' he said. 'Yeah. Yeah. ATLANTIC CITY!!!!'

The last two words fell onto the table like a dead duck blasted from the sky. Mike listened further, all sense of smugness dispelled, a heavy frown on his face.

'OK,' he continued, with a dejected tone. 'Understood. We'll go manual on the manifests. OK. Thanks. Keep me posted if anything else comes up.'

He disconnected the call and paused, collecting his thoughts as searched for the best words to use in the report he was about to give. Carlos looked on expectantly. John looked down at his hands, which were clasped together on the table. John could feel the tension building, a room in need of guidance. After a further moment's reflection, Mike was ready. Here goes...

'It seems the little shit-nuggets made it to an airport,' he said meeting Carlos's gaze evenly, trying to maintain a level of authority that his heart knew was no longer appropriate.

'This is an unexpected and unwelcome development,' was Carlos's icy response. John slowly wrung his hands.

'Correct,' Mike continued, his confidence eroding marginally with every word. 'The idiot called his mother from an airside payphone at the Atlantic City airport. We'd put every number we could find that the kids might call onto the N.S.A.'s monitoring lists. Their computers take an hour or so to process payphone data. There are so few public phones left that the government has given them a low priority, so they're prioritized behind all other phones. What kind of a moron uses a public phone these days anyway, when there are untraceable SIM cards for sale at every electronics store?

'Anyway, we'll check the manifests of all flights that left within two hours of the call to find them and see where they're heading next. It's only five or six flights, so it shouldn't be hard.'

'So how the fuck did they get to Atlantic City? And how did they get past the T.S.A.?' asked John, feeling that his questions were entirely reasonable even if the force he put behind the delivery was excessive. He slipped his hands under the table and gently wiped the sweaty palms of his hands against his pants legs. Time to take some control of the situation. Assume a position of leadership. Before Carlos does…

Before Mike could reply, his phone rang again. Mike's phone identified the number and told him it was Enrique Riojas, who was back from lunch and was calling Pointer exactly one hour and ten minutes after he'd called Charlie DiCarlo.

The conversation was short, but the impatience that grew in the room during the call was uncomfortable for everyone. After listening to Enrique's report, Mike updated him on the call the N.S.A. had intercepted at Atlantic City, confirming everyone's fears that the kids had escaped Manhattan.

Mike concluded the call curtly and paused once again to summarize his thoughts before addressing the room.

'The N.Y.P.D. team may have figured out how they're able to travel. We've completed an inventory of Eric's apartment. It seems we underestimated him. We found a commercial grade printer which can be used to produce driving licenses.'

'What sort of operation are you running?' John screamed, working hard to keep Carlos out of the conversation. 'It takes you three hours to notice a professional I.D. printer?'

The tension in the room had notched up considerably. Mike and John glared at each other. John knew the situation was spiraling violently downwards, and that he and Carlos were now dependent on resources they didn't control. Resources which they were effectively borrowing from a Government agency through their relationship with Mike. Mike knew that he was in a precarious position, both in the room and back in his day-job. But to get information he was dependent on the goodwill of the N.Y.P.D. and the technology of the N.S.A.

Mike wanted to correct John, to point out that while he could influence the actions of the F.B.I., he wasn't in control of the other agencies involved in the chase. Once they'd had to widen the net when they'd failed to capture the kids at Penn Station or at Crick's apartment, that had been the inevitable consequence. They were intertwined in this situation, co-dependent on finding a resolution and would only be freed once their quarries were in custody. Or dead.

John glared at Mike as the tense stand-off continued for a moment. Both John and Mike were surprised to have their intensity broken by Carlos, assuming the unusual role of pacifier.

'We can do nothing about the past,' he said. 'Only the future.'

'Good point,' Mike said, a little too enthusiastically, relaxing his shoulders a little as the adrenaline dissipated from his body. He looked at John, who also appeared to be relaxing. Deep down they both knew that their futures were linked whatever happened, and the opening up a rift between them would serve no benefit. Passions were running high because the stakes were extreme, but there was nothing to be gained from fighting.

'We'll quickly be able find the names Crick printed on the fake cards from his machine,' Mike continued. 'But he's a pro. They're using an über-geek from the N.Y.P.D. to crack the security. It's some of the tightest they've ever seen. We'll get them.'

John and Carlos absorbed this information, realizing that they were powerless to speed the process up as they were reliant on the resources of others.

'Correct,' confirmed Carlos. 'We'll get them.'

Charlie had arrived at La Guardia airport with a plan in his mind. He'd received a second call from Enrique as the taxi was pulling into the airport. Enrique relayed the news he'd received from Mike Pointer that the kids had travelled through Atlantic City airport that morning. This information made up his mind.

Working forwards from the time of the gunfire in the alley outside Eric Crick's apartment, he'd allowed three to four hours for them to get to Atlantic City. There were eight flights that had departed from that airport within two hours of the time he projected that the kids had arrived there.

Of these eight flights, four were to airports in Florida, which told him a lot about the clientele in Atlantic City. He thought they would be unlikely destinations for the kids to choose as they'd actually end up farther from Guam than they had been in Atlantic City.

Two further flights were to Philadelphia, which he discounted as it would have been an easier airport to reach from Manhattan than the one they'd chosen. Charlie also discounted the flight to Boston, as that was once again taking them away from Guam rather than towards it. Which left the flight to Detroit. Which easily connected to a flight to San Francisco, and from there Honolulu and Guam.

Charlie thanked the genius that had developed kayak.com and left the taxi, looking for a Delta ticketing desk, where he would buy a ticket for the flight that departed for Detroit in forty minutes. Another Smartphone application had told him that his chosen plane was scheduled to depart on time.

Carlos was growing frustrated, and he was struggling to contain it. They knew Lucas and Amber had been at Atlantic City airport. They knew they were flying somewhere, and because it was a mercifully small airport, they knew they were likely to be on one of only a handful of flights. How hard was it to find them?

When Carlos raised his concerns, Mike's explanation was emphatic. Without a name, they were on a fishing expedition. Mike's team had quickly procured the manifests of the five flights. 707 people had been on those flights. Out of this total, there were 454 people who'd checked in as a couple, representing 227 pairs of travelers. In addition, 109 single male travelers and 38 single female travelers had boarded, giving another 38 possible couples if the kids had booked their travel separately. That made 265 possible couples, far too many to be meaningfully investigated without more data to narrow the search.

The basic manifest data didn't include ages, which would have been the most useful data to have access to, as a lot of these couples would be elderly couples gambling their pension money away on vacation. The F.B.I. team was gathering age data, but that was a laborious and time-consuming task to complete, and Mike knew from experience that it would almost certainly be quicker to allow the N.Y.P.D. computer geek to do his job and crack open Crick's security.

It was frustrating, but Carlos accepted the explanation. He knew he could do nothing but wait.

Chapter Thirty-two

As Charlie DiCarlo's plane left La Guardia airport, Lucas and Amber's plane was arriving at Detroit's Wayne County Airport, a little over two and a half hours after they'd pushed back from the gate in Atlantic City. They had skipped the first-class breakfast, still recovering from their feast at Harrahs, and instead had taken a nap, finally able to relax even if it was for a short period. The flight had even been on time.

They had been the first passengers to exit the plane into the airport concourse, as was the privilege accorded to first class travelers. They had been delighted to find that there was no welcoming committee for them at the gate. They quickly found the first class lounge and settled into a quiet corner to pass the three hour wait for their connecting flight to San Francisco.

'So we've got a few hours here,' Amber said, feeling somewhat refreshed by her short sleep. 'There's a hair salon downstairs. We should spend some of that time getting our hair done.'

She looked up at Lucas's hair and smiled.

'What style do you want?' she asked playfully. 'A Clooney? A Pitt? A Gaga?'

Lucas smiled, appreciating the attempt to lift the mood. His mind was still in a place where relaxation was not easy.

'I think we should stay right here,' Lucas said somberly. 'Do you want a coffee?'

Amber nodded assent, and Lucas walked to the buffet, looking around him anxiously, fearing detection at any second. As Amber watched Lucas cross the room, she felt the complete horror of their situation sinking in. They really were in a whole heap of trouble. She hadn't enjoyed being shot at, but was thrilled to have survived the encounter. She realized that they may not be so lucky if they crossed paths again with the two killers.

Lucas returned, carrying two coffees, but his smile faded as he sensed Amber's distraction. He quickly put the coffees down on an adjacent table and scanned the room.

'What's up? Is someone onto us?'

'No,' Amber replied. 'Well yes. We're wanted by the F.B.I. and God knows who else. And some African heavies are trying to kill us. But I think we're safe here for the moment.'

Amber smiled at Lucas, attempting to introduce some black humor into their predicament but she quickly saw that it was still too soon for Lucas to share any sense of amusement.

'Something's been nagging me for the last hour or so,' she continued, getting back to the serious business of remaining alive. 'With Eric, well, gone, there's no guarantee this will actually go away. In fact, I can't see a way that it can go away without having someone on our side pulling for us.'

'Are you thinking we should give ourselves up?' Lucas responded thoughtfully. 'Perhaps surrendering to the F.B.I. and trusting the justice system might be better than allowing those murderers to catch up with us. After all, we haven't actually killed anyone.'

'That's an option. But you saw the F.B.I. report at Eric's. They've got circumstantial and physical evidence that we killed Ralph. And I'll bet that by now they've manufactured something similar that says we killed Eric.'

'But we didn't do anything,' Lucas protested.

'Your trust in the justice system is fantastic. But I'm starting to worry that GoldRock's got someone inside the F.B.I. working for them. How else could they have got our DNA on the gun that killed Ralph? I've not been near a gun, any gun, in years.

'We know someone was in my apartment, and I'd bet that they'd also bugged your place. Either GoldRock has someone inside the F.B.I., or they've got some really high-tech equipment available to them which the F.B.I. has been too gullible to question.

'So let's assume the F.B.I. is being strung along. The other alternative is too rough to consider. If we gave ourselves up and trusted the system, it could take a year or more for our case to get to trial, and I doubt we'd get bail. So do you really want to spend a year in jail, destroy our careers, our prospects and our finances trying to get out of a GoldRock frame up? With there being no guarantee we'd actually succeed?'

Lucas reflected on this in silence. He retrieved his coffee and took a long sip.

'I sure don't want to run forever,' he added, his voice cracking slightly as the emotion of their predicament caught up with him again.

'I'm happy to have staying alive as my goal until we get out of the States,' Amber responded, sharply. Her statement reminded them both that the game they were playing was for the most serious stakes possible – their lives.

Their eyes resumed their vigilant surveying of the passengers around them, their brains deep in thought.

'It takes something like this to remind you how good it feels to be alive,' said Lucas, looking at Amber with a hopeful smile. 'We do have each other, don't forget.'

Amber thought she detected hopefulness in Lucas's words that she knew would only complicate matters if she acknowledged it.

'If we get clear of the country, we can go to the media, the local authorities, lots of people. We can contact Eric's father. We'll have lots of options.'

'I agree,' said Lucas. 'Surrendering isn't an option. Getting out of the country is step one.'

Charlie DiCarlo sat in his seat yearning for the seatbelt sign to be extinguished. He knew it would still take several minutes for those passengers seated closer to the door to file out of the plane, but there was something about achieving a standing position that felt good.

Charlie had realized on his flight that he'd never been to Detroit before, not that he'd have any opportunity to explore the city as he planned to turn right around and fly back to New York the second he'd been able to talk to the kids. Assuming of course that they were there.

Charlie's plane had taken forever to taxi from the runway to the terminal complex. There was a further delay as the plane needed to be towed the final few feet to the gate for reasons which Charlie didn't understand and the pilot didn't explain.

If Charlie's deductions were correct, the kids' connecting flight wouldn't be leaving for at least another hour, which should give him plenty of time to track them down and talk to them. But every minute he spent trapped in his cylindrical metal prison was a minute he'd not be able to spend with the kids. They knew something crucial to his investigation that he had to download. He knew he could also help them piece the puzzle together. He just needed to find them.

Finally, the magic "ding" echoed through the cabin indicating that the seatbelt light was extinguished, and the race for the exit began. Charlie was on the concourse within two minutes of the doors opening, a few passengers having felt the point of his elbow as he navigated the plane's aisle, making sure he was courteous to anyone who shared the profile of an air marshal. Charlie couldn't afford to be detained.

Once out of the plane, Charlie quickly found a terminal map and was pleased to see he'd arrived into a gate only a few yards from the first class lounge, in which he hoped to find Lucas and Amber. He'd figured that they would seek out a quiet area to wait in, and the discretion provided by the elite lounge would be the best place to find the privacy they sought.

He reached the door within a few seconds, and the power of the Police badge worked to circumvent the usual restrictions on entry. He thought he may have detected a wisp of a smile from the attractive agent who waved him through, which he might otherwise have noted for follow-up, but the stakes were too high to accommodate distractions like that on this occasion.

Once in the main body of the lounge, he paused to take stock. He knew what his targets looked like, or at least what they'd very recently looked like. There was a limit to the superficial changes they could have made to their appearance, but their height, weight, eye color and skin tones could not have all changed significantly in such a short time.

Conversely, they'd probably had enough opportunity to take a good look at him too, but he was prepared to wager that the adrenaline of the situation in which they were thrust together would have interfered with their memories such that he would be able to approach them incognito.

So assuming he was able to get close enough to engage them in conversation, what would he say? He needed to avoid a loud confrontation at all costs, and the worst case scenario would be for a scuffle to break out which may draw in other passengers or members of the security team. No, his approach needed to be stealthy, but needed to achieve the goal of engaging his targets in quiet conversation. He needed to win their trust.

Chapter Thirty-three

Davie Eason slipped nonchalantly into the chair beside Lucas. Lucas looked around sharply, sensing a presence beside him. Meeting Lucas's anxious glance, Davie smiled back politely, two weary travelers passing the time of day. Lucas did not recognize Davie, which surprised Davie a little, given they'd locked eyes in the coffee shop the afternoon before, after which Davie had tailed them through New Jersey's transport system for nearly two hours.

Davie waited a full three minutes before making his next move. He passed the time by idly flicking at a magazine that had been left on the table. His eyes periodically swept the room, assessing the tactical situation in an attempt to discern if there were any other agents present, friendly or unfriendly. One could never be sure, but after a couple of minutes Davie was as comfortable as he could be that it was safe to make his approach.

'Excuse me,' he said, turning towards Lucas.

Amber and Lucas immediately tensed, uncertain of what was happening. Lucas glanced at Amber. In all probability this was just a civilian, asking an innocuous question, or starting down a convoluted path to obtain Amber's telephone number. It would certainly draw unwanted attention to them if they created a scene, so they knew they had to play it cool. For now at least.

Lucas looked back at the stranger and smiled in encouragement.

'You're innocent and I can prove it,' Davie said, loud enough for both Amber and Lucas to hear, but quietly enough that no-one else would. It was certainly an unusual sentence for strangers to be exchanging in an airline lounge.

Lucas heard the words and was instantly conflicted. The form of the words denoted the speaker as a threat. He knew who they were, knew they were in trouble and knew enough about their plans to have found them, two needles in the massive haystack of the U.S. airport network.

But the substance of the words gave hope. They *were* innocent, and if this guy believed it, and could help them prove it, he could be the salvation they were seeking. But the questions remained, albeit with subtly different consequences. How did he know who they were, and how did he find them and how did he recognize them?

Before they could respond, Davie continued.

'GoldRock is laundering drug money, but I need you to tell me what you know so together we can figure out exactly how they're doing it.'

Amber and Lucas exchanged glances. This was the kind of sentence they'd longed to hear since they'd left John's office in New York the day before. But who was this guy, and how was he involved? And wasn't he taking a huge risk by assisting wanted felons?

Amber noticed that the stranger was sitting silently, waiting for some reaction from them. In that instant, she noted that his body language was extremely passive. His hands were cupped, empty and motionless in his lap, representing no immediate threat. She doubted he'd be armed airside of the T.S.A. control points, and anyway, the positioning of his hands didn't suggest he was on the brink of drawing a weapon.

He was sitting well back in the chair, which was a recliner seat with a very low base, which resulted in his backside being only around eight inches off the ground. His shoulders were relaxed and his legs were crossed at the ankles, all of which combined to suggest that he'd really struggle to leap out of the chair and onto his feet if they moved to run.

His face was calm, with the suggestion of a smile forming on his lips with a slight furrow to his brow indicating an earnest interest in their response. All of this had been planned by Davie to project the image of passive support, which was the impression Amber formed from her observations. She was inclined to trust him.

'Who are you?' she asked.

'Thanks for not running,' he replied. 'My name is Detective Charlie DiCarlo of the N.Y.P.D. And for the last six months I've been working undercover in GoldRock's organization as Davie Eason, building a case against them. You guys can help me blow it open, if you'll trust me.'

Amber and Lucas had listened to Charlie run through a brief chronology of his time spent undercover.

Amber had then taken five minutes to explain their frustrations about not being allowed to see any gold in Africa, and the resistance they'd met every time they raised the issue. She told Charlie of their belief that there actually wasn't any gold. Finally she recounted how they'd been followed from Africa by two thugs who'd tried to abduct and then kill them after they'd voiced their concerns to someone who turned out to be part of the conspiracy. That somebody was now dead, and they were wanted for his murder.

Charlie had synthesized the stories and was having a "Eureka" moment of enlightenment.

'So it's a question of supply and demand. The drugs enter the U.S. through whatever channels the importers use. That's not been the focus of my investigation – the D.E.A. has jurisdiction over that and is much better positioned to investigate that side of the operation. The drugs are distributed by GoldRock's illicit wing to the street-level drug dealers to sell. They ironically call those guys the "talent" of the operation.

'The dealers sell the drugs, and get cash. That's what I've been interested in – you can often crack a case by following the money. The talent hands the cash to Runners, who give it to Collectors. I've had both of those roles in the organization over the last year or so, so I'm very familiar with the processes. The Collectors hand it up the chain, where it ends up with people they call Buyers, who take the cash to jewelry stores owned by GoldRock's legitimate wing.'

'I'm still not clear on why they want to kill us,' said Lucas, a little impatient with the detail of the lecture, but still optimistic that his and Amber's salvation lay at the end of the story.

'There's a little more detail that you need to know,' Charlie continued, undeterred. 'I think the key is this. These Buyers buy jewelry and get legitimate receipts, but don't take any inventory out of the store with them. I had to become a Buyer earlier today, when their usual guys were redeployed looking for you.

'It was one of the oddest things I've ever done. I had a budget, went in, and browsed the store. One of their salesmen helped me pick out stuff I liked. I chose some necklaces that came to a little over the cash I had. The guy rang it up, after which a manager came over and gave me a discount for cash, which coincidentally brought the total down to exactly the amount I had on me. The manager must have known exactly how much I had to spend before I got there.

'They printed me a receipt, and then the sleight of hand took place. The manager said he needed to remove proprietary security devices from my purchases, so he took them out of my sight into an office behind the counter. When he came back, it looked as if he'd gift-wrapped the purchases and put them in a bag. After leaving the store I was supposed to drop the purchases straight off with my contact. Of course

I opened up the gift-wrapping and I found that the packages were empty.

'I've thought a lot about whether they'd gone through that gift-wrap rigmarole because I was an unfamiliar face. Or perhaps there were security cameras that required them to make the transaction look legitimate. Or it might have been because the salesman was straight and had no idea he was participating in a money laundering transaction. Perhaps it was all of the above. Either way, they got their cash into the system in a way that looked one hundred percent legitimate to me, the salesman and anyone looking on. It would certainly look legitimate to any accountants and auditors looking at the books.

'The key is that jewelry all looks the same, or at least gold jewelry does. Simple necklaces, bracelets and rings, for example.

'So the store shows a record of considerable sales, but doesn't give their customers any inventory. But if they showed sales in their books with no purchases, they'd look like they made one hundred percent margins. So they need to show the purchase of large amounts of inventory to create this "cost of goods" which is what makes their accounts look reasonable. So they create records which make it look like they're buying product from a wholesaler.'

Amber leaned forward eagerly.

'Let me guess,' she said. 'The wholesaler is also owned by GoldRock.'

'Exactly,' Charlie confirmed. 'The wholesaler is one hundred percent legitimate for all intents and purposes, as are the jewelry stores. That wholesaler looks as if it buys its raw materials from your mine.'

Amber smiled enthusiastically. The final piece had fallen into place. Lucas was still a little behind.

'I still don't get it,' he said dejectedly.

'The mine in Ghana fakes the production of gold,' said Amber, taking the lead. 'It looks like a mine, operates like a mine and carves enormous holes in West Africa. But there is no gold, just as we suspected. But now we know *why*. Ignoring all the intermediate steps, the gold they're pretending to mine turns into jewelry in New York, which is "sold" over and over again to these runners, who are in fact buying the product with drug receipts.'

'Not just New York,' added Charlie helpfully. 'I've confirmed they own stores in Boston, Washington and Baltimore. I'm sure we'll find they also own stores in a lot of other places.'

'Wow,' said Amber. 'The whole thing is an elaborate money laundering ring. And we stumbled into the middle of it. We must be talking about huge amounts of cash.'

'We are,' Charlie replied. 'Tens of millions of dollars, in my estimation.'

Lucas suddenly perked up.

'Remember that polystyrene cube at the mine in Ghana?' he asked. Amber nodded enthusiastically. 'It represented the gold they'd produced in the last year. Well Carlos said it was worth six hundred million dollars.' He looked at Charlie, nodding hard.

'Wow,' Charlie responded. 'That could make this the biggest money laundering ring in history.'

Amber had been thinking while Charlie spoke.

'Hang on, I think it's even bigger than that. Six hundred million dollars is their cost of purchases. If they have any sort of margin in the books of the wholesaler or retailers, then that figure needs to be grossed up to produce a gross revenue number. Retail and wholesale margins are often well over fifty percent.'

Charlie did some simple mental arithmetic.

'Jesus. That means they could be taking over a billion dollars a year off the streets through these jewelry stores.'

All were silent for a moment in contemplation of the gravity of this situation.

'That's enough money to motivate people to commit murder, and enough to pay them to do it,' Lucas noted sagely.

'And you guys figured it out,' Charlie said gently. 'This could bust the biggest drug ring in history.'

'But we didn't figure it out,' Amber noted.

'True. But you figured out enough to scare the hell out of them,' Charlie continued.

'Now you have figured it out,' Amber said, 'you should assume they'd want you dead too.'

Charlie nodded at this sobering observation, resolving to trust the F.B.I. even less for as long as Mike Pointer was on the scene. He couldn't resist sweeping his eyes around the room one more time in an attempt to detect enemies. The same crowd of fatigued travelers met his gaze, reinforcing his earlier conclusion that they were safe for the moment at least.

'There's still one thing I don't understand,' Lucas said, still catching up with Charlie and Amber. 'They're spending a stack of money on operating that mine. On operating the jewelry stores. Presumably also on operating the wholesalers. That's a hell of a high price to pay to legitimize their money. Isn't the whole idea of money laundering to make money, not to spend it?'

'Yes, but their margins are fantastic,' Amber replied, after looking quickly at Charlie and receiving a nod of approval for her to continue. 'It costs, what, three hundred bucks for them to get each ounce out of the ground? Wasn't that what we found? They'd sell each ounce to a wholesaler for over twelve hundred dollars, which could generate two or perhaps even three thousand dollars in retail sales in the jewelry stores. Even if operating those stores costs another three hundred bucks an ounce they'd still be making a, er, a seventy percent margin,' said Amber.

Charlie looked on, pleased that he had won the trust of the two kids. He was impressed at the speed that Amber had conducted the mental arithmetic to support her last sentence. As Amber looked around the small group triumphantly, he found an opportunity to add some perspective.

'That's great,' Charlie said. 'Gold mining can be one of the most profitable businesses on the planet, if you can keep costs low. In my experience, which is better than most, crime syndicates are delighted to get perhaps fifty cents on the dollar if they launder cash domestically. But that's what they'd get for relatively small quantities of cash, a hundred thousand dollars perhaps. Laundering a billion? Hell, that would be just about impossible. They'd be happy to get twenty cents on the dollar. But here, they could be getting seventy. That's several hundred million reasons why they go to the trouble of faking a gold mine.'

All three sat in silence for a moment contemplating the consequence of the discovery. All three found themselves looking for some chink in their logic that could produce a different answer, an answer with less fatal consequences for the three of them than the one they were facing. Lucas's aversion to lengthy silences overcame him again.

'So how do we get ourselves out of this?' said Lucas, bringing his and Amber's mind back to the predicament they faced.

'Well, it's going to take me a few days to assemble the evidence we have and to convince my bosses that you're innocent,' Charlie said carefully. 'The N.Y.P.D. isn't scared of having a pissing contest with the F.B.I., especially if there's a mole in the F.B.I.'s ranks who gets exposed as a result. But there are some scary warrants out for you guys that won't go away without me producing some serious evidence. And even more persuading.'

'You've got to stay alive while you do that too,' Amber added.

'Yeah,' Charlie said. 'My gut tells me it's time to retire Davie Eason. I'm worried they've noticed that I tampered with the gift-wrapping on the packages I bought today. But then again, disappearing Davie so soon after winning their trust might raise other issues.'

Charlie paused to contemplate his dilemma for a moment. Davie could still be useful, but Charlie needed to spend every waking hour documenting his case rather than standing idle on street corners.

Very little of Charlie's work had been documented to the level it would need to be, as was typical for undercover cops. Firstly, they didn't usually know what was worth documenting until the case broke open. Secondly, it was demanding and exhausting enough to get through a day undercover without having your cover blown. Going home and documenting everything that had happened was too great a burden, especially as Charlie had been putting in ten hour shifts as Davie, up to six days a week. Charlie did his share of hours in the office, but preferred to spend that time researching the background to his investigation rather than reliving interactions that might prove to be irrelevant.

Amber snapped his thoughts back to the present. He knew he'd have time to think about his predicament on the flight back to New York.

'We think we have a way of getting out of the country without setting off any alarms,' Amber offered. She figured that a sufficient level of trust had been established to allow her to share this information, even if she concealed the details. They were in the same boat now…

'Really?' Charlie replied with skepticism.

'Yeah. Don't ask us how, but I think we should clear the country until you've had a chance to straighten things out.'

Charlie was intrigued to know what this cute girl was planning, but knew better than to ask right now. He'd find out once this was all over.

'You haven't told us how you found us,' Lucas said, breaking the silence again.

'You're big news. The F.B.I. asked the National Security Agency to put a trace on phone numbers you might call. Parents, siblings etc. The N.S.A. picked up your call to your mother, which they traced to the airport in Atlantic City. I was then able to look at the flights out of the airport – the one closest to the call was to Detroit. So I gambled and found you.'

'No shit?' asked Lucas.

'Yes, shit,' replied Charlie. 'As I said, you're big news. And in case it isn't obvious, don't do that again.'

Chapter Thirty-four

Back in New York, Mike, John, Dirk and Carlos were sitting in John's office. The tension was thick, another few hours having passed since their last significant update.

The time had passed slowly. John had ordered in some food, which had distracted them for fifteen minutes. Carlos had made a handful of calls to persons unknown. The tone of Carlos's voice, along with the time Carlos spent talking relative to the other person, suggested to John that Carlos was talking to his superiors. Carlos spoke in a language, or perhaps a dialect, that John did not recognize but his conclusion was that the conversation had not gone well. John could only speculate on who commanded Carlos, and didn't want to think about the power they might wield if they grew impatient with the team's handling of the situation.

Mike had continued to doze periodically. He'd made a few calls, but had repeatedly been assured that there were no updates and any news would be passed along immediately.

Dirk had arrived about two hours earlier, having been driven back to midtown by George after lying low for a few hours in the immediate aftermath of the shootout. Dirk had reported on the details of the confrontation in the alley, leaving out a few of the details. Specifically, he'd omitted to report that he'd had four opportunities to kill or wound his targets and had missed every time. That fact might come up when the N.Y.P.D. forensic analysis was completed but that would worry him another day. Besides, Dirk was not at all certain that all four bullets would be found given the size of the alley.

George remained in the car, his presence not required at such a high-level gathering. This suited Dirk, as even though George was Dirk's asset, he couldn't rule out George blabbing about Dirk's wayward shooting if put under pressure by a skilled interrogator like Carlos. Best to save that discussion for another day.

Mike's phone rang, Enrique Riojas calling again. Mike answered it before the end of the first ring. All eyes swung to observe him.

'Larry Shelton and Abigail McNally,' he said. John noted the names on a legal pad.

'Atlantic City to *Detroit*...,' Mike added, pausing to emphasize the last word. John and Carlos exchanged knowing glances and both raised their phones, poised to make calls once the next piece of information was delivered.

'They fly to San Francisco in an hour or so,' Mike continued. 'Then to Honolulu, then Agana. Where the fuck is Agana? OK.'

He hung up, his eyes scanning the room for support from his colleagues. Dirk's eyes were impassive, staring deep into

Mike's soul, causing Mike a moment's discomfort. John and Carlos were already engaged in their own calls.

Charlie pulled his phone from his pocket to check the timing of flights back to New York. He was irritated to notice that he'd neglected to turn it back on when he'd deplaned in Detroit thirty minutes earlier. To his greater annoyance, he saw three missed calls from Enrique when he'd powered the device back on.

Enrique called for a fourth time seconds later.

'Yeah,' answered Charlie.

'Where've you been, brother?' asked Enrique.

'Long story. What's new?'

'We've got names. Larry Shelton and Abigail McNally. We've got an itinerary. Atlantic City to…'

'Detroit,' interrupted Charlie.

'How the hell… Where are you?'

'Detroit,' Charlie replied calmly.

'If you're holding out on me…' Enrique said, a note of threat creeping into his voice.

'You're going to have to trust me on this one, but if anyone will understand, I figure you will. I've been infiltrating the GoldRock organization for six months, and these two kids hold the key to blowing open the biggest money laundering ring we've ever seen.'

'Wow. Seriously? Did you find them?' asked Enrique.

Charlie had an instant to make a huge call. If he admitted that he'd spoken to the kids, he'd face a barrage of questions if he failed to arrest them then and there, as there were warrants out for their arrest. The worst case would be a suspension, which would seriously crimp his ability to bust the crime ring open.

If he lied to Enrique, he'd buy the time to square his facts away. God knows how many arrest warrants would fly out of his case when the dust settled. Enrique would understand. Undercover agents are professional liars. And besides, Enrique had gone along with him over his request to drip feed information to Mike Pointer and the F.B.I.

'No,' said Charlie, simply.

'Hmmm,' Enrique replied, obviously not convinced by Charlie's response. 'Detroit's not that big an airport, is it?'

'It's big enough. Look, you have to trust me. I need you to pass as little information as possible to Pointer at the F.B.I. I'll explain why when I get back to New York.'

'Too late brother. When I couldn't reach you, I called him. Told him what I just told you.'

Charlie swore to himself. In an instant, a cascade of dominos fell in his head. The F.B.I. knew the kids were in Detroit's airport, about to fly to San Francisco. They'd bring the hammer down, and Charlie risked being caught in the follow through.

Charlie needed the kids alive, and out of the F.B.I.'s care for at least a couple of days. Aiding and abetting a felon wasn't such a bad deal if the felons you aided turned out to be innocent and by helping them, you end up nailing the real bad guys.

'OK,' Charlie said, looking at his watch. 'I understand. There's a flight back in forty minutes so I should be back in New York by five.'

Back in New York, Mike had received a further call which energized everyone in the room.

'Gate thirty-five,' he said. 'The two thirty flight to San Francisco. Get every man there. Take them down – they're dangerous fugitives.'

Carlos looked on. A smile threatened to form at the corner of his mouth.

Charlie turned to Amber and Lucas, a stern expression on his face. He breathed slowly in and out for a moment, gathering his thoughts. Amber and Lucas edged forward in their seats.

'Right,' Charlie said. 'They've figured out your itinerary and the names you're travelling under. They think you're in this airport, and we have to assume they'll be doing something about that soon. Perhaps in minutes.'

Lucas lifted his hands to his temples, as the comfort he'd felt when making progress across the States was replaced by an all too familiar need to run. Amber was frowning in thought.

'I believe you, and as I'm sure you heard, I didn't tell them I'd spoken to you,' Charlie continued. 'I agree that getting out of the country is the best plan. I think I need to get scarce, too.'

He looked up at the screens above them which indicated departing flights.

'You have to get out of the country, but first you need to get out of this airport,' he said. 'Find a ticketing counter and buy new tickets. It'll take me two hours to fly back to New York, so find a flight of a similar length. Somewhere that's an international hub with lots of flights. Then call me when you get off the plane.'

Charlie offered Lucas a business card, but as his head was still in his hands, Amber took and pocketed it.

'Why don't we just fly to Canada?' she asked. 'It's only an hour's flight to Toronto?'

'Bad idea,' replied Charlie instantly. 'The U.S. cooperates too closely with the Canadians. The heat will be just as extreme up there as it is down here.'

'Yeah,' said Lucas. 'Eric said his trick would work on America's system. He didn't say anything about it working in Canada. I only want to have to cross a border once.'

'Agreed,' said Charlie.

'Alright,' she said. 'But when we're not on the plane to San Francisco they'll check the airline systems and find Abigail and Larry in seconds. They'll be waiting for us at the gate wherever we land…'

'You're thinking like a policeman should,' Charlie said with a nod. 'Most aren't that smart. Use your real identities. You're airside so you won't have to pass through T.S.A. checkpoints, and they're the ones with the scary systems, not the airlines. We'll have to gamble a little that they'll be looking for Abigail and Larry and won't think to look for

Amber and Lucas. But as long as you can deplane safely, you should be able to get on an International flight using your passport trick, whatever that is.'

Amber nodded enthusiastically. Even if they were captured, they now had an ally who could help. Perhaps they'd get out of this situation after all.

Chapter Thirty-five

The Detroit Police Department maintained a S.W.A.T. team just outside of the airport. A sensible contingency, their resource planning committee concluded, given the significance of the airport to Detroit's economy and the likely prominence of the facility in terrorist minds. The surrounding neighborhoods weren't strangers to armed robbery either, meaning that the squad was one of the busier tactical firearm units in the department.

Every time the call came in for the squad to be deployed, the surge of adrenaline gave the squad's members chills. Overwhelmingly, the squad came back without firing a shot and every member of the team hoped to come back with as many bullets as they left with. Yet they lived for the call, knowing that the drama unfolding around them would be far more thrilling than any extreme sport.

The call was for an airside takedown, which was unusual, as it meant that a T.S.A. control had failed at some point. Known criminals had reached the airside portion of the airport system. Back in Atlantic City, the administration manager had already received a call indicating that his boss was keen to have a discussion the following morning, which was never good news.

Airside takedowns were good and bad. On the plus side, it was very unlikely that the suspects would be armed with anything more dangerous than a blunt object. Even if the T.S.A. had allowed them through their security checkpoints, it was very unlikely that they'd let them through with guns. There was always the fear that terrorists could be reunited with weaponry airside, stashed somewhere by a crooked airport employee. But this remained unlikely as the screening of airside employees was just as stringent as it was for passengers passing through the facility.

The downside to an airside takedown was spectators, particularly with an urgent takedown such as this. There wasn't time to clear the terminal, and issuing an alarm would alert their targets, almost certainly resulting in them vanishing into the crowd being evacuated. So any action would have to be taken in front of a potentially large crowd with the ancillary dangers that the public's presence would bring. Lines of fire would be hard to determine and the risk of collateral damage was extreme. Police departments had even received opportunistic lawsuits from people claiming hearing loss from being within one hundred feet of a discharged weapon.

As the squad moved purposefully through the terminal, they experienced the usual mix of interest and anxiety from the members of the public they passed. Some shrank back in fear, while others moved forward, intent on following the squad to see what eventuated, deadened to the reality of police activity from watching too many episodes of Cops.

Each member of the squad kept his eyes fixed firmly ahead of him, but every one of them loved being the center of attention. Wearing black body armor emblazoned with the magic letters "DPD", earpieces provided a constant stream of information from their squad leader and the support team back at base.

Behind them, actually several paces behind them, followed a small delegation from the airport security team. Obliged to participate, eager to rubberneck, but wary of getting too close to the action, every member of the team would exaggerate this episode when recounting it to loved ones. To a man, they'd make their peripheral responsibilities of crowd control seem like they'd singlehandedly taken down a major terrorist.

The squad noted that the gates they passed were incrementing steadily, odd numbers to their right, even numbers to their left. They were familiar with the terminal having trained extensively both through simulators and in the real world, in the wee small hours when the public's presence wasn't a concern. They knew that gate thirty-five would actually be facing them at the end of the terminal where the building opened up into a circular rotunda, housing the final six gates.

As they drew nearer to the rotunda, they could make out that the gate was mostly deserted. A gate agent manned the door to the plane, which was open with an electronic sign overhead reading "Gate 35 – San Francisco – Last Call."

The leader of the squad frowned, noting that boarding must nearly be complete. Their tactical advantage behind the takedown narrowed as they would be now looking at an on-plane extraction. Access would be limited – they'd have to enter the plane one by one rather than as a group. But escape options for the bad guys would be limited. At least the on-board air marshal would be able to help. The squad leader began to update his team on this development through their intercom system.

As the squad closed on the gate, a latecomer ran up to the counter from the squad's right. In her anxiety to make the flight she hadn't noticed the intimidating S.W.A.T. team bearing down on the gate. As she paused for her boarding card to be swiped through the machine, she noticed the gate agent looking over her shoulder with wide eyes. She spun to see what was holding his interest and nearly passed out as he saw the S.W.A.T. team, all guns and body armor, marching towards her.

She did pass out when one of the team pointed at her, then pointed emphatically to the side, indicating they wanted her to move. As she'd turned, the squad leader had immediately recognized that she was not a target and had communicated this to the team. However they could not surrender their tactical advantage by allowing a distraught passenger to board the plane alerting others to their presence. The squad member deftly caught her before she hit the ground, and motioned for a member of the airport's security team to care for her away from the gate entrance.

The squad leader handed a piece of paper to the gate attendant, detailing the names of Larry Shelton and Abigail McNally.

The agent clacked at her terminal and quickly was able to report that these two passengers were no-shows.

The squad leader reported this to his team and they instantly fanned out around the gate, scanning faces and scaring children. Their assumption was that their quarries could be arriving at the gate any moment, yet the reality was that anyone as dangerous as their targets would have vanished into the crowd on seeing the S.W.A.T. team.

One hundred feet to the north, at gate thirty-eight, two passengers were surprisingly unperturbed by the goings on at gate thirty-five. Superficially unperturbed at least, as in reality their hearts were pumping at epic rates as they fought to keep their hands steady and to walk in a straight line.

Lucas presented their gate agent with his and Amber's boarding passes, which snapped the agent's attention back to the two hundred and seventeen passengers waiting to board the flight. The agent looked at the two first class boarding passes and he the scanning machine remained silent as the cards swept effortlessly through. Handing the boarding passes back to Lucas, he motioned for them to board the plane.

As they passed through the door onto the finger connecting the plane to the terminal, Lucas glanced with relief at the sign above their heads. It read "Gate 37 – Dallas/Fort Worth – Pre-Boarding Only."

* * *

Charlie watched the S.W.A.T. team retreat down the terminal concourse with mixed emotions. He hated to see his fellow police officers tasked with such a wild goose chase. Even more so as he believed that the squad was prepared to use live rounds to subdue their targets, which may have resulted in a tragic miscarriage of justice. But he had his own case to build, which brought with it its own complications and challenges.

He could now see the extent of the conspiracy and the depth of the involvement from the participants. Breaking up the conspiracy may be the greatest success of his career. He was now certain that Mike Pointer was a crooked F.B.I. agent, which would make things complicated. Throwing that kind of accusation at a federal agency was never easy nor was it usually well received. The F.B.I. tended to build momentum when pursuing cases such as this and showing Pointer for the criminal he was may not immediately slow that momentum. That would be a difficult conversation to have with his superiors, given the antagonism between the two law enforcement agencies. Besides, Charlie had no actual evidence of wrongdoing yet, except for a series of hunches and a glimpse of something suspicious reflected in a broken window.

A boarding announcement snapped his thoughts back to his current situation. He'd been pleased to see Amber and Lucas slip onto the plane un-noticed by the D.P.D., but he knew he had to get back to New York.

He reflected that Amber and Lucas seemed to be decent, honest citizens who'd been in the wrong place at the wrong time. It was tough luck. He wondered idly on the relationship between them, wondering whether it had developed beyond the collegial level they'd presumably started at. He found himself to be a little surprised at a wave of jealousy that surged through his body thinking about Lucas being with Amber. Silly boy, he thought. Pull yourself together.

A few minutes after he watched Amber and Lucas slip onto their plane unnoticed by the D.P.D., he was walking down his own jet way onto his plane back to New York.

He'd expected to spend much of the flight thinking through the developments he'd experienced that day, but fell asleep as soon as the plane took off, a deep sleep from which he had to be roused by a stewardess as they began their final approach into La Guardia airport.

On his awakening, Charlie quickly realized that he felt quite refreshed by the short sleep. The adrenaline he'd felt from confronting Amber and Lucas had not compared to the surge he'd felt numerous times when undercover, but it had still tired him out enough to produce a deep sleep in an upright aircraft seat.

Charlie had learned from his error in Detroit, so made a point of switching his N.Y.P.D. Smartphone back on as soon as the plane's wheels touched the runway. As an afterthought he also switched on the pay-as-you-go phone he used when posing as Davie Eason. Davie had had his day-off interrupted once already that day so Charlie thought it very unlikely that Davie's phone would ring again.

As Charlie stepped out of the jet way into La Guardia's busy concourse he was surprised when Davie's phone rang.

Shit, he thought. There are a thousand reasons to not answer the call. But there's one reason why I should.

I'm still Davie, and I can still use that to my advantage. Now I know the extent of the criminal activity, Davie may be getting close to retirement, but I can still use him in the short term to gather data. The trust I'm developing within the organization may allow me to take the pulse of the conspirators while Charlie was building the case against them.

Thinking quickly, Charlie quickly found a quiet corner of an adjacent boarding gate and answered the phone.

'Yeah,' he said, summoning as much tiredness into his voice as he could. He'd learned long ago to not use a false voice when undercover as it became a nightmare to maintain and was an easy chink in the armor for the bad guys to exploit. Rolling exhaustion into his voice was not hard for him given the exertions of his last sixteen hours.

'It's Jorge,' the voice replied. 'I have to bother you again.'

More respect from Jorge. Could this day get any more revealing?

'That's OK, boss,' Charlie replied. 'I was taking a nap.'

'Yeah. We'd like you at a meeting at Carlo's Pizzeria on eighth avenue and twenty-seventh street at six this evening.'

'Sure. No problem. What's up?' Charlie decided to risk a quick fishing trip, given the hold he now seemed to have over Jorge and the fact that Davie could now disappear in seconds if required.

'We've got another tracking job for you. You did well trailing those kids, we've got another one. Same pay as last time.'

'Sure. Thanks Jorge. See you soon.'

Jorge disconnected the call without responding. Charlie slipped the phone into his pocket and rubbed the back of his neck. He worried that he was wearing the same clothes he'd had on for their meeting earlier that day, which may look odd as Jorge knew he'd just been asleep. Jorge would have to live with it though, because he wouldn't have time to change them if he was going to battle through the rush-hour to make the meeting on time. If he didn't make it, Davie could just disappear.

Charlie knew he had to really move it to make it downtown, but again he paused. He'd learned over the years that an undercover cop is at his most exposed when he's tired, unprepared and uncertain as to what was going on. Charlie realized he would be all three at the upcoming meeting, which made him nervous. For a moment he seriously considered skipping the meeting, effectively killing Davie off. But the opportunity to gain more intelligence from the inside was too good to pass up. He knew he'd have to take the risk.

Who would he be asked to tail? Why would he be tailing them? Would the meeting reveal another conspirator? It was too good an opportunity to miss, considering the intelligence that might emerge.

His final concern was the kids. They were scheduled to arrive into Dallas/Fort Worth airport at 5:45pm Eastern time, but any delay to their arrival would mean that they'd land after he'd have to switch off his N.Y.P.D. phone to get into his Davie persona. He had no way of communicating with them while they were in the air or even when they were on the ground, as they would be calling him. Charlie realized that this would only be a problem if their plane was delayed, so he retrieved his Smartphone and checked their flight. Sure enough, their plane was scheduled to now land at 5:05pm Central Standard Time. Five minutes after his meeting started in Manhattan.

Charlie looked again at his watch and sighed. He had to go. He set off towards the terminal's exit at a brisk jog.

Chapter Thirty-six

Charlie was still jogging when Davie Eason covered the last two blocks to the rendezvous. He'd been able to grab a cup of triple espresso on a station platform when he changed trains which made him feel a little stronger. A little jumpiness wouldn't hurt the image he was trying to project either, he thought.

He'd agonized about what to do about the kids and had made a snap decision. He had decided that the simplest option was to re-record his voicemail message, leaving a clue in his words for the kids to pick up on that hopefully would seem innocuous to anyone else calling him. The message had been simple:

'Hi. This is Charlie DiCarlo, N.Y.P.D. I believe I'll be in meetings until seven pm Eastern, six Central, so please call me back after that time, or leave a message now. Thanks.'

The reference to believing and adding the central time stamp would be enough for the kids to pick up on, he was sure. Amber certainly would, even if Lucas might miss it.

He arrived at the restaurant at two minutes to six. There were two large guards monitoring the doors and Charlie's trained eye could tell that several of the parked vehicles were occupied across the street from the restaurant. He had his hoodie pulled over his head, partly to protect a little against the light drizzle that was falling, but partly so his face would be remembered by as few people as possible.

Two other guys were ahead of Charlie in line to enter the building, being screened by the guards before they were allowed to enter. He didn't recognize either of them, but it made Charlie speculate as to how many people were going to be in attendance. More than this morning's gathering between himself, Jorge and Nigel. If so many people were going to be gathered and would therefore have the opportunity to see their colleagues, something serious must be brewing. That wasn't how the organization operated.

Charlie recognized one of the guards as the guy who regularly patrolled Charlie's drop-off locations, so he eased his hood a little up his forehead to allow the guard to recognize him, which he quickly did, waving Charlie through. Charlie looked hard at the other guard, hoping he'd have a recognizable face that would allow Charlie to identify him later. Charlie's goal was to remember as much information as possible, as he was increasingly certain that this would be Davie's last outing.

Charlie entered the restaurant, and quickly realized that this was no ordinary meeting. His memory would be at full stretch to recall all of the faces he'd encounter today.

Perhaps twenty-five people were present, half a dozen of whom Charlie quickly recognized. Charlie's usual handlers, Jorge, Juan and Nigel were all present, as were a couple of guys Charlie recognized as Runners from his old patch. Charlie hadn't seen either of them for some time now which suggested they'd been promoted to Davie's current rank of Collector.

Of the faces Charlie didn't recognize, Charlie speculated from their dress that they were probably other Collectors, pulled temporarily from the street to swell the ranks of the trusted in whatever endeavor was being proposed.

One guy stood out by wearing a suit. He was overweight, somewhat disheveled with graying, thinning hair plastered to his head. He was deep in conversation with Nigel, and had his back turned to the room, which Charlie quickly concluded was a ploy to minimize the number of people who got a clear look at his face.

Charlie's instinct told him that this was a significant player in the organization, someone who wouldn't regularly fraternize with the troops, hence his reticence to show his full face. Something nagged at Charlie's mind that the man was familiar but he wasn't immediately able to place him without seeing his full face. He's probably uncomfortable to be in attendance, thought Charlie, but he has to be present to pass on the necessary information. Charlie's anticipation as to what would be discussed grew yet further.

At a few minutes past six, after another three people had been admitted, Nigel broke his huddle with the suited guy and called the room to order. The guy in the suit discretely slipped through a back door, which Charlie assumed led to the kitchens. Charlie had caught an oblique glance at the face from which he was able to connect the face to a name. He'd just seen John Showers, GoldRock's U.S. General Manager.

This was a major breakthrough for Charlie, as it meant he could now definitively link GoldRock's most senior U.S. manager to the illicit gathering of drug runners taking place in a dingy restaurant. Charlie's heart nearly beat out of his chest as he realized the significance of making this link. Whatever happened next, giving Davie this one last outing was going to pay huge dividends.

The people in the room shuffled around a little to be able to hear Nigel. Some sat at the dining tables, others leaned against a wall. Charlie took what he considered would be a strategically intelligent position, leaning against a wall close to the door. Charlie reasoned it would give him an excellent chance to be the first to leave, which would minimize the interactions he had with others as he departed.

Another advantage of the location was that, in the unlikely event that the situation turned against him, he'd be able to exit the building quickly. Of course he'd have to take his chances of getting past the twin slabs of security positioned outside the door, but a small, fast guy unexpectedly blasting past ought to give him enough surprise to be able to dodgy any clumsy swings at him that they took. But that scenario was unlikely, as he'd no reason to believe the situation would turn bad.

'Attention, everyone,' said Nigel, authoritatively. 'I'll be brief. We've experienced some losses in recent weeks. Some of you have assisted us in tracking down those we believe were responsible. They have been dealt with.'

Nigel looked directly at Charlie. Charlie knew he was being updated, and he boldly and evenly returned Nigel's stare. I know exactly how you *wanted* to deal with them, Charlie thought, even if it didn't exactly turn out as you planned.

'But a problem remains. Someone leaked information. We believe our operation has been infiltrated by an undercover cop,' Nigel continued.

Charlie's blood ran cold. His shoulders tensed and his eyes fell to the floor. Charlie quickly realized that this was the most critical moment of his career, perhaps of his life. It was incredibly unlikely that any other agency would have infiltrated an agent into the organization, so they had to be referring to him. But how could they possibly know?

Charlie's rational brain kicked in. He looked back at Nigel, concerned that by dropping his eyes so rapidly he may have communicated guilt. To his relief, Nigel had shifted his gaze and was looking towards the other side of the room.

Think, Charlie, think. They wouldn't have invited you to attend if they knew it was you. They'd have summoned you to an empty restaurant, and cornered you right away. Charlie didn't pause to contemplate what might happen if he was cornered. No, by gathering so many people together they couldn't know who they were looking for. Charlie breathed a little more easily as he realized that he still had a chance to wriggle out of the situation.

Charlie thought more. By making such a revealing statement in front of so many people, Nigel was effectively confirming they didn't know who they were looking for. Admitting such a security concern to so many people would be madness if they already knew who they were looking for. Intimidation and control of information were two cornerstones of the organization, and this was a major admission of weakness that wouldn't have happened unless they were really desperate. Desperation was not good news. Really bad things happened when people were desperate. Charlie casually raised his hand to his head and subtly pulled his hood another inch forward across his forehead.

Charlie sensed rather than heard the door opening to his right. He became aware of a latecomer positioning himself against the wall between Charlie and the door. Charlie wanted to check the face, to file another associate in his memory banks, but was nervous of making any movement which may draw further attention to him.

From Charlie's position, using only his eyes and without moving his body, he could see his neighbor's legs and hands. He was big, and appeared to be wearing a pair of casual runners, and black colored jeans. His hands appeared to be clasping a stack of documents, and Charlie relaxed when he saw a large signet ring on the pinkie finger of his neighbor's left hand. He instantly knew that the hand belonged to the security guy who's granted Charlie entry to the meeting. The guy who usually policed the drop-off meetings at the end of his shift.

Alright, thought Charlie, calm down. Not a newcomer. Nigel was still speaking.

'I want you all to keep your eyes and ears open,' Nigel continued. 'We have a name and we're getting a photo.'

Charlie sensed his neighbor moving his arm as he processed the words from Nigel. Dread refilled Charlie's soul as the words sank in. He turned his head an inch or two to the right and stole a glance at the documents his neighbor was holding. He was mortified to see that the sheet contained only one detail. The photograph from Charlie DiCarlo's driving license. He was trapped in a room with twenty-five of his greatest enemies and they were all about to be given his photograph.

Chapter Thirty-seven

Amber and Lucas passed the flight to Dallas in a state of mild shock and looming terror. The three hours felt like an eternity, but they knew the die had been cast and there was nothing they could do to change the outcome. Either they'd walk out of the plane into the anonymity of the terminal or they'd be apprehended. Neither wanted to dwell on what being apprehended might be like, or how much it might hurt.

The pilot reported that the plane had been put into a holding pattern by air traffic controllers, which immediately panicked Lucas as he assumed this was being done so the authorities could prepare for them. However, the pilot's explanation that it was the busiest time of day at the airport seemed entirely plausible to Amber.

The plane eventually landed and after an eternity of taxiing, the door opened. Amber and Lucas remained in their seats, deciding on this occasion that it was best for them to forgo the deplaning privileges of travelling in the first class cabin, preferring to leave the cabin as one of the last passengers so as enter the concourse amid as many people as possible.

As they stepped from the jet way into the main terminal they were both braced for action. Lucas gasped as a flashbulb went off to his right. He breathed again when he realized he'd been startled by a mother capturing a snapshot of her daughter at play as they waited to board their plane. Looking around them, while they saw plenty of people milling around the busy terminal, there were no police. No S.W.A.T. teams. No guns.

Exchanging a quick glance of relief, Amber grasped Lucas's hands and pulled him at speed away from their arrival gate.

Back in the Italian restaurant, Nigel motioned to the security guard standing beside Charlie. The guard moved to cross the room to hand the stack of photocopied sheets to Nigel.

Charlie tensed. Now could be his chance. The obstruction between him and the door was moving. It would take him perhaps three strides to reach the door, perhaps two seconds. Doable.

There was other good news. With one of the security guards now in the room, there'd only be one left to dodge outside. Charlie remembered the people he'd seen in the parked cars and there was a risk they'd left the cars and were now manning the doors. That may give him a small crowd to break through if he made it through the door.

No, thought Charlie. It was more likely that they were just observers, monitoring attendees, perhaps photographing them. That would be what Charlie would do. Gather some photographic evidence of participation in a criminal activity that could be used against people down the road if they needed to be reminded where their loyalties lay. If he got past the remaining guard, he'd be well clear of the restaurant before anyone would be able to get out of the car to challenge him. He could be really fast when he needed to.

There was yet more good news. The photo came from Charlie's driving license, and thus had been taken perhaps ten years earlier. Charlie struggled to remember exactly how long ago it had been taken, but quickly realized it didn't matter. He had a different hair color and style. His skin tones were lighter, having spent so much of the last few years indoors. He considered that there was a good chance that the six or seven people he'd interacted closely with wouldn't immediately recognize him. It didn't seem that the security guard had recognized him, as Charlie was sure he'd have glanced at the photos when he'd taken possession of them. Perhaps he'd be able to leave the room without incident after all?

But could he take the risk? Rely on an old photo in a room full of people who'd seen him before, some of whom had seen him regularly? And they'd seen him without his hoodie, his full face exposed. Charlie quickly concluded it wasn't a risk he could take. He'd have to leave. Now…

Charlie tensed the muscles in the thighs of his right leg, which he'd bent, resting his foot against the wall behind him for comfort. He would use his right foot to push himself away from the wall, pivot off his left foot and head for the door. He flexed his fingers, preparing to deliver a punch to the security guard outside the door if confronted. The guard was a big man, so big that Charlie considered it unlikely that he took regular exercise. He'd have size and power, but probably would not have the control or anticipation of a regular fighter. Charlie was starting to fancy his chances.

His attention was snapped back to the present by Nigel, who'd noticed the movement of the security guard with the photographs.

'Just hand them round,' Nigel said.

The guard stopped dead, barely a pace from the wall, leaving Charlie no space to navigate behind him to the door. Worse, he started to turn towards Charlie. Charlie felt crushed. He was trapped and it looked like he was going to stay that way. People would have the photograph in seconds and he'd have to tackle the first guard in order to get to the door, then the second guard outside if he made it that far. But scuffling with the guard inside would only alert the guy outside. Dammit.

The guard split the stack into two piles, and handed one to Charlie, who took the stack without looking up. The guard paused, deciding what to do with the other half, before deciding to hand them to the person sitting at the table directly in front of Charlie. The intention was to have a schoolroom hand-around. Take one, pass it on.

Charlie needed to take a decision. Tactically, he was in a tough spot. There was a guard between him and the door who was now facing him with his hands free. His own hands were now full of papers.

All eyes in the room had turned to look at the hulking security guard, anxious to see the photo of the imposter they'd been tasked to find. Many of those eyes would also be looking at him. In that instant, Charlie decided to ride things out for a moment longer. Perhaps the guard would go back outside, having completed the job of passing out the photographs. People would be distracted by passing on the papers, then by looking at the picture on their copy. There'd certainly be a better opportunity to bolt in a few more seconds. Charlie took a sheet and passed the rest on. He held up the sheet to pretend to look at it, but actually used it to partially shield his face as he observed the other people in the room.

A murmur of chat had broken out as Nigel had fallen silent, obviously waiting for the photographs to circulate before continuing to speak. Charlie looked at the man sitting in front of him and his heart fell when he realized it was Jorge. The one person in the room with whom Davie had spent the most time. The person who'd had the longest face-to-face conversations with Davie, as recently as this morning. The person who had the greatest chance of recognizing him, even from an outdated photograph. The worst person to be receiving the photograph first.

As Charlie watched, Jorge took the stack from the guard and took one without looking at it. He was distracted by a conversation he was having with the person sitting next to him, to whom he handed the rest of the stack. Charlie watched Jorge, hoping beyond hope that he'd continue to ignore the sheet until the guard had left. The person next to Jorge took a sheet and looked at it before passing the rest on.

Then, just as a car crash seems to happen in slow motion, Charlie's life began to disintegrate in front of him.

The guard turned towards the door, making as if to exit.

Jorge laughed at a comment from his neighbor, and his eyes fell onto his sheet.

Charlie sensed his moment was now, and tensed his muscles, using his right foot to push his body away from the wall.

Jorge emitted a loud yell of recognition and began to rise from his seat.

Charlie landed on his left foot, and pivoted to his right, having the intention of taking the guard by surprise, nipping around him and beating him to the door.

The guard paused, alarmed by the sudden shriek from Jorge.

Jorge pivoted around, towards the position Charlie had been occupying against the wall, raising his arm to point.

Others in the room gasped in response to the disturbance. Everyone's eyes swung in the direction of Jorge's pointed finger, searching out the infiltrator.

Charlie took a step onto his right foot, looking to his left in an uncontrollable reaction to Jorge's exclamation.

The guard began to turn to his left, back towards the room. Seeing Charlie approaching, the guard braced and lowered his shoulder.

Charlie, still looking at Jorge, did not see the guard's turn and collided with him, his chin squarely hitting the guard's lowered shoulder.

For Charlie, everything went black.

Chapter Thirty-eight

Amber and Lucas had agreed during the flight down from Detroit that they would avoid any first class lounges in the future. Amber's suggestion that they avoid being cornered in an area with only one exit made excellent sense to Lucas.

Walking through the busy terminal, they quickly found a vacant gate where they could get some privacy. Even better, the vacant gate was shielded from its neighbor by a bank of credit card operated phones. This created a dilemma for them. They had to call Charlie, but should they use one of their cell phones, which they were certain would be traceable, or should they use a payphone, which Charlie had warned them to avoid? And if they used a payphone, they'd either have to find one which accepted coins, or they'd have to risk using one of their credit cards.

Lucas voted to risk a credit card, but Amber had a better plan. Time to use some of the feminine wiles she usually refused to accept she had.

She tucked her t-shirt deeper into her pants, which increased the fabric's tension across her breasts, creating a look she knew would be effective. She picked her mark, a middle aged businessman seated alone a few rows down from the bank of payphones.

Lucas looked on with interest as Amber walked towards the man, accentuating the roll in her hips as she covered the short distance. The businessman quickly noticed her approach and was thrilled to be engaged in conversation with such a hottie.

Amber returned to Lucas a moment later, holding the businessman's cell phone. Lucas had been watching the businessman's face closely and he could see the disappointment when he'd realized that Amber wasn't travelling alone.

'I thought the damsel in distress routine would work, particularly here in the south,' said Amber by way of explanation. 'People are too nice. I told him my cell phone was dead.'

Lucas smiled as he drew Charlie's business card from his pocket and handed it to Amber. Amber dialed the number.

'It's a voicemail,' she reported as Lucas leaned in eagerly, trying to overhear.

Lucas retreated on this news, as Amber listened intently to the message. To Lucas's surprise, she hung up at the end of Charlie's recording without leaving a message. He looked at her quizzically.

'He'd left a message for us in his message. Call him back after six pm.'

Lucas looked at his watch. Another forty-five minutes of nervous waiting.

'Do you mind giving that guy his phone back?' asked Amber.

Charlie came round with a jolt. A wave of almost pleasant fogginess washed over him as he regained consciousness. It quickly evaporated, as the jolt of adrenaline generated by his reanimated mind reminded him why he'd lost consciousness in the first place.

As Charlie's mind regained its functionality, he really didn't know what to expect. He hadn't been knocked out since the fifth grade, when some big kid with an inferiority complex had decided to make an example of a much smaller Charlie. Charlie had still got a number of good shots in before succumbing… Since then he'd made it a policy to avoid being punched.

Suddenly the events came back to him. A room full of drug runners looking at a photograph of his face. A brave dash to the door. Blackness. He hadn't seen a fist, but something pretty solid had hit him.

His thoughts briefly swung to the kids, who should be sitting at the airport in Dallas, trying to call him. He hoped Amber would keep her cool.

His thoughts turned back to the room and although he knew he was sitting in a chair, he found that he could move his arms and legs. He fought off a wave of surprise as he realized he wasn't tied to the chair. Interesting…

He also determined that he was still fully clothed, but raising his hand to check his pockets, he found that his wallet had been taken. He'd travelled to Michigan and back with his N.Y.P.D. shield and he'd had no opportunity to dispose of it between La Guardia and the restaurant. So they had his police identification. No point denying it then...

He hadn't had time to seek and receive approval to take his weapon with him to Detroit so at least there was no gun for them to discover. That may count in his favor: at least he hadn't turned up to their meeting packing a piece.

Both of his phones were also gone, Davie's pay as you go and his own N.Y.P.D. Smartphone. That could be bad news...

He sensed that he was alone. The chair was oriented to face a wall against which were stacked cartons of vegetables. Charlie assumed from this that he was still in the restaurant, perhaps in a storage area at the back of the kitchens. That would make sense, he thought, as they'd not want to drag an unconscious body through New York streets at sunset.

Charlie turned his head through as wide an arc as he could and could see no-one. He moved to rise out of his seat but a pair of large hands clamped down on his shoulders, restraining him in place. OK, I'm not alone, he thought.

The grip was released and he then heard a knocking on a door, presumably a signal from his captor that he was now conscious. A moment later he heard the door open. A number of people entered the room, perhaps three, maybe four, thought Charlie, trying to count the footfalls. That now made a maximum of five people, if there'd only been one guard in the room with him to start with. Too many to overpower on his own, for certain. He'd have to talk his way out of this.

Suddenly, he felt the large hands of his captor grasp the chair where the seat met the back of the chair, and he and the chair were both effortlessly swung through one hundred and eighty degrees to face the new arrivals. What he saw made his heart sink.

Before him stood four people. The guard, who'd been the linebacker Charlie had collided with. The guy in the gray suit who'd briefed Nigel, who Charlie could now positively identify as John Showers, GoldRock's U.S. Manager.

The third person was Mike Pointer, the F.B.I. agent who Charlie could now prove beyond a shadow of a doubt was crooked from his very presence in the room. And a fourth guy who Mike did not recognize, but who was small and wiry. Charlie quickly concluded that he looked like a real nasty piece of work. Charlie noted that he was carrying a small canvas bag, and stood half a pace behind Mike and John.

Charlie was concerned to see these individuals lined up before him. It meant that they were not afraid to show their faces to him. They knew he was an undercover police officer, something he could not deny given they had his police shield. Having an F.B.I. agent present at a criminal gathering was one hell of an admission of guilt. Same with having the manager of an apparently legitimate international mining operation. Charlie was not thrilled with how this was turning out.

Seeing that the situation was under control, the guard slipped quietly out of the room leaving Charlie alone with Mike, John and Dirk.

'Well this is awkward,' Mike offered, breaking the uncomfortable silence.

'Awkward for us all,' Charlie replied, deciding that offense was the best form of defense.

'Indeed,' Mike replied. 'Right. First of all, some logistics. Don't try to escape. If you get past us three, there's an entire battalion of our resources outside that door, which is the only door out of this room. I could be bluffing, but I'm not. Besides, you won't get past us. We haven't bothered to tie you up as you're a smart guy and we want to converse like adults.'

Charlie nodded. As he'd thought.

'OK,' John said, taking over the lead role in the interrogation. 'We know you are Charlie DiCarlo, an eight year veteran of the N.Y.P.D. For the last six months or so you've infiltrated our organization as Davie Eason.'

'Correct,' Charlie said. 'And for the record, you're all under arrest.'

Mike and John exchanged glances and laughed heartily. The small wiry guy also broke into a crooked smile. Even Charlie found himself smiling.

'Thanks for that,' John said. 'We needed a laugh.'

'I didn't mean it to be funny…' Charlie added, killing the smile that was rippling around the edge of his mouth as the laughter from the others subsided.

'So you'd have seen and heard a lot of things that would be highly detrimental to our operations if they became public knowledge,' Mike continued, bringing the conversation back within the parameters he'd agreed with John before entering.

'Very detrimental,' John added.

'So I assume you're going to kill me?' Charlie asked. 'Because if you are, you can at least let me know how you found me.'

'You assume correctly,' was John's even reply. 'About killing you, I mean. As to how we found you, that was Mike.'

'We met at Eric Crick's apartment,' Mike said. 'The F.B.I. had established jurisdiction over the case, and so there was no reason for an N.Y.P.D. detective to be snooping around the crime scene. I spoke with the officer who was organizing the C.S.I. work and he mentioned you saying you had an interest in the case. That obviously piqued my interest. You can imagine I've learned to be very cautious given my conflicting responsibilities.'

Charlie nodded. He'd no reason to be angry with Enrique. While they'd both considered the F.B.I. agent to be rude and highhanded, Enrique had had no reason to suspect that Pointer was actually crooked.

'So I looked at your file,' Mike continued. 'One of the benefits of being with the F.B.I. I found out that you had built a somewhat stellar career by working undercover. You had been infiltrating a crime syndicate for the last six or seven months. It didn't take a genius to figure out that it was our operation you were infiltrating. Which explained your appearance at that particular apartment, which we had to link to GoldRock in order for me to get jurisdiction over the crime scene. What clinched it was when a charge hit your credit card this morning for a flight to Detroit.'

'We decided this afternoon to roll the dice and put out a wanted notice for you amongst our team,' said John, taking over the narrative. 'Imagine our surprise when you were actually in the room with us when we did it.'

'So you guys were responsible for killing Eric, not those kids you are trying to frame,' Charlie asked.

'Of course we were. Or to be specific, Dirk here was,' John said, indicating the third man in the group with the mysterious canvas bag.

Charlie looked at Dirk, memorizing the face out of habit. The man certainly looked like a killer, although at that particular moment he was giving Mike a look which suggested that he wasn't thrilled about having been identified as a murder in front of a police officer. Perhaps there is a hope that I'll get out of the room alive, Charlie thought, given the small man's apparent annoyance.

Charlie looked back to Mike and reflected on his words. They knew too much – he was in deep trouble. He decided to change tack.

'Killing some computer geek is in a completely different league from killing a sworn law enforcement officer,' Charlie said reasonably. 'You really want to make that leap?'

John paused and appeared to be contemplating his answer.

'You make a good point. But it's a necessary step,' he replied. 'We've killed government officials before but I'll grant you, not in the United States.'

'And besides, you're undercover as a drug dealer,' Mike added. 'Drug dealers get whacked all the time. We'll make it look like a drug deal gone bad. I wouldn't worry about that.'

'The explanation you give for my death wasn't my primary concern,' Charlie replied, dryly.

John and Mike laughed again.

'You may kill me, but you're all still all going to jail,' Charlie said, deciding to take the initiative. 'I know the entire story. I know how you fabricate gold production in Africa to supply jewelry stores with phantom product which you use to launder drug money off the streets. I know you framed those kids for the first murder. I saw you take a sock from the apartment, from which you'll extract Eric's DNA. You'll use that to frame the kids for the second murder too.'

Mike frowned at this, realizing that his theft had been noticed. He was sure the cop had been looking out of the window when he lifted the sock. He'd taken a calculated risk which it would appear didn't completely pay off. But he had to get something from the apartment before the C.S.I. team locked it down and did their work, after which all evidence would be held at the N.Y.P.D. precinct under lock and key. Mike realized that the situation had just grown a little more complicated.

'I talked to the kids in Detroit and was able to tell them to avoid the San Francisco flight,' Charlie continued. 'It was fun to see the S.W.A.T. team flapping around. And no I don't know where they've gone, so don't make this worse by trying to torture that information out of me. I also know who's helping them now. And everything I know, my bosses know, including the fact I was coming here this evening. If they don't hear from me within the hour he'll come down on you all with the force of God before the day is over.'

Charlie leaned back and folded his arms, presenting a facade of security and self-assuredness. He knew that big chunks of his statement were a barefaced bluff, but he hoped there was enough truth scattered amongst the lies to slow down his adversaries and give them a reason to reconsider their next move. Even if they stepped out of the room to confer and left him alone for a few moments he'd have some opportunity to attempt an escape. Even if the guard returned, he'd be one-on-one with a guy he felt confident he could take down in a hand to hand fight. He just had to interrupt their current momentum and regain some of the initiative.

John and Mike looked at each other, thinking silently. Dirk stared at Charlie with a barely perceptible tilt of the head which suggested that he was evaluating the best way to kill him.

'Well, I very much doubt that all of that is true,' Mike eventually said to John, temporarily ignoring Charlie. 'Remember, we've seen his files and there's minimal documentation of anything.'

'So, if he's bluffing, we've still got a great chance of getting this back in the bottle. So we'd stick with the plan,' John replied. 'On the other hand, if he is telling the complete truth, we can't let him testify against us. We'd be well in the shit tomorrow, but it leads us to the same place this evening.'

'So either way we end up at the same conclusion,' Mike replied.

Charlie watched this interaction with a sinking feeling in his chest. It began to dawn on him that he really was not leaving this room alive.

'And if the reality is somewhere between those two extremes,' Mike continued, 'it still takes us to the same place. So we're agreed?'

'Agreed,' John replied, turning to Dirk. 'If you'd do the honors please.'

Dirk nodded and opened up his canvas bag. He drew a silenced gun from its depths and stepped forward.

'Wait, we can talk about this,' Charlie said, a sense of desperation rising up from within him.

Dirk slowly shook his head, not wanting to be subjected to the petty babbling of a desperate man. He much preferred killing people when they weren't expecting it, or better still when they were gagged. Looking his victim in the eye didn't faze him, but mindless blithering got on his nerves.

Dirk quickly silenced Charlie with four closely grouped shots to the chest. Mike flinched as the bullets extinguished the police officer's life. John had already turned away.

Chapter Thirty-nine

Amber and Lucas had nervously waited out their forty-five minute hiatus. The businessman had moved seats as soon as Lucas had returned his phone, realizing that his fantasy of banging Amber in a restroom before his flight back to Podunk, Arkansas were just that. A fantasy.

Lucas's thoughts had been uncoordinated. He'd caught himself reenacting the horrors enacted upon them in the last twenty-four hours, and in particular the tragic murder of Eric. Deep down he knew this wasn't a constructive use of time, but his mind clearly wasn't ready to let the memories fade into the background.

When not thinking about the past, he found himself working through wild scenarios about the future. A year in a federal prison? Vindication? A frantic flight to Honduras? Who knew? He was pleased to have Amber beside him, someone he could trust and someone who was proving to be handy in difficult situations. And maybe, after this, something more than a friend.

Amber's thoughts were more structured. An angel had appeared, literally appeared beside them, with an outstretched hand offering redemption. He'd offered a miracle, something almost too good to believe. But an angel had come and gone before, in the somewhat un-angelic form of Eric Crick. He'd shown them a path to freedom, which they'd embraced, but it had been cruelly snatched from them before they could even leave his apartment.

Amber wanted above all to believe that Charlie would get back to New York, make a few calls, and summon them back to their homes where confetti and balloons would magically fall from the ceiling in celebration of their freedom. But she knew that was not guaranteed. Charlie was up against formidable opposition in the form of a multi-billion dollar company desperate to keep its secrets hidden. A company that had the resources and immorality to do just about anything to defend those secrets. Combine that with a crooked F.B.I. agent who would bring the full force of the U.S. government down on them, including the N.S.A., and Charlie succeeding didn't seem that likely. The N.S.A. for God's sake! How could Charlie compete against that?

Amber's thoughts had lingered on the beacon of hope that Charlie had extended, but she'd also spent time thinking about what she'd do if Charlie's beacon was extinguished. And those thoughts were complicated because she had to take Lucas with her. She respected Lucas's professionalism, his intellect and his work ethic, but he was proving to be a less than perfect counterpart when difficult decisions needed to be taken.

At two minutes to six, Amber rose, stretched her t-shirt across her chest one more time, and left Lucas sitting by the bank of payphones as she walked away to find another sucker. She was back with another phone at the stroke of six, and she anxiously re-dialed the number. Lucas leaned in eagerly.

'Hello?' replied a voice on the second ring.

Amber paused. She'd spent perhaps thirty minutes in Charlie's company and had a decent appreciation for his voice. Despite the distortion of the phone connection, this didn't sound like Charlie.

'Charlie?' she asked, more in hope than expectation.

'No, this isn't Charlie,' the voice replied. 'Charlie is, well Charlie is indisposed.'

Amber gasped. Lucas hadn't been able to clearly hear the response to Amber's question but he recoiled nevertheless from the shock of Amber's reaction.

Amber thought she heard a snort of laughter in the background in response to the mystery voice's comment. Amber decided to deploy the tactic of silence, and was surprised when the voice quickly filled the void.

'Yeah, Charlie, Davie, whatever. Both of them are going to be indisposed for quite some time, actually.'

Amber's heart sank, as she realized her worst fears were being realized. Biting her lip as her emotions built, she fought to remain silent, not wanting to give the voice the pleasure of a reaction.

'And thanks for calling. It'll make finding you so much easier.'

Amber's mind was filled with cinematic images of computer tapes whirring as the N.S.A.'s super computers swung into action to trace the call, using all manner of satellites and algorithms to launch a cruise missile at her.

'Charlie's voicemail registered a call from a guy who lives in Mississippi about an hour ago. No message though. I guess that was you? The phone is switched off right now so I guess the owner is on a plane. But as soon as he lands, we'll find out where you two little fuckers are and we'll get you. Then we'll rip your fucking heads off and shit down your…'

Amber disconnected the call, her pulse racing. Lucas looked on. It was clear the call had not gone well…

Amber paused for a moment, gathering her thoughts. She wasn't a religious person, but she prayed the first businessman whose phone they had borrowed was on a really, really long flight. She turned to Lucas, struggling to convert her thoughts to words.

'Charlie's, well… They said Charlie was "indisposed". Permanently…'

Before she could gauge Lucas's reaction to this devastating news, she jumped as the phone in her hand rang. She looked at the screen and was appalled to see it was Charlie's phone calling. She quickly realized that they had figured out that she'd called them from a borrowed phone. They were trying to contact the phone's owner to discover where they were!

Amber thought quickly.

'Lucas,' she said. 'We actually now have to commit a crime.'

Lucas looked at her quizzically. Amber deftly flipped the phone over and quickly identified the flap hiding the phone's SIM card. She levered open the flap with a thumbnail and slipped the card from its housing.

After closing the flap, she snapped the card in half. The phone's owner had taken a seat close by and was waiting patiently for his phone to be returned. He frowned a little as he saw Amber fiddling with his phone. Lucas nodded in understanding. Amber decided that she needed to return this phone personally....

Mike redialed the number for a second time, and heard the call connect to a voicemail. He listened closely but the message left no clues as to the phone's owner, beyond the fact he was called David and had a southern accent. His face was still red from his earlier outburst.

John stood beside him, trying hard to not look at the slumped body of the police officer who'd rolled out of chair onto the floor. Dirk stood by impassively, dismantling the gun he'd used for the murder, which he would now dispose of. He didn't want to be in possession of a weapon that had killed an American police officer for any longer than was necessary. Dirk didn't care if Mike wanted to use the weapon to frame anyone. This gun was going in the Hudson.

Mike calmed himself a little, and drew his own phone from his jacket pocket and dialed a colleague who'd be able to track down the owner of the second phone Amber had used. They'd already tracked down the first phone owner's wife, who had thought her husband was at a conference in Boston. She'd seemed surprised when Mike had reported how unlikely that was.

'We're so close,' said John, expressing what they all thought.

The second businessman had taken his phone from Amber, focusing on the languid wink he'd received from her rather than on the phone. Amber had held the man's adoring gaze as she whispered a "thank you" in the strongest southern accent she could muster, and she was thrilled to see the man hold her gaze as he slipped the phone into his jacket pocket without looking at it.

She regretted her actions, and felt bad for the guy as she turned back to Lucas, but she knew what she'd done was necessary. She also knew they needed to now get scarce before the guy realized his phone was dead and called the authorities on them. Getting busted for stealing a SIM card would be an ironic end to their hopes of freedom, especially when the arresting officer ran them through his system and saw the warrants they had hanging over them.

Amber steered Lucas down the terminal building, deciding that being in a crowd was now an advantage. They stopped in the central atrium of the terminal, speaking quietly as they looked up at the departure board.

'We're screwed,' Lucas said. 'Totally screwed.'

His voice was breaking as the full emotional consequence of Charlie's death sank in. He'd been down this path before with Eric, but this time it felt worse. Now they knew more about what they were up against. Now they knew the full extent of the conspiracy. And Charlie had been a police officer, while Eric was only the son of one.

Amber patted Lucas's arm maternally, as she scanned the departure board.

'C'mon,' she said. 'Hold it together. This isn't over yet. Not by a long shot.'

Lucas immediately perked up.

'Do you have a plan?' he asked with hope in his voice.

Amber paused, then smiled.

'You know, I think I might,' she said with a wink.

Lucas looked at her with wide, dependent eyes. For a brief moment, Amber felt real sympathy for him. Lucas was just a simple guy, caught up in a surreal drama. She found herself perversely enjoying the control she now had over him, which felt unnatural given their professional relationship. Seeing Lucas's dejection, she knew that taking command was essential for their survival.

'I had some inspiration while we were waiting by the phones. In case Charlie, well in case Charlie failed.'

Lucas nodded enthusiastically, eager to hear the punch line. Amber felt the need to take her time.

'A large corporation is trying to kill us,' she continued. 'They have huge power and the assistance of someone in the government. So, who can we go to that's bigger and more powerful than that large corporation? That also has ample resources and can be motivated to help us?'

Lucas shook his head, hanging on every word.

'Simple,' she said she felt that her hesitation had teased and tormented Lucas for long enough. 'We go to a bigger company. And specifically, I think we go to the world's biggest mining company. Elemental Resources.'

A smile quickly spreads across Lucas's face. They have a plan. Whether it's a good plan or not was impossible to tell, but having a plan beats drifting across the country waiting to be caught.

Amber pulled her passport from her bag.

'I think it's time we risk these,' she said. 'Eric's been right about everything so far. We have to get moving before they figure out who owned the phones we used.'

Lucas smiled again. 'So another flight?'

'Exactly.'

'But where?'

Amber swept her arm theatrically up, pointing at the destination board suspended above their heads.

'There,' she said.

Chapter Forty

Sydney, Australia is many people's idea of paradise. A seemingly endless harbor of sparkling blue water, a glorious subtropical climate and friendly people at every turn combined to make the city a regular fixture in lists of the most desirable places to live.

The nineteen hour journey from Dallas via Brisbane is often considered to be an excellent a reason to not make the trip. The sixteen hour first leg to Brisbane was actually the longest flight that can be taken on a Boeing aircraft anywhere in the world.

Eric's remaining cash had not been adequate to afford a First Class ticket but was sufficient for Business Class seating. They'd experienced a few moments of anxiety when purchasing their tickets as the Australian government required all visitors to obtain an electronic visa before embarking on a flight down under. Fortunately the Qantas ticketing desk had sensed their anxiety and had offered to procure the necessary approvals for them. Qantas's policy was to not allow something as trivial as an electronic visa to interfere with the sale to two full-fare business class tickets. Once again, no alarm bells rang.

Amber and Lucas were finally able to relax once the plane took off, certain in the knowledge that they would have half a day of unmolested rest. Their Business Class accommodation had provided them with fully flat beds and enough food and wine to satisfy even the most obese businessman. Amber and Lucas both slept for over ten hours.

The hour before landing in Brisbane had been spent preparing for the next stage of the process. Amber's plan was better than nothing, but it had still lacked some detail. Between them they had been able to fill in some of the bigger gaps, so they knew what to do if they successfully made it through immigration into Australia.

Their tension levels escalated when faced with uniformed authorities at the immigration desk on arrival, but they'd passed through without incident. Having only hand luggage, they were able to bypass the baggage reclaim system and in minutes they were seated at the departure gate for their connecting flight to Sydney.

The flight to Sydney, their fourth in exactly twenty-four hours, was similarly uneventful. Amber started to feel that there was a real chance that they'd slipped the net, for now at least. The flight from Brisbane was a routine domestic flight so after landing they walked straight out of the terminal without encountering any security checks, and before they knew it they were hailing a cab in the warm fall morning.

A thirty minute drive through quaint suburbs brought them to the heart of downtown Sydney, and they found themselves having to stroll around the picturesque Circular Quay for an hour until nine am rolled around. That was the time at which it felt appropriate to take the next step down what they hoped would be the path to vindication. Despite the early hour in Sydney, Amber's body clock was still on east coast time where it was time for dinner, so she was thoroughly enjoying an ice cream.

'Not a bad spot, this,' commented Lucas.

'I wish we were here under better circumstances,' Amber replied, slurping on the ice cream.

They paused and leaned against a railing by the harbor. The Opera House shone in the morning sun to their right, while their view of the Harbor Bridge was partially obscured by the imposing cruise ship docked at the downtown passenger terminal.

Their eyes met and held. Amber broke the gaze, uncomfortable at the yearning she thought she could detect in Lucas's eyes. Too complicated...

'Worrying about toxins for a living is never going to be the same,' she said, bringing both of their thoughts back into the moment.

'I'm looking forward to getting back to it,' Lucas replied. 'Never fancied being Indiana Bond.'

Amber smiled at this, turning her eyes back to Lucas to share her amusement at his joke. She was decidedly bothered to read from Lucas's straight face that no joke had been intended.

Lucas looked at his watch.

'Nine,' he said.

'Right,' Amber replied, taking a last mouthful of ice cream and discarding the balance in a trash can. 'What's the guy's name again?'

'Peter Johnson. Head of Risk Management. I met him at a conference a couple of years ago. He should remember me.'

'Let's do it.'

They turned and walked across the plaza to the door of a very smart looking office building. Ever the gentleman, Lucas held the door open for Amber to enter, and followed her in.

New York was almost exactly ten thousand miles from Sydney, almost literally half a world away and at that time of the year, fifteen hours behind, given the influence of the international dateline which Amber and Lucas had crossed mid-way through their flight from Dallas.

John's office was beginning to resemble a war-room. Empty food and drink containers were scattered around the desk and meeting table. Luggage was stored in corners. Maps and charts had been pinned to walls.

John was there with Carlos and Dirk, and they had been joined by George who'd grown bored of sitting in a car in an underground car park. He had proven very useful for fetching food for the group, which he didn't object to as he was able to take a "miner's commission" from every dish procured in the form of a hearty mouthful. Mike was absent.

Dirk was examining an array of unusual objects which had been assembled on the desk. The items had been taken from Amber and Lucas's apartments, and were being held by GoldRock in case they needed to be augmented to link their owners to additional crimes they hadn't committed. Dirk was leafing through a rolodex.

John stood to address the room.

'Look. All is not lost. No-one will believe two murderers' bullshit stories about phantom gold. We'll catch them. For sure.'

Carlos was quick to respond, less emphatically. 'Perhaps. Our investment in Mike seems to have paid off, although he had delivered less than he promised. I will go back to Ghana. There is no more I can do here – Dirk and George will stay to, to tidy things up.'

John glanced at Dirk, concerned as to what further tidying up might be required and worried that he may one day fall under that classification. Dirk responded with a large fake smile.

Almost on cue, Mike strode into the room, positively radiating success. The room turned as one to listen, their spirits lifting appreciably in response to the positive energy Mike was exuding. He moved to speak, but noticed Dirk and the rolodex.

'Careful – that's evidence from the kids' office,' he said to Dirk. 'Try not to get too many fingerprints on it.'

Dirk responded with a look that hovered between disgust and hatred, but he thought better than to amplify the confrontation and respectfully pulled his hands away from the card file.

Mike turned to Carlos. 'We found them. Eric Crick pulled some bullshit stunt in a Government database so the bells didn't ring when they used their passports – they used their real names which we weren't expecting. Cute. My bosses are going absolutely nuts. If Dirk hadn't killed Eric I think the Director of Homeland Security probably would have done so herself by now, barehanded.

'Anyway, they landed in Sydney, Australia an hour ago. Once we'd figured out they'd been in Dallas, we had to eyeball manifests until we found them. We started with the shortest international flights and worked outwards. We didn't expect them to go all the way to Australia. It took a while…'

Carlos greeted the news with a frown, which unsettled Mike. Undeterred, Mike continued with his rehearsed report.

'Yeah, that's right. It's great news. The Aussies are highly disposed to help. We'll have them extradited by the weekend.'

John was swept up by Mike's enthusiasm and hadn't detected Carlos's hesitation.

'That's great news, isn't it Carlos?' he said, turning to Carlos. He immediately felt his spirits sag as Carlos failed to reciprocate the excitement.

The room fell silent, all eyes on Carlos, waiting for his reaction. After a moment, he spoke.

'Perhaps. But we should ask ourselves a question. Why Sydney? Convenience?'

John and Mike reflected on this and their enthusiasm also sank as they realized the path Carlos was taking them on.

'No,' John replied with a sigh. 'It's a ridiculously long flight, I've done it and it's not convenient for anyone. Mexico, Canada, two dozen other countries are closer.'

'It's much easier to get fake papers in Central America than Australia,' Carlos added. 'No, they went to Sydney for a reason.'

Carlos rose from his seat and moved across to the window. John and Mike exchanged glances, thinking through the implications of Carlos's theory.

'OK,' Mike said. Not exactly back to square one, but close. 'We'll check family trees. See if they've got relatives there.'

Dirk silently slipped a card from the Rolodex, then rose and walked across to Carlos. He could not avoid looking theatrical in doing so, but he didn't care. He still resented being tagged as a murderer in front of that N.Y.P.D. guy. Not cool…

He handed the card to Carlos.

Carlos studied the card for a second.

'We continue to underestimate our prey,' he said.

Carlos smiled, producing an expression that conveyed respect as much as amusement. He walked back to the meeting table and placed the card between John and Mike, both of whom leaned in, eager to see what the card contained.

It read:

Peter Johnson
Head of Risk Management
Elemental Resources
1 Circular Quay
Sydney

Chapter Forty-one

The offices occupied by Elemental Resources shouted success. With a grand entrance directly off Circular Quay, every floor commanded views of the harbor, opera house and bridge. The building housed the most expensive commercial real estate in Australia, and the location told the world that Elemental Resources wanted to be taken seriously, and deserved to be.

The lavishness was not confined to the location of the office and its views. Every feature of the tenancy had been designed to amplify the prestige of the office, from the desks and chairs right down to hinges on the closet doors. After all, Elemental didn't pay people to spend all day looking out of the window. They paid them to make money for the shareholders.

Amber and Lucas were greeted by a receptionist, and after some imploring by Lucas that to Amber, bordered on begging, they were shown to the reception area for the executive office suite on the seventh floor. After a short wait spent looking through the floor to ceiling windows watching

318

the traffic gracefully circulating below on the harbor, they were shown into Peter Johnson's office.

Peter was a smart man, mentally and physically. A graduate of Sydney University, Oxford and Harvard, he was one of the brightest men of his generation. Elemental Resources had spotted his talent early and had snapped him up after completing his MBA, able to offer him as much money, travel and excitement as he could handle.

Peter's choice of clothing reflected his mental acuity in that he also dressed smart. Very smart. His suit alone cost more than many people earned in a year at some of the mines he'd overseen through his career. A platinum Rolex glinted against the sixteen hundred thread count of his tailored cotton shirt, which protruded from the sleeve of his Merino wool jacket.

He rose to greet Amber and Lucas as they entered his office. He did indeed remember Lucas from a conference in Colorado the previous year. Peter had attended mostly in a public relations capacity, a senior executive from the world's largest gold miner, there to be mentally poked and prodded by anyone prepared to pay the registration fee. Not a growth opportunity for him personally per se, but valuable for the business and that was what ultimately mattered. He'd been convinced to attend as there'd been unusually good snow in the Rockies that year, which had provided a pleasant weekend for Peter after the conference. It had made the travel and the jetlag bearable.

Lucas had been seated at Peter's table during one of the conference's formal dinners, and Peter remembered him to be a smart individual with an interesting job but with virtually no personality. Their conversation had been entirely focused on business, Lucas showing great interest in the tedious details Peter worked hard to delegate to others.

Peter had been very surprised to discover that Lucas was in Sydney, unannounced and with a companion. He agreed to the meeting when many of his better instincts screamed not to.

'Lucas,' he said, waving them to sit down. 'You're lucky to catch me. I should be on a flight to Perth but you say this is "life or death"?'

Peter succeeded in suppressing a note of cynicism when using the words "life or death". He truly understood what that phrase meant, but doubted whether Lucas did. Peter noted that Lucas was shifting anxiously in his seat, eager to speak.

'We really appreciate your time,' Lucas said. 'You must hear this.'

'You've got ten minutes.'

Mike Pointer and John Showers were sitting alone in John's office. Both chewed distractedly on a sandwich. The luggage and much of the trash had been removed.

'This really is a class A fuck up,' John offered, apropos of nothing.

'These kids are good,' Mike replied. 'Or lucky. Either way, it ain't over yet.'

'Your confidence never fails to amaze me. I hope you're right. I've got too much invested for this to fail.'

Mike reflected on John's first comment, unsure whether to take it as a complement or a criticism. He decided to push back a little.

'And you think I haven't?' he said. 'When we get them back to the States I've got a kick-ass murder-suicide ready for them. Watertight. My best work yet.'

Mike leaned forwards, his body language emphasizing the confidence of his statements. John leaned farther back, growing a little tired of the ceaseless optimism given Mike's lack of delivery so far. Certainly they would have compelling evidence against Amber and Lucas and certainly he may be able to engineer a murder-suicide to solve all of their problems if they got them into custody. But that was the point – they didn't have them in custody. So far they'd effortlessly evaded the clutches of every U.S. agency involved in travel, domestic security and law enforcement.

'Look, I need to level with you,' John said. 'I feared something like this would happen one day. So I've got a plan. I have a bolt-hole set up in the Cayman Islands. My family left this morning.'

The rush John received from confiding in Mike was unexpected. They'd worked closely together for many years and John felt they'd developed a bond that allowed him to make this confession. Any admission of weakness was usually forbidden within the organization.

Mike received this information with a mixture of disappointment and excitement. This was not what he'd expected John to reveal to him, but it presented some intriguing opportunities.

'Why are you telling me this?' he said cautiously after a moment had passed.

'I think we should team up. Help each other out. I'll shout if I see it all going tits up. You do the same. Then you can come and hide out with us until it blows over. In the Caymans. Until things quieten down.'

'You seriously think Carlos won't find you? Or us? This kind of catastrophe doesn't just "blow over", not when people like Carlos get hurt.'

'But he wouldn't find us,' said John, deploying Mike's tactic of absolute confidence. 'There's no paper trail, no link. Hey, if there's one thing I've learned over the years, it's how to move money and assets around without leaving a trail.'

'I still don't understand why you're still sitting here, if you have this all planned. You could have run days ago. Weeks even.'

'I still believe in you. I still think we'll get them back to the States and be able to put the lid back on this. Then we can carry on.

'We both make a lot of money, but I'm greedy. I want to make more. This bolt-hole was always meant to be a contingency, but I'm not going to take stupid risks. If I have to cash out now with what I've got, that will be OK.

'You see, I think you'll see the shit starting to fly before I will. So I think *I'll* need *your* help to time an exit more than you'll need mine. But I can offer a refuge. So it feels like a fair deal.'

John smiled, hoping to build a connection with Mike that could take both of them beyond the current crisis into the next chapter of their lives. Mike leaned back in his chair and looked deep into John's eyes.

Many, many thoughts jostled for primacy in his mind. He was impressed by the initiative John had shown. He was disappointed that his colleague didn't fully share his optimism about bringing Amber and Lucas home. The Cayman Islands wouldn't be his choice, but what other options did he have? At least it was warm there. Eventually, he decided on his response.

'Look, we've worked together for a long time,' he said. 'Done a lot of stuff, particularly in the last few days. Made a lot of money. But we've not made as much as Carlos has and certainly not as much as Carlos's bosses, whoever the hell they are. I sure want to be around to spend what I've got if I'm not going to be making any more. And I don't particularly want to meet Carlos's bosses if this all goes to shit. Neither am I excited about federal penitentiaries. OK. You've got a deal.'

John rose triumphantly from his chair and shook Mike's hand vigorously.

'We'll still get them,' Mike warned. 'Don't start to seriously think we won't because Carlos will sniff doubt out of you, even from back in Africa. But if I see the wheels starting to come off, I'll let you know. And you'll do the same?'

John nodded vigorously. He moved to his desk and drew a sheet of paper from a drawer.

'Here's the address,' he said. 'Take it now, just in case. Commit it to memory, then destroy it.'

Mike took the paper, maintaining his eye-lock with John. 'Thanks,' he said.

Amber and Lucas's report to Peter had taken considerably longer than ten minutes. Peter had interrupted them twice. The first time he asked his assistant to cancel his flight to Perth and to clear his diary for the next three days. The second time he asked his assistant to gather a group of his colleagues in the boardroom. Immediately.

Amber and Lucas were now in that boardroom. It was lavishly appointed, as were all the rooms in Elemental's head office. The walls sported the same style of geological map that they'd seen in Ghana and in New York. It must be a mining thing, they'd thought to themselves on entering.

Peter was standing by a whiteboard, on which Amber had drawn an elaborate schematic of how they understood the GoldRock fraud to operate. Lucas was sitting at the table looking on, offering the occasional comment.

Also at the table were three of Elemental's most senior managers, including the most senior, Chief Executive Officer Brian Carney.

Brian was old school. Clothes were to keep you warm, and his, while expensive, didn't quite fit. Food and wine was to be savored, exercise not so much. So he was a little tubby but could tell a '96 vintage Penfold Grange from a '98 from its bouquet alone. Language was to be used to communicate, not to make friends, so he didn't mince words. Old school all the way.

Throughout Peter and Amber's presentation, Brian had sat uncharacteristically quietly, not usually one to miss an opportunity to contribute to the goings on in *his* company. This was partially in response to the unusually aggressive nature of Peter's summons, which indicated that the matter at hand was truly serious, but mostly it was because his current girlfriend, twenty-six years his junior, had been a very naughty girl the night before and he was unusually fatigued that morning. Thoughts of his girlfriend had quickly been dispelled when Peter and Amber had got into the meat of their presentation.

'So there is no gold,' said Amber, wrapping up. 'And we're on the hook for a double homicide.'

Silence filled the room. One by one, eyes turned to Brian, anticipating his reaction. The attendees didn't have to wait long. When it arrived it was characteristically robust.

'Fuck me,' he said, everyone hoped rhetorically. 'That's fucking ingenious. Hey, Jackson, why the fuck aren't we doing this? Would add millions to the bottom line.'

Peter looked Brian square in the eye, something few people had the courage to do. After a beat, Peter laughed which triggered a domino of giggles around Elemental's representatives in the room. Thank god, he was joking, they thought. Amber cracked a smile, but Lucas maintained his grim expression, still bothered by Amber's concluding words of "double homicide."

'Yeah, you're right,' Brian continued, feeding off Peter as his straight man. 'That's a bit aggressive. Even for us.'

'Thank you for believing us,' Amber offered, genuinely. 'So what do you think we should do?'

'Well, I'm focused on the millions of dollars of gold sitting under a Ghanaian mine that the current owner doesn't seem to be interested in,' Brian said. 'You're best option is to let us convince them that we know what they're up to. Which should make that mine's owner very willing to make a deal. From which we'd all win.'

Peter nodded throughout Brian's statement.

'I agree,' he added, pointing at one of the geological maps. 'We'd wondered about this location. We have a mine close by, so we monitor our competition to benchmark our performance against them. Our understanding of the geology suggested that the bulk of the gold is deeper than GoldRock's digging had reached. But their production levels were very strong. Reportedly. Now we know the reason for the discrepancy.'

He turned to Brian and with a knowing look added: 'We have another property just over the border in the Cote D'Ivoire.'

Brian smiled broadly, the significance of this being lost on Amber and Lucas but being obvious to Brian.

'You fuckin' genius,' he added generously. 'I knew there was a reason why I hired you. And it's the Ivory Coast – don't go all French on me.'

Amber took a seat next to Lucas and both were able to relax a little as they sensed a definite momentum building around them. They looked at each other and they both realized that they once again had someone on their side. People who had the ability to help them.

Chapter Forty-two

The next hour passed quickly. Amber and Lucas's sense of relaxation and security grew as they felt the Elemental family scrambling to support them. They were smart enough to realize that this swaddling of them was driven purely from Elemental sensing the opportunity for profit, not for any altruistic reason to do with helping two innocents in need. But neither Lucas nor Amber cared, provided they stayed safe, remained alive and ended up exonerated.

A number of conversations had taken place around them in the meeting room and many more had been kicked off in other offices around Australia and at Elemental's neighboring property across the border in the Ivory Coast.

Eventually, Brian called people to order as the final plan was agreed. Amber and Lucas listened attentively. The invite list to the meeting had swelled over the previous hours, such that eight Elemental executives were now present, none of whom had been introduced to Amber and Lucas. Amber couldn't help but notice that none of Elemental's leadership team was female, certainly none of them present that morning. She'd concluded that working for Brian was a tough gig, but surely there were some females in Australia capable of holding their own against his personality?

'OK people, there's a mine waiting for us,' Brian said. 'We're agreed. Barry is going to get with the Ghanaian Minister of Mining and tell him that his sexual peccadilloes will be all over C.N.N. unless he endorses our takeover of the GoldRock mine.'

The executive presumably named Barry took a note and nodded to his boss.

'Jason will talk to the manager of our neighboring mine and tell him his job just doubled,' Brian continued. 'And you'd better find out what his name is and whether he's up to it.'

The executive presumably named Jason took a couple of notes and nodded to his boss.

'Peter, we'll do the Sierra Leone maneuver,' Brian continued.

'Yeah,' added Peter, feeling the need to elaborate the point to his colleagues. 'There's a three kilometer buffer zone between properties with just some dense bush and an international border between. Nothing to worry about.'

The executives nodded and a brief mumble of assent filled the room. Amber and Lucas looked at each other wondering what was meant by that cryptic guidance. Amber was feeling brave. They were part of this, after all...

'Excuse me,' she interjected. 'What's the Sierra Leone maneuver?'

Every eye in the room swung to regard her. She momentarily felt very uncomfortable by this, feeling a sense of persecution that people would react adversely to her daring to question the great leader. The lack of other women in the room didn't help her self-confidence in the face of wall-to-wall testosterone. But as she returned the glances she was surprised that many faces bore smiles of encouragement. Was it possible that she was being complemented rather than castigated? Was it possible that half these people had no idea what the "Sierra Leone" maneuver was either, but had been too scared to ask?

'No worries,' Peter said. 'It's something we did a few years back a little farther up the coast. Just like Sierra Leone in the mid Nineties, the Ivory Coast has been in a state of Civil War for several years.'

'For fucking ever if you ask me,' injected Brian.

'Quite,' Peter replied calmly. 'Well, we run the largest mine in the country, as we did in Sierra Leone. Our taxes have been propping up the government for years. *We* had to pay to train *their* national army so they were capable and equipped to defend *our* assets. There's nothing the rebels would like more than to get control of our site, and its revenues.'

'Which is not going to happen,' Brian added. 'Didn't happen in Leone and it ain't gonna happen on the Coast.'

'I'm with you so far,' said Amber encouragingly.

'So the government owes us. They did in Sierra Leone back in the nineties, and the Cote D'Ivoire, sorry Brian, the Ivory Coast does now. In ninety-seven we called in a favor and borrowed Sierra Leone's army to help us with a small problem we had over the border at a property in Guinea,' Peter continued.

'It was the least the ungrateful bastards could do,' Brian added emphatically.

Brian and Peter looked at Amber as if this was the kind of everyday transaction common to international business. The executives around the table murmured a little between themselves, and Amber's intuition told her that this was the first time many of them had head of the Sierra Leone maneuver. It was probably not something that had been reported in the staff magazine, she thought.

'So we'll borrow the Ivory Coast's army, and take over the mine in Ghana,' Peter continued, attempting to ignore Brian's narrative help, but having to respect his bosses right to participate. 'The Ghanaian government will agree to the transfer the prospecting license to us.'

'The mining minister enjoys his trips to the Philippines a little too much,' said Brian helpfully, pointing at Barry, who shortly before had been tasked with pointing this issue out to the minister in question. 'I knew we'd get a return on that investment one day.'

Peter paused, and sighed imperceptibly. He battled on.

'When we have control of the mine and we have received the Government's license to operate it, we unveil two guys that we know GoldRock have framed for murder. GoldRock will implode in about five minutes and we all make a fortune.'

'Hell yeah,' shouted Brian.

Lucas looked on with incredulity.

'You're going to "borrow" the army of a sovereign country to use it to invade its neighbor? For your own financial gain?' The shock in Lucas's voice was easy to appreciate.

'Fucking A. You're a genius mate.' Brian's praise was somewhat hollow.

'You can't do that,' Lucas persevered.

'Yes we can,' Brian said. 'It's Africa. We can do pretty much what we like. Elemental's annual revenues are bigger than the Gross Domestic Product of the Ivory Coast and Ghana combined.'

Lucas was silenced. Amber had noted something that Lucas seemed to have missed, which she felt the need to return to.

'You said you'll "unveil" two guys there,' Amber said. 'I assume you mean us?'

'No-one else around here has been framed for murder. Not recently, at least.' Brian snorted with laughter at some recollection the others in the room prayed he wouldn't share.

'And you know the layout of the site and where the boss sits in the office complex,' Peter added reasonably.

'We're not going back to Africa,' Lucas said emphatically. No way! No we're going to stay right here where it's safe.'

Perfectly on cue, there was a gentle tap on the door and an assistant let herself in. She easily caught Brian's eye.

'Mr. Carney,' she said. 'Sorry to interrupt. There are some federal policemen downstairs. They say we're harboring two Americans wanted for murder and would like to speak to you about it. They seem quite impatient. Shall I show them in?'

Lucas leapt from his seat, looking around anxiously. Amber stayed in her seat but her body tensed noticeably.

'Show them up,' Brian said. 'Fuckin' cops.'

He turned to Lucas with a smile. 'Still want to stick around buddy?'

'Where's the plane?' Lucas asked with urgency.

'You're a fucking genius, son.'

Seven stories below, six of the Australian Federal Police force's finest men stood waiting for an elevator. They'd responded quickly and efficiently to America's request for assistance, as Australians generally did.

That request had come through an unusually senior channel, which had annoyed the Commissioner of the Federal Police who'd been fast asleep in a Perth hotel when the call came in. He'd previously observed that Americans never had the courtesy of figuring out the time difference before making calls like these. His anger was assuaged a little when his American counterpart had explained the seriousness of the crimes the individuals had been accused of, and the importance being placed on their swift capture. Federal agents around the world share a special bond, particularly when it comes to murderers.

The six officers standing in in the office lobby in Sydney were being chaperoned by the assistant who'd earlier interrupted Brian's meeting. They carried their usual side arms, but hadn't felt the need to bring a SWAT style approach to the situation, this being Australia after all. Six officers were confident of taking two targets into custody in a downtown, professional environment without a shootout.

The elevator opened with a gentle ping, and there was a moment of jostling as all six moved to enter the elevator simultaneously. Manners quickly prevailed however, as they stood back to allow their female escort to enter first. This was Australia after all…

As the elevator door slid quietly to a close and the squad began their ascent, the other elevator door slid gently open. Peter, Amber and Lucas emerged into the reception. Peter was calm and smoothly turned towards the exit doors to Circular Quay. Amber followed his lead, moving quickly but efficiently. Lucas looked around frantically, moving initially in the wrong direction before seeing the others moving and jogging to catch them up.

Chapter Forty-three

The nine thousand, nine hundred miles between Sydney and the airstrip at Elemental's mine in the Ivory Coast was almost exactly twice the distance from GoldRock's mine in Ghana to New York. Elemental's Gulfstream 550 was designed to operate into and out of small airstrips such as that at the mine, but it's range of seven thousand seven hundred miles necessitated a refueling stop in Durban in South Africa. Amber and Lucas had been surprised that their landfall on the African continent was so far south, but they hadn't appreciated the nuances of the great circle routing taken by their plane.

Peter had driven Amber and Lucas to Sydney's airport himself, and they'd taken off as soon as a flight plan could be prepared and approved. Amber and Lucas spent the bulk of the first segment of the flight to South Africa deep in sleep, enjoying the first real sense of security they'd experienced since Amber had spotted George outside GoldRock's office in New York, two days earlier.

The six hours of flying time from Durban to the Ivory Coast passed slowly, as the anticipation of what would transpire once they were back in West Africa began to grow. Amber realized that this was her only real shot at escaping the grip of the conspiracy lined up against them. The stakes could not be higher.

She stared out of the window, watching the African continent slip past, the browns of the desert prevailing until they'd crossed the tropic of Capricorn, to be replaced by the greens of the rainforest as they passed the turbulent equatorial zone. Once again she took no photos, this time because she had no camera. The in-flight map told her that they crossed the African coastline again over Gabon, before looping north across the Gulf of Guinea.

On arrival in the Ivory Coast, Lucas had been expecting some border formalities, as he wanted at a minimum to get an immigration stamp from the Ivory Coast in his passport to prove he'd been there. Peter politely informed him that given what they were about to do, they'd probably want to deny that they'd ever been in the country. Lucas reflected on this for a moment before agreeing that their purpose for visiting the country would be hard to explain on a landing card.

Leaving the aircraft to refuel for what they hoped would be a speedy return flight, they'd initially driven to the Elemental Resources administration block, where they had been given twenty minutes to shower and freshen up after the flight. They also changed into clothing that was an unusual blend between army fatigues and casual clothing.

The materials were cotton, which made them comfortable and easy to wear, even if they sported an unfashionable green and brown camouflage pattern. Amber and Lucas noted that their sizing had been communicated ahead of them, so they had a range of sizes to choose from, from which they were quickly able to find an outfit that fit them perfectly. A sign of professionalism from their hosts that they had not expected but which was most welcome.

Wearing their new outfits, they regrouped by the jeeps. Amber immediately noted that Peter had also changed, from the smart formal suit he'd worn throughout the journey into a similarly militaristic outfit. Amber's attention was drawn to Peter's torso, which was pleasantly on display given the tightness of the outfit Peter had chosen. Her thoughts briefly travelled to a very happy place, far away from their current location, but she was quickly pulled back into the present when it was time to board the vehicles.

They then travelled by jeep a very short distance to a staging post on the outer edge of Elemental's property.

They first encountered a security detail made up of guys from Elemental's mine security team who were guarding a roadblock at the perimeter of the site. Guns were prominent, which drew Amber and Lucas's immediate attention, but looking past them they noted that there were some clear differences between this squad and the guards they'd encountered at GoldRock's facility over the border.

Elemental's team were clothed in uniforms that looked new, and looked as if the individual's size and shape had actually been considered when allocating the uniforms. The sleeves sported convoluted insignias, indecipherable to an uneducated onlooker such as Amber, but obviously meaningful to the team. This encouraged Amber greatly as it was a sign of order and professionalism, two things she prioritized highly amongst a group of people charged with keeping her alive.

The squad politely challenged Peter in a non-confrontational way, which showed the new arrivals that they were armed but didn't suggest they were on the brink of using them. The squad leader easily identified Peter and the barrier was quickly lifted, allowing the group to pass.

After driving a short distance along a narrow road which been hacked through a dense area of jungle, they entered a much larger clearing. There, they found a motley band of accomplices waiting for them.

Their jeeps parked, and as they dismounted they immediately noticed a squad of soldiers, who turned and looked with interest at the newcomers. Wearing lighter uniforms than the mine's security detail, these were obviously the brigade of the Ivory Coast's army that Elemental was "borrowing".

During the flight when they had not been asleep, Peter had explained that Elemental had lavished financing on an elite band from the Army to cover this eventuality. The group was usually tasked with high profile jobs such as guarding the Presidential palace or escorting visiting dignitaries. Their skills, training and discipline were significantly superior to the rank and file in the wider army, and their loyalty had been demonstrated time and time again.

Numbering about forty, Amber and Lucas saw that they were well equipped with large automatic weapons and hanging from their belts were what looked remarkably like grenades. Lucas frowned a little when he saw the firepower. Surely they wouldn't be needed? What exactly were they getting into here?

Once Amber and Lucas's eyes had taken in the squad of soldiers, they noticed a man standing beside the squad. The man had a white face that was oddly familiar. Lucas struggled to place the man, and looked on with a frown as he moved quickly across the clearing to greet Peter. Peter and the stranger embraced heartily, obviously close friends from previous adventures.

The stranger turned to them and extended a hand to Amber.

'Hello again,' he said, with an accent which was clearly Australian, mixed with years of international travel.

Amber frowned, also struggling to recognize the face. The unusual accent caused triggered a spark of recognition and a smile quickly spread across her face.

'Yeah,' the stranger continued with a sly smile. 'We met at Accra Airport, a week or so back. You were checking in for the Washington flight behind me. Small world isn't it. Welcome to the world of "Private Security".'

On hearing these words, Lucas caught Amber up and recognized the man. They'd been in line at Accra airport behind him when they'd left Africa a week ago. The air of mystery the businessman had given off had been a little intoxicating to Lucas, and he smiled at the irony of them being reunited in such different circumstances.

'Looks like you're going to earn some of your own stories that you can never tell anyone,' the businessman added with a strong wink.

'Well, it looks like you've already met Steve,' Peter interjected, a note of perplexed amusement on his face. 'Not sure how, but anyway. Steve, well Steve helps us out on special projects around the region.'

'"Special projects"?' asked Amber as she shook Steve's hand.

'I'm a freelancer,' said Steve, smiling at Amber's question and shaking Lucas's hand. 'Peter brings me into projects like this that require my specialist skill set. Some might call it "plausible deniability" but I prefer "dependable discretion".'

As Steve spoke, Lucas noted that one of the Army soldiers had peeled away from the group and was walking across the clearing towards them. Lucas noted that his sleeve was particularly cluttered with insignia, including a number of nested chevrons, from which Lucas deduced that the guy was a senior member of the squad. Lucas found himself gently backing away from the soldier when he noticed that he was carrying three of the large weapons.

Peter noticed Lucas's subtle retreat, and looking behind him spotted the approach of the soldier. He shook the soldiers hand warmly after which he received a sharp salute from the man.

'Ah, good to see you Major,' he said. Turning to Amber and Lucas, he continued: 'This is Major Kouame of the Ivory Coast's famed Leopard squadron.'

The Major nodded his head respectfully to Amber and Lucas, smiling at Peter's complement. Using flattery to build rapport was a universal tactic.

'He will lead the team over the border,' Peter continued. 'We'll stay well behind his team, but we need to be prepared for any eventuality. Do either of you have experience with firearms?'

Peter gestured to the guns carried by the Major. Lucas sharply exhaled, unheard by Peter but noted by Steve, who frowned and gently shook his head.

'I used to go hunting with my father,' Amber offered brightly. 'Not with one of these though…'

Lucas was growing tired of being trumped by Amber, and decided it was time to contribute.

'I went paintballing once on a management development course,' he offered confidently.

It was Steve's turn to respond audibly, this time with a brief snort of amusement. Amber and Peter looked from Steve to Lucas in response to Steve's outburst, but Lucas took the high road and chose to ignore the slight.

'OK. Good,' Peter said with a moderate slice of sarcasm. 'The Major will show you the basics. If an eight year old rebel guerilla can master it, so can you. As I said, we'll be well behind the column, but preparation is everything in this kind of operation.'

Amber and Lucas nodded, Amber confidently, Lucas nervously, as the Major swung his spare weapons from his shoulder and offered them to his new trainees. Amber took hers smoothly, and used the strap to swing it onto her shoulder in a fluid movement that could only instill confidence amongst those around her. The Major smiled at Amber supportively.

Lucas took his from the Major as if it was smeared in shit, held it briefly between thumb and forefinger before he fully appreciated the weight of the object., after which he stood it on the ground between his feet, butt down, balancing the barrel against his thigh with one finger.

Steve observed this with growing amusement. Exchanging glances with Peter and the Major, he quickly slipped his game face on and commenced the detailed briefing.

'Right,' he said. 'We've already crossed the mine's perimeter. The border is one klick that way then it's another two to the mine perimeter. The border is basically a line in the jungle, and as far as we know it's unmanned this far from any of the major roadways.

'When we reach their mine, we don't expect any resistance. Our intelligence is that their security force is an unmotivated rabble, poorly paid and barely trained. When they see the Leopards we're expecting them to step back and let us through. They'll probably ask us for a job as we pass.

'In case we're wrong and they do show some spine, we've got several thousand American cigarettes which are probably more useful in this scenario than bullets and grenades.'

'Once we've secured the mine perimeter,' Peter continued, 'we'll call you two forward to guide us through the administration complex to the head honcho. We ad-lib from there.'

Amber had listened attentively through this and nodded encouragingly at the end. Lucas looked on in shock, noting Amber's growing enthusiasm and barely believing it.

'OK – we move out in ten,' Peter concluded. He and Steve moved away.

Lucas looked at Amber with a frown of disbelief on his face. This was the kind of thing he read about in novels and occasionally in the Economist, but now he was in the middle of a scene from Apocalypse Now. Armed, part of an illegal military operation which may cause an international incident and wanted by the F.B.I. for numerous murders he didn't commit.

Amber was coping much better with the drama than her colleague. You can't do anything about the past, only the future. And while she shared every thought Lucas was wrestling with, she'd discounted all of it and was focused on the future. Going along with Elemental's plan was the only way she could see of extracting herself from the perilous situation they found themselves in. She patted Lucas gently on the arm, and then turned her attention to Major Kouame as he moved forward to instruct them on how to operate their weapons.

Chapter Forty-four

The squad moved quickly through the kilometer of bush on the Ivory Coast's side of the international border. Major Kouame's troops were very familiar with the conditions and only found themselves slowed by the inexperience of the amateurs following them.

Amber and Lucas brought up the rear of the column, flanked by Peter and the Major. Lucas was perspiring freely, weighted down by the triple onslaught of the heat, humidity and the stress of being on the brink of an armed engagement. Amber was more relaxed, as she'd realized that the chances of a firefight were slim, and even if one broke out, the chance of Amber and Lucas becoming involved was so remote that she had comfortably discounted the possibility.

They followed an overgrown trail through the jungle, which had once been a major smuggling route but which had become overgrown and neglected since the outbreak of the civil war. People had had more pressing concerns in the war-torn country in recent years than on making a few extra dollars from bootlegging Johnny Walker.

Major Kouame's troops rotated their positions at the head of the column, and those at the very front of the group carried machetes to quickly clear any branches or tendrils of jungle plants which threatened to impede their progress. They were well trained, and knew that one scenario had them retreating back along this path at speed. That scenario was unlikely, but it incentivized them to invest more energy on clearing the path than would have been the case under other circumstances. To Peter, it confirmed the wisdom of using a high quality military unit such as the Leopards, rather than a lesser unit that may not have recognized the value of the investment of energy.

After a relatively short time, the trail broadened into a small clearing, at the far end of which was a thin fence, which Amber realized must be an indicator of the international border. The fence was no more than a few wires stretched between posts hammered into the ground, and peering into the jungle, Amber could see that the fencing petered out a few yards from the trail. Amber had once vacationed in San Diego with her parents and had visited Border State Park, which was a small publically accessible picnic area sandwiched between the international border with Mexico and the expanse of swampland that marked the southwestern-most point of the Continental USA. She was struck by the contrast between that heavily guarded and fortified border and this scrappy jungle clearing.

Amber noticed a small geographical marker which had been hammered into the ground at the center of the clearing, a relic of an old colonial administration when precise borders mattered more. That indicated to her that the border was several meters closer to the center of the clearing than the fence, but the fence served to make a clear point nevertheless.

The group paused in the last few feet of the Ivory Coast's territory, and the mood became more somber. Crossing the border into Ghana would be a technical breach of international law and the chance of meeting resistance, while still small, would increase significantly once they crossed the line. The squad checked their weapons one last time. Cigarettes were quickly finished and canteens were drawn from.

After a few moments, the Major gave a signal to Peter and he turned to Amber and Lucas.

'Ready to invade Ghana?' Peter asked with a smile on his face.

'Not particularly,' Lucas replied honestly.

'Remember, we're to stay well behind the head of the column but we cannot be so far behind we lose contact,' Peter continued, growing a little tired of Lucas's negativity. 'It's up to us to keep up as the focus will be on looking forward for threats rather than looking back for stragglers. Our reconnaissance suggests that the jungle gets a little thicker between the border and the mine perimeter, so concentrate on your footing as we don't want any twisted ankles.'

Amber nodded and took a step across the geographical marker on the ground.

'Welcome to Ghana', she said proudly.

* * *

Kofi Sarpong had a cushy job, or at least he'd had a cushy job until the events of that morning. As Chief of Security for the GoldRock mine, he had status and prestige, plus the position granted him innumerable opportunities to skim, coerce and occasionally steal funds from his employer.

His career in the Army had been respectable, helped by the good fortune of having his father and uncle a couple of ranks ahead of him up the hierarchy. He'd worked as diligently as he'd had to, he'd received the promotions that were due and he'd polished his boots as hard as anyone. He'd enjoyed the opportunity to keep fit, particularly from playing soccer regularly on well-maintained pitches.

He'd been fortunate to leave the Army before Ghana's contributions to regional peace keeping missions became anything more than token gestures, so he'd avoided the inconvenience of lengthy stints in the Congo or Liberia. Both would have been difficult postings for an entrepreneurially minded soldier like himself.

After completing his commission, he'd easily transitioned into the private sector, initially working as a security guard, but quickly using his family connections to build a respectable resume.

He'd established his own company six years earlier, expressly for the purpose of bidding for the contract to protect the GoldRock facility. As his father had promised, he'd won the contract, and he set about recruiting a band of loyal, reliable but inexpensive men to provide the mine's security. With his father's army connections, he knew that his entrenchment in GoldRock was assured, so he'd scrimped and saved at every opportunity, for example buying second hand uniforms and weapons. Of course his employers thought they were getting top quality former servicemen, and were certainly paying an appropriate premium for the men. But that façade was just bolstering Kofi's profit margins, which were swelled further by the service charges he levied on various suppliers and other local agencies for safe passage into and out of the mine.

He was sure his bosses must know the extent of his nefarious activities, but they'd never shown any great interest in them and besides, he'd kept the mine safe, which was ultimately what they were paying him for.

Today, all of that had changed.

His first warning that things were going awry was when he received a garbled message over the mine's ancient radio system from a man patrolling the western border of the facility. He'd reported that he'd been disarmed at gunpoint by a unit of the Ivory Coast's army, and specifically the Leopard unit. He'd received a carton of Marlboro cigarettes in compensation for surrendering his gun, and had been told to leave the mine and find another job. The man knew that there were many Sarpongs in positions of power around the district, so he'd been inspired to call in the episode before he headed home to his village for a good smoke.

Kofi initially attributed the report to a hallucination, probably brought on my drinking too much bush whisky, although his instinct told him that it was a little too early in the day for that, even for his team. His second warning was when a very similar message was received by his deputy commander. This message was received from a guard who had been patrolling the ore mounds a few hundred meters inside the mine's perimeter. That guard had run past the deputy commander clasping a carton of Marlboro's while shouting about an invasion.

Kofi's well-appointed office was located at the lower end of the administration block, and was the closest building to the smelting hut. Despite his fog of incompetence, Kofi recognized the smelter as a significant asset to the mine. As he'd walked briskly down the hill, determined to get to the bottom of the confusion, he was stunned to see a squad of soldiers taking positions around the smelting shed. Their weapons were very real and very modern and were no match for his teams antiques.

Kofi had neglected to bring his own rifle with him from his office, and so was not regarded as a threat by the Leopards. His military training had not completely deserted him, so he was able to positively identify his adversaries as members of the Leopards from the Ivory Coast. For once, he was speechless.

Later, after a few beers back in his village, he would reflect that this inability to speak may have saved his life. As with his team, his own uniform lacked any form of insignia or identification. As he was so well known around the mine he hadn't bothered to stitch anything on to mark his seniority. That morning, his interceptor had assumed he was just another ragtag guard and had babbled something at him in a dialect he didn't understand before pointing him towards one of the other soldiers, who was bringing up the rear of the column carrying a large sack.

Just as he thought his ability to speak was returning to him, he was dumbfounded again when the guy with the sack withdrew a carton of cigarettes and handed it to Kofi, with a jerk of the thumb that unequivocally meant "get lost". Never one to pass up an opportunity, Kofi had hesitated, which resulted in the guy reaching into the sack for a second carton. Kofi's friends would laugh about that for years to come, he thought.

Chapter Forty-five

Carlos sat in his office at the mine site. He'd been back in Africa for a day, growing increasingly impatient with the lack of progress from his team back in the States. Despite this, he still remained optimistic that the countermeasures they'd put in place would prevail.

The kids were still wanted for the murders of Ralph West and Eric Crick, that hadn't changed nor would it. Mike reported that the Australian Federal Police were co-operating fully with the manhunt. Funding had miraculously been found to close the passport loophole and America had quietly instructed its closest allies to do the same. Australia was one of those allies, so there was high confidence that Amber and Lucas were cornered in Australia. Carlos knew that Australia was a big country with lots of hiding places, but they'd eventually be captured and brought back to the U.S.A.

They'd decided against adding the murder of Charlie DiCarlo to the kids' rap sheet. John and Carlos felt that they'd had enough evidence to make the charge stick, but Mike had insisted that it would have required them to make assumptions as to the kid's movements that may have ended up being proven false at any trial. Instead, Charlie's murder had been represented as a random drug killing, albeit a particularly unfortunate one as the victim had actually been a highly decorated undercover agent.

Carlos was uncomfortable at how interested the press had become in the case, which John had downplayed as an entirely normal consequence of such a juicy story landing in their laps.

Dirk had set-off on the circuitous return journey to Africa that was his normal modus operandi after such an eventful trip, especially one which involved a number of capital felonies. He'd last reported in having crossed the Canadian border and would be back in Africa by the weekend. Dirk had reported that George had been an asset on the project and he would be happy to partner up with him again if required. Carlos received this news positively, but was a little concerned to hear that instead of returning to Africa with Dirk, George had decided to visit Disneyworld.

The issue of the environmental certification that Amber and Lucas had been working towards had been resolved very satisfactorily for Carlos. Given the tragic death of the consulting firm's senior partner, and the associated embarrassment that firm was experiencing given that two of their associates were wanted for his murder, the remaining partners felt that the inconvenience GoldRock had experienced from being dragged into the vortex of media speculation was extremely regrettable.

John had pointed out that signing off on the review was the very least they could do to rebuild their client's confidence. The firm agreed, and the necessary certification had quietly been lodged with the E.P.A., after which a discrete line had been drawn under the project by all involved. The surviving partners agreed that Amber and Lucas's documentation had been exemplary, even if there were some trivial issues outstanding. Carlos's operations could therefore continue without intrusion for another two years, until the next certification would be required. Two years was a long time.

Carlos's Ghanaian office was still immaculate, uncluttered by paperwork as if it was business as usual and the current crisis was not happening. He was talking to John on the phone.

'So it's been forty-eight hours and still no contact? And they still haven't contacted Elemental Resources?'

He listened to the response with a heavy brow. He gently shook his head as the seemingly perpetual lack of information angered him, delivered as it was wrapped up in excuses and apologies. Heads were already rolling, and more would follow, he knew it. He even felt uncomfortable for the first time in many years, as even his bosses were becoming impatient.

Carlos remained very proud that the concept of a fake mine had been his idea, despite the difficulties he'd faced in the last two weeks. He'd taken his idea to his Colombian brothers seven years ago when he was running their distribution operations on the East Coast. He'd grown tired of seeing two thirds of his proceeds disappearing as the cash passed through the laundering process. To Carlos, the mine had been a logical solution.

After spending two years getting the operation up and running, Carlos was thrilled that over four billion dollars had been laundered through his system, with a staggering 38% average cost ratio. This was probably half the leakage of cash he'd have faced laundering his proceeds in traditional ways. He'd enriched his bosses by over a billion dollars, and they'd enriched him in return.

He was still riding the wave of goodwill his concept had generated, which he amplified with his ruthlessly effective management style. This style was typified by his regular employment of people like Dirk Bekker, amongst others. But even Carlos was growing nervous that his reserves of goodwill were being eroded as the crisis lengthened and deepened.

His thought stream was abbreviated by a sharp knock on the door. Carlos looked up angrily, having left instructions not to be interrupted. His closed door ought to be enough of an indicator, he thought. Who would have the impertinence to knock on his door?

'I have to go. Check-in again in two hours.'

He disconnected the call, but before he could summon his visitor into his office, the door swung open. Carlos's anger at the intrusion was immediately replaced by a look of dumbfounded astonishment when he saw Peter walk into his office, brandishing a large rifle which he had carefully pointed straight at Carlos's chest.

Carlos recognized Peter from the files he kept on all of the legitimate mining operations that surrounded his property. His memory placed him as Peter Jackson from Elemental Resources. Why was he here? What the fuck did he want? Where was the security detail? He'd been promised his security detail was made up of only the finest guys, poached from the elite ranks of the Ghanaian army.

Carlos's mouth flapped as he struggled to form any verbal response to the events unfolding before him. He was closing in on coherence when he was further shocked to see the large frame of an African soldier entering his room. His brain struggled to answer the question of whether the uniform he was wearing was from the Ivory Coast? What the fuck?

He looked past the soldier and his confusion was compounded when he began to see ghosts. He blinked furiously, but he could swear that the crazy boy and girl that his crack international team had repeatedly failed to capture had just entered his office.

As he stopped blinking, he realized the ghosts had to be real. He frowned in bewilderment as he observed that the bitch Amber was standing confidently at Peter's shoulder, also pointing a gun at him. How dare *she* point a gun at *him*? What impertinence… But wait, was she actually wearing camouflage paint on her face? And what was the bastard Lucas doing? Was he actually attempting to hide behind the soldier?

Peter snapped his attention back, front and center. 'Carlos Vasquez, I assume?' he said.

Carlos found himself unable to speak. Thoughts were careening through his head but the interface between his brain and his mouth seemed to have failed for the first time in his life. He stared at Peter. He shifted his gaze to stare at Amber, who returned his gaze with a confidence completely inappropriate to her position in Carlos's world.

'You know who I am?' Peter continued, undeterred.

Carlos processed the question, and shifted his gaze to Lucas. Lucas nervously returned the gaze over the shoulder of the soldier. At least one person was showing some respect, Carlos's beleaguered mind thought.

Carlos turned back to Peter and nodded.

'OK,' Peter continued. 'Here's the deal. Earlier this morning, the Ghanaian government transferred your operating license to us. This is now Elemental Resource's mine. This afternoon, you'll issue a press release saying we've acquired it from you for an undisclosed sum. We all know that that sum is actually zero, but we have shareholders, so we need that kind of statement. I've taken the liberty of drafting that press release for you. OK?'

Carlos could only nod mutely. Peter drew an envelope from his pocket and extended it to Carlos, making sure he maintained his weapon's unwavering aim on Carlos's chest. Carlos leaned forward and took the envelope dejectedly.

'Next,' Peter continued. 'You clear my two mates here from any involvement in those murders. Frame someone else, offer up whoever did kill them, we don't really care. You also pay one million dollars each to the families of Eric Crick and Charlie DiCarlo in compensation. We don't really care about Ralph West as he was on your team anyway. Agreed?'

Carlos was in a surreal world of pain. Never before in his life had someone talked to him like this. Never before in his life had someone *been able* to talk to him like this. He was getting some idea of how he had made countless people feel over the years. He did not like it.

Again he nodded, hoping his shattered memory would retain all of these details. He knew that delivering everything he had promised would be essential to his long-term survival.

'You then fuck off back to whatever shit-hole you crawled from,' Peter continued without pause or remorse. 'If you want to try this game somewhere else, make sure it's nowhere near any of our operations. But I wouldn't recommend it. Congratulations, you get to live. And if any of your Colombian mates decide to play silly buggers, you forfeit that right. Not them, but you. OK?'

Peter lowered his weapon and extended a hand, with a broad smile. Carlos looked from Peter's face to the hand, across to Amber then back to Peter. His overriding emotion was joy, given his realization that he was going to leave the room alive. He would live to fight another day. His business was critically, perhaps fatally wounded, but he'd have a chance to rebuild. He leaned forward and extended his hand to grasp Peter's, shaking it enthusiastically.

Carlos released Peter's grip and stood looking at him for a moment. His lips flapped as he again attempted to form words appropriate to the situation.

'Which part of "you fuck off" did Peter not make clear?' Amber said helpfully.

Carlos looked at Amber in shock, then his brain and central nervous system reacquainted themselves with each other, which jolted his body into motion. Clutching the envelope, he deftly sidestepped to the left around Amber's still raised gun barrel, after which he stepped to the right to avoid the soldier, who had stood by impassively throughout the conversation. With a hard stare at Lucas, who Carlos figured was the only person in the room he could still intimidate, he left his office.

As Carlos's rapid footsteps receded down the corridor, the tension in the room eased. Amber lowered her gun and looked appreciatively at Peter. Lucas stepped confidently around the Major and raised his hand, requesting a high five from Peter. Peter did not notice the gesture as he'd turned and reached into his pocket for his cell phone. Lucas turned his open palm into a fist and punched the air in celebration.

Chapter Forty-six

Back in New York, Mike Pointer and John Showers had been together in John's office when they had both received calls at precisely the same moment. Mike had ducked into a neighboring office to take his; John had remained in his office to take his call.

The calls lasted similar durations, and as Mike returned to John's office, he was surprised to see that John's face carried a look of shock that was as profound as his own.

'You're not going to believe this,' said John.

Mike made to protest as he was sure his call had been more shocking, but the investigator in him kicked in and he deferred to hear John's report first.

'That was Carlos,' John reported. 'People from Elemental Resources turned up at the mine. With the two kids. Supported by an army unit from the Ivory Coast. They took the mine without a shot being fired. They confronted Carlos in his office and told him to fuck off.'

Mike sank into one of the visitors chairs, contemplating the gravity of this news, his eyes fixed on the carpet.

'Carlos was humiliated,' John continued. 'There were further terms he had to agree to. He didn't elaborate but he's on his way here. Flying commercial.'

'He's not going to like that,' Mike replied. 'Not gonna like that one bit.'

Mike raised his eyes to meet John's. Simultaneously they pictured Carlos crammed into a commercial airliner, being offered chicken or fish as he ran in disgrace from a fake mine he'd spent years building, or to be more accurate, digging. A mine which had been destroyed in an afternoon. Despite their horror, both men slowly, but emphatically began to laugh.

As they saw the other man laughing, their amusement grew further until they were both locked in a monstrous, tension-relieving bout of hysteria.

After a moment, as the laughter subsided John decided to exploit the bond he felt he'd just forged with Mike.

'We've got about twelve hours until he gets here,' John said. 'He said we should start afresh. Somewhere new. Chile perhaps. Bolivia.'

Mike nodded, allowing John to continue to talk, withholding the details of the disturbing news he'd received on his call. He rose from his chair and moved slowly across to the window, looking at the morning sky over New York.

'Look,' John continued. 'I don't know if I've got the guts to do this again. Or the balls.'

Mike nodded, his back now turned to John.

'You're right,' Mike said. 'I think it's time to get going.'

Mike turned, and as he did he smoothly drew a gun from a holster under his armpit. He pointed the gun at the center of John's chest.

John's shoulders sagged in exasperation.

'Oh, come on!' John said. 'We're in this together. We agreed!'

'My call was from a Graham Crick. Eric Crick's father. He's a special agent in charge of the agency's Boston field office.'

John's face fell further as the news sank in.

'It's over,' Mike continued. 'That Charlie DiCarlo must have been telling us the truth, and he did tell someone everything before we killed him. Or the kids have got someone to listen to them. Either way, Crick is onto us. He was polite on the phone, trying to arrange a meeting to discuss the murder of his kid. But I could read the undertones. He knows.'

'So let's go!' shouted John, rising from his seat. 'Come with me…'

'While you've been playing your corporate games, I've been working for Carlos while trying to be a decent F.B.I. agent. D'ya think I've had time to get a new identity? Buy a bolt-hole? Of course not. So I'll take yours.'

'But my family!' John protested.

'Don't worry – I'll take care of them. And you.'

Mike fired once. He was not even remotely concerned about splatter.

* * *

Amber and Lucas were standing alone in the Boardroom of GoldRock's mine in Ghana. Lucas looked on with amusement as Amber's wiped the camouflage paint from her face.

'I get the feeling you actually enjoyed that,' he said.

'You know, in a crazy way, I did,' she replied. 'We've trained for years to manage risk. To anticipate it, to mitigate it. Ultimately to avoid it. You end up arranging your life so nothing is unexpected. There are no surprises, so you experience no emotions. But emotion is what separates us from the furniture. I've realized from this that I don't want to spend my life avoiding emotions. You forget what it's like to be alive.'

Lucas listened closely, reflecting on every word.

'Seeing Eric die in front of you can't be an emotion you enjoyed,' Lucas asked gently.

Amber turned to face Lucas directly.

'Of course not,' she replied, conscious that Lucas and Eric had been close friends. 'But for most people around the world, death, even violent death, is not that unusual. We're lucky that it's so unusual for us.'

Both stood in silence for a moment, remembering Eric. Lucas broke the silence.

'Well I like avoiding risk. It's going to be strange going back to work after all this, but I enjoy what I do.'

'Perhaps this has come at the right time for me,' Amber replied. 'This whole experience has been the best career guidance I've ever received.'

Lucas found himself moving closer to Amber, physically and emotionally. He longed for her to move closer in response, and his heart surged as he recognized that she was. He gently closed his eyes and puckered his lips to meet hers, and was shattered when she wrapped her arms around him and pulled him close into a tight embrace. With his head resting on her shoulders, their hearts beating just inches apart, Lucas knew in that instant that they would never be together.

He knew they'd always be close as a result of experiences they'd shared, but he realized that she was now a different girl from the one he'd grown to love through their time together. A girl for whom adventure and excitement was an attraction not a threat. As his head rested on her shoulder, smelling the dusty perfume of her hair, Lucas smiled.

They held the embrace as Peter entered the room. Amber and Lucas parted, not embarrassed to have been found together, and united in the bond that had formed.

'Helluva day, eh? Peter said.

'Sure was. Kinda fun though,' Amber replied. 'Good guys triumph, bad guys vanquished and all that.'

'Fun, eh?' Peter replied. 'That's one word for it. It's not like this every day, though. Vanquishing the bad guys can be kinda fun though. Hey, you should think about joining us. We could always do with smart people like you.'

'Well I really don't think I'd...' Lucas replied formally.

'Mate, I wasn't really thinking of you,' Peter interrupted with a kindness and gentleness in his voice.

Peter turned his eyes to Amber and held her gaze for a moment. Amber was pleased to sense that she wasn't blushing. She'd earned the compliment and she was comfortable about accepting it. Not only that, but a compliment from a real man like Peter, too. A rugged, handsome man at that. Amber noted that she'd avoided the warm sensation of embarrassment when receiving Peter's initial compliment, but was starting to feel that sensation as she thought about Peter himself. She changed the subject.

'I am happy no-one got hurt here,' she said. 'It's a shame I didn't get to fire this though.'

She indicated the gun, which lay on the meeting room table. Peter nodded and paused for a second. With a knowing look he nodded his head towards the cube of polystyrene gold that still sat on the table at the end of the boardroom.

Amber read his thoughts, and smiling at the irony of having nearly died over a mine with no gold, she picked up her gun and flicked off the safety. She swung the barrel to point at the yellow block and unloaded her magazine into it on full automatic.

As the smile spread across her face and the cube exploded into a million shards of fiber, she felt reborn as a new life opened up before her. She did not notice Lucas diving for cover under the boardroom table.

About the Author:

Matt Elham was born and raised in England. At school, he was equally good at English and Mathematics, but correctly decided that Mathematics was where the money was. After studying Economics at Exeter University, he qualified as a Chartered Accountant with Arthur Andersen (may they rest in peace...)

Over the next twenty years he worked for major corporations in industries such as mining, hospitality, banking, distribution and retail. His ambition to become a C.F.O. was overachieved in 2008 when he was appointed Chief Financial and Operating Officer of America's largest retailer of outdoor living products, based in Carlsbad, California.

Throughout his career, Matt was dogged with the criticism that he was too funny and creative to be an accountant. So having achieved the goals he had set himself in the world of finance, he has decided that it is time to pursue the other branch of his personality as a writer.

Matt's other love is travel, having lived in 5 countries on 4 continents, becoming an Australian citizen on the way. He has visited more than 100 countries and every US State. He currently lives in London but isn't entirely sure why.

Printed in Great Britain
by Amazon

31863767R00211